REDNECK

by

CLAYTON WILLIAMSON

ISBN: 0-692-53023-1

ISBN-13: 978-0-692-53023-8

Also available as a Kindle eBook

Cover Art by Jennie Rawlings

Visit claytonwilliamson.com for stories and updates.

For Vanessa.

(Love and biscuits.)

ONE

I WORK FOR A LIVIN'. I know that might offend you. A lot of people don't think country men like me can do anything besides install drywall and drive trucks and watch shit TV in their mobile homes. But those same people also think starin' at a computer and writin' a story counts as an honest day's work. Huh. A lot of them people, beatniks especially, like to start their stories off with somebody gettin' murdered with a shovel or a guy jackin' off behind a curtain. It's the only way they can keep you readin' their smut. Fuck that piss. I'm a workin' man, and I don't need no goddamn shocks to keep your pecker at full tilt.

But when my manager begged me to write a memoir, I told him I'd start with that time I saw that live show in Los Mochis featurin' Alejandro the Muff-Divin' Donkey. He didn't even let me explain how Alejandro grabbed the carrot out of that showgirl before he said "Dammit, Reggie, stop being a jackass." He didn't even let me point out his pun before he threw this here voice recorder at me and told me talk into it so some writer can make me sound like a halfway-intelligent person. My manager don't laugh very often.

My name is Reggie Dunn, and I always thought I'd be a contractor or a truck driver or maybe even own a farm like my daddy. But apparently I'm a rock star.

TWO

MOST EVERYTHING OF THE PAST YEAR can be traced back to the day I met Keith Neck. All the bullshit, all the fury, all the success. Keith Neck. Sayin' his name makes me want to eat a pile of shit. But that little fucker made some sound business moves, I'll give him that. And those moves opened the door for me, so I could shine my own brand of hellraisin', even if my success won't his intention.

It was El Paso, Texas, on a springtime Sunday mornin'. I had just re-entered the U.S. border from the Bridge of the Americas, carryin' a couple of handmade Mexican blankets under my arm. I loved the desert heat; all the sweat made me feel like I'd been workin' hard just from being outside. And I liked ol' Juarez for a quick visit, even if the cartels kept tryin' to piss all over the place every chance they got. I don't blame illegals for wantin' to escape all that bullshit neither. If they're willin' to work hard, I couldn't care less. No immigrant ever called me a puta, so I ain't got no quarrel.

El Paso was the fifth-to-last city in a twelve-week tour of coffee shops, bars, and churches across America, and my wife Ruby Naris and I were the headliners. My guitar and her sweet, sweet voice was the reason I had traded in my pickup truck for an old, wood grain minivan with nary a gripe upon my person. She had told me we needed to gain tourin' experience if we were ever going to become professional musicians, and I was plum tickled when she proposed the idea. Money won't no object.

Not a thousand feet from the border stood the Baptist Bible Church of El Paso, the latest venue for the Ruby and Reggie showcase. I walked past the sign out front that read WELCOME RUBY & REGGIE in changeable block letters. I beamed with pride until I looked toward our minivan, parked near the front door of the sanctuary. The trunk door was in the air, and somebody was rustlin' through the back of the van.

The tour had been a DIY proposition thus far, and we had been careful not to let anyone handle our expensive ass equipment without permission. We never hired or asked for help, and I sure as hell knew it wasn't Ruby going through the back of the minivan, cause she wasn't built like a twelve-year-old boy.

"Hey!" I hollered.

The kid kept his back to me, his head still rootin' around the back of the van.

I stomped across the parking lot toward the van, and made sure my boots scraped against the asphalt with the proper gritty noise. "Who the hell are you?" I asked.

The skinny kid turned around, holding our one and only amplifier in his hands. He had brown parted hair and wore a white tanktop with jeans. He stared at me, confused.

"Put that down!" I yelled while I dropped the Mexican blankets and charged him. But before I could reach him, he tossed the amp back into the van and took to runnin' like a gazelle. I chased him along the side of the church until he jumped through the tall prickly bushes at the end of the church property.

I stopped at the bushes and listened. I couldn't see him no more, but I could still hear his footsteps poundin' further and further away from my homemade justice. Just as well.

I went back to the van and draped the Mexican blankets over the rest of the gear. The twelve pack of Neptunes hadn't been touched, thankfully. If that kid had tried to steal my beer, hoo boy, I would've turned into a damn dragon. I took the amp and slammed the trunk door shut good and hard.

As I walked up the stairs to the church entrance, I looked to the cross hangin' above the double doors. "So why weren't you lookin' after me and my Ruby this time?" I asked aloud. "Hmm?"

I didn't get any kind of response. Another one-sided conversation with nothin'.

I entered the air-conditioned foyer and saw my Ruby in a handsome green dress, standin' on the sanctuary stage, messin' with her acoustic guitar. I stood at the threshold of the empty sanctuary and watched and listened.

There aren't nothin' like a Baptist sanctuary, cause it's one of the dullest places you'll ever see. Aside from the few dozen padded pews, the sanctuary lacked any decorations or fancy frills, save for a lone stained glass window behind the choir loft. A Baptist's three favorite sayings are 'No fun', 'No games', and 'When can we eat?' But my Ruby made that vanilla sanctuary special just as she did anywhere she breathed. She hummed a wordless melody, her eyes closed and her head swayin' to her own metronome.

My Ruby Naris. My darlin' person. Goddamn she was built like a woman. Healthy curves in all the right places. Legs that could squat my own weight. Long brown hair, done up in a ponytail. And the cutest damn face I'd ever had the pleasure of tonguing. It didn't matter she was only 5'9; my darlin' commanded the stage. And her voice - oh, her voice - filled that empty sanctuary with an absolute purity. She could turn a tired hymn into a wondrous anthem worthy of a dyin' man's final moments.

Her melody wasn't familiar, and she kept trying different chords every time she repeated her progression. It must've been one of her works-in-progress.

She pressed her palm against the vibratin' strings and her melody ceased. Her eyes opened.

"Did that sound all right?" she asked, her words echoin' across the sanctuary.

"Sounded good, what I heard," I said. "Keep messin' with it."

She nodded and looked to her long fingers on the fret board. Mmm, them fingers could press and grip and squeeze.

I set the amp by the bottom step of the stage and wiped the sweat from my brow. "The lock on the trunk ain't no good, apparently. I caught some runt in the back of the van trying to steal the amp."

Before Ruby could even process this new development in the decay of America, the kid with the brown parted hair walked through the choir loft door, covered in sweat and dirt.

"That's him!" I pointed and climbed the carpeted steps of the stage to close the distance, but Ruby put her hand on my chest.

"Whoa, baby," she said. "Hold tight, now."

The kid froze and stared at me while he breathed through his mouth. His hair still looked perfect, believe it or not.

"The little glue huffer can't leave well enough alone," I said.

Ruby kept her hand on my chest while she looked at the kid and waved him down from the choir loft. He vaulted over the loft wall and stood next to Ruby, but kept the preacher's lectern between me and him.

"You goin' after the offering plates, little weiner?" I asked.

The kid handed Ruby a set of keys. The set of keys with a familiar Tennessee shaped keychain. Ruby's keychain.

"I asked Keith here to bring in some of the gear to give you a little break," she said. "I figured you could enjoy the mornin' a little longer." She gave me a kiss on the cheek and her lightnin' ran down the small of my back.

"Your husband gave me quite a scare, Miss Ruby," the kid said. He grinned at me and held out his hand over the lectern. "You're pretty fast for a big guy. You bout near got me." He laughed to himself.

I looked down at his hand and back up at his dirty face. The fuck was this kid?

Ruby looked at me and slapped my chest before I could run my mouth anymore. Her brown eyes got me every time.

I cleared my throat and shook the kid's hand.

"My name is Keith," he said. "Keith Neck. Good to meet you."

His handshake reminded me of a young, dead catfish: tender and floppy. But he held eye contact. He had that.

"I'm Reggie Dunn," I said and put my arm around Ruby's shoulders. The runt won't much bigger than Ruby, and he had the babyface of a harmless teenager. He was a girl's first crush, before she realized she wanted a man instead of a boy. But he was what some ladies might've considered handsome, and he smiled like he knew it. Now me on the other hand, I had a little stubble and a bit of a workin' man's gut but I was otherwise an attractive piece of ass. I didn't win Ruby over just cause I could earn a paycheck. She liked her men tall and strong.

"So how long till you reach high school, Keith?" I asked.

"Actually," Keith grinned and ran his hand through his brown hair like he was some damn heartthrob. "I graduated high school a few years ago. Heck, as of last month I can buy you a beer, Mister Reggie."

Holy piss. A man-boy. Ruby pinched me on the rump before I could snicker. She knew me well.

"Keith here was just tellin' me he wanted to make country music, Reggie," said Ruby.

"That's right." Keith nodded. "I wanna learn everything about the country music business. Even the grunt work: cables, amps, everything." He grinned again. "I'm already good enough to be a roadie."

"Country music, huh?" I said. "Hold out your hand for me, there, Keith." He extended his hand over the lectern, and I rubbed his soft palm. I sucked my teeth. "Have these hands ever seen a hard day's labor?"

Keith laughed again. "I work data entry at this car insurance place downtown."

I held out my own palm and made the 'come on' motion with my fingers. He rubbed my hand like he was feelin' for lumps. "Feels like sandpaper," he said.

"That's what country feels like," I said. "If you ain't never worked like a dog day in and day out, how do you expect to make genuine country music?"

Instead of a thoughtful response, he just laughed again.

A voice came from sanctuary floor. "Excuse me, Miss Ruby?"

The Preacher climbed the steps of the stage, his black suit and bald head just a shinin'. "Ah I see you've met Keith! Our resident musician." He shook Ruby's hand and said "Miss Ruby, I know you're setting up for the service, but I've got a fun offer I hope you and Mister Reggie will consider. Our Sunday School teacher for the 8-9 year olds is always looking for new ways to teach the children about living the Christian life, and I was hoping the two of you could talk to the class about your cross-country musical journey."

"Absolutely, Mister Guzman!" said Ruby as she tapped me on the shoulder. "Reggie and I would absolutely love to talk with the kids. Let me and Reggie finish settin' up and we'll head right over."

"I'll do it for you, Miss Ruby!" said Keith. "I know how to set everything up."

"Oh, how nice of you, Keith," said Ruby. "Thank you!" Ruby started walkin' to the back of the Sanctuary with Preacher Guzman.

I stood on the sanctuary stage with Keith, with the big ol' preacher's wooden lectern still attached to the floor.

"All right, let's move this thing real quick," I said.

"No, I got it, Mister Reggie," Keith replied as he kneeled underneath the lectern. "You've got a class to meet."

"This looks mighty cumbersome. Let me help me you."

"I'm positive I've got it. I won't let Miss Ruby down."

"Reggie!" Ruby's voice echoed across the sanctuary. "Keith can handle it. Come on."

There was no need to argue. I walked toward the back of the sanctuary and listened to Keith grunt and struggle as he tried to loosen the lectern from the stage.

I just knew I'd end up movin' that damn thing anyway.

THREE

I COULD HEAR 'EM through the door. Runnin' round. Knockin' over things. Hollerin'. Ruby and I stood at the closed door of the 8-9 year-old Sunday School class and my stomach lurched.

"I really think I should be settin' up the gear, darlin'," I said.

"No, you should be right here with me." Ruby squeezed my hand. "Keith said he can handle it. There isn't much left to set up anyway."

I breathed hard.

"Don't huff. We've always wondered about having youngins. Let's jump in the deep end, huh?" She turned my head towards her.

I kissed my Ruby and smiled. "You're lucky I love you."

"I know." She quickly squeezed my hand and opened the classroom door.

My only thought was 'damn'.

The youngins were all over the room, spinnin' around in circles tryin' to make themselves dizzy or doin' jumpin' jacks or drawin' on their Sunday clothes or just hollerin' at each other just to hear themselves holler. A middle-aged lady walked around a beat-up wooden table, placin' napkins and little halves of toaster pastries in front of each of the table's mismatched chairs.

9

"Oh hello," she said over the noise. "You must be Miss Ruby and Mister Reggie. I'm Miss Sanders, and we're delighted to have you as our guests." She shook our hands with a firm grip. "Well let's get started." She walked to the blackboard at the front of the room.

I guessed the Preacher really recruited me and Ruby for crowd control. Hot damn, without us, Miss Sanders was gonna need five minutes just to round up the class and calm them down for-

Miss Sanders suddenly screamed like a goddamn banshee. Her fists clenched, her eyes bulged and she stood like she was ready to deadlift three hundred pounds. I was too fuckin' terrified to breathe but those kids dropped whatever shit they were holdin' and went straight to their chairs. She finally stopped screamin' once the kids sat down and gestured for us to have a seat with a smile on her face. Ruby gripped my hand harder than the time she was fitted for her IUD.

The kids didn't say a word. They just nibbled on those toaster pastries in silence. All I could hear was a dozen youngins chewin' on brown sugar snacks and my own goddamn heart poundin'. But they weren't upset or anything. All of 'em were really drawn in by their snack.

I had to say somethin'. "Th...thank you for havin' us this morning," I said as Ruby and I sat in some kid-sized chairs.

All the kids looked at me and Ruby, still chewin' away. Miss Sanders smiled. "Thank you for being here, Mister Reggie. We're delighted to hear about your amazing journey across the United States. Class, say hello to Miss Ruby Naris and Mister Reggie Dunn. They're a married couple that sings for churches across the country."

"HELLO MISS RUBY NARIS! HELLO MISTER REGGIE DUNN!" The whole class greeted us with a loud burst and I jumped in my little chair. That damn banshee screech bout near gave me PTSD.

Miss Sanders held up an illustration for the class. "But first, we're going to study the story of Jonah and the whale. It's about trusting and obeying God's plan instead of following our own desires. Before we get started in our discussion, would Mister Reggie please lead us in opening prayer?"

"Uh, all right, then," I said, closed my eyes and took Ruby's hand. "Dear Lord...thank you for bein' the Lord...and thank you for lettin' me and Ruby-"

She squeezed my hand, her long fingers laced through my own.

"-for lettin' me and Ruby meet with this class of youngins. Help us through the lesson of Jonah and the whale, cause we're gonna need all the help we can get. You've got a man gettin' eaten up by a whale and then barfed up three days later."

A couple kids giggled when I said barfed.

"I know you've got miracles and all, but I remember readin' somewhere that the biggest whale You ever made only had a throat the size of a beach ball. Now Lord, as you know, I'm a grown man, and my shoulders ain't never gonna fit through a hole that size. And I ain't dumb, Lord, but-"

I cracked open an eye and looked down at Ruby's weddin' band, the gold metal pressed between my fingers. Her thumb gently rubbed my knuckles

"-but you know better than us, don't you, Lord? Thank you for the toaster pastries. Amen."

The class echoed the amen. Ruby patted my hand for a job well done.

A black-haired boy on the left side of the table raised his hand. "Miss Ruby?"

Ruby beamed. "Yes? And what's your name?"

"My name is Spencer." He giggled into his hands. "I...have a question. Are you two really married?"

Ruby nodded and took my hand again. "Yes, Mister Reggie and I have been happily married for almost three years."

My heart pattered. Mmm mmm mmm.

Spencer raised his hand again. "But if you're married...why do you have different last names?"

"Well, Mister Reggie and I both enjoyed our names as they were, and we decided there was no need to change them."

But Spencer didn't leave well enough alone. "But doesn't that mean you aren't really married? My mom and dad have the same last name and everybody knows it. So I don't think you're married."

I leaned forward, propped my left elbow on the table and held the back of my hand towards Spencer so he could see it plain and clear. I pointed to my gold weddin' band with my other hand. "What's that say?"

Spencer leaned in close to my weddin' band and squinted his eyes.

"It says none of your business," I said and pulled my hand off the table. Spencer fell back into his chair and giggled to himself again.

Ruby rolled her eyes and smirked.

FOUR

THE SERVICE HAD ALREADY STARTED by the time Ruby and I finished with Sunday School. We sat on one of the front pews as the choir dragged through *Peace Like A River* with all the zest of a deer carcass. The preacher swayed back and forth on the wooden lectern, his eyes closed and right hand raised in reverence to the ceiling. Keith tapped me on the shoulder and gave me a thumbs up. Despite changin' into a blue polo and washin' his face, he still had sweat stains on him. I nodded and turned back to the preacher and his bored choir. True joy offended God, apparently.

The guitars and amps and cables looked good on stage. Our guitars were on their stands, and the cable connections seemed to have the proper strain relief, but the damn lectern was still attached to the stage floor. I turned around to Keith and pointed to the heavy ass obstruction he had failed to take care of. He shrugged and whispered "I couldn't get it unhooked from the floor."

"It ain't that complicated, you little weiner," I whispered back as the choir hit an off-pitch high note and drowned me out.

Keith pointed to his ear and shook his head. I turned back around.

The preacher kept his sermon brief and irrelevant. He went on about Noah's call to save the animals despite everybody doubtin' the comin' flood. A few of the old timers in the choir napped. Others stared ahead, lost in thoughts. The Preacher didn't bring up the part where Noah got drunk and yelled at his youngins for findin' him naked. I always found that part pretty funny.

Luckily, the preacher only wasted ten minutes of everyone's time before Ruby and I took the stage. I unlatched the lectern from the stage in less than ten seconds and hoisted it to a corner while Ruby strapped on her acoustic and the choir left the loft.

"Morning, y'all!" Ruby called out. "Mind if we play for a bit?"

The congregation approved with claps and an "amen" or two. Those poor people had been starved for music if their choir was any indictation. I equipped my guitar and led the count into the upbeat *Paul and Peter Walked*. That locomotive tempo always got toes a-tappin' like a good country song should. Ruby took lead vocals and rhythm guitar and I picked the licks and provided backup vocals where needed. We shared a microphone, so we had to bunch up close whenever we had to harmonize or sing counter-melodies. I'd known that woman almost five years by that point, and those cheek-to-cheek brushes always kept us electric.

We had burned through most of our six-song set when the preacher stood on one of the stage steps and asked for a special offering to be taken up on our behalf. A few ushers got up and passed the silver plates amongst the pews.

"Thank you so much," Ruby said into the mic. "Y'all have been mighty kind to Reggie and me, and this collection will help us to keep sharin' the Lord's blessings. Every little bit helps."

The congregation signed checks and folded greenbacks into the plates, a welcome sight for two road warriors like us. "Before out last song," Ruby said, "I'd like to thank Mister Keith Neck for his help in setting up our gear this morning." A mild round of applause emerged for Keith, who clasped his hands and shook them above his head. I just kept still.

"We're gonna do something special for our last number," Ruby said, "and if you listen closely, you'll hear the beauty of God's house. Thank you for having us." She set her guitar down and I unplugged my own, and we walked down the stage steps to the center of the primary aisle. We faced one another and Ruby counted us into her favorite original song *A Fantastic Color.* It was a quiet anthem of joy, and her melody and my guitar filled that hall with the wonder of Ruby's creative mind and lyrics on a color so great no one can comprehend its splendor. People usually thought the song was about meetin' God in Heaven, but she wrote it butt naked not ten minutes after we did it on the bathroom floor one night. (Actually, I don't know why I just told y'all that. How I sex up my wife ain't none of your business, to be honest.)

Anyway, on the closin' note of the final riff, the congregation let the note fade into silence before they launched to their feet and cheered for a good, honest music. Ruby and I half-bowed to opposite sides of the sanctuary and took hands. I loved hearin' a group of Sunday Baptists almost abandon their buttoned up ways because they want to hoot and holler like a pack of roughnecks. Besides, a standin' ovation for a few seconds is better than none. The preacher stood to give the closin' prayer, and me and Ruby walked out of the sanctuary.

That performance buzz surged through me like it always did after a show. Dadgum alchemy is what our music was. Sound and energy transformed into glowing praise, and I felt invicible.

My world was good.

Me and Ruby stood in the church foyer and spoke with the congregation as they left the sanctuary. We met a lot of families, old folks and excited youngins keen to share their joy. I also heard Ruby tell everyone "Have a blessed day!" about fifty times. Even Spencer jumped around with a big grin on his face, eager for more.

✻ ✻ ✻

Within an hour, Ruby and I had packed up the minivan and gratefully accepted the $229 offering from the church. We were about

15

to drive out of the parkin' lot when Keith knocked on my window. I hit the brake and rolled down the window.

He was grinnin' ear to ear under his tan cowboy hat. "You two ain't no joke! Man, y'all were good."

"Thank you Keith," said Ruby. "Mighty fine of you."

I couldn't speak for Ruby, but I soaked in that runt's praise like a damn junkie. Didn't matter where it came from. It felt good all the same.

"And thank you for helpin' with the set up this morning," Ruby said. "It saved us a lot of time."

Bullshit. Movin' that lectern just before we played made us look unprepared. But Keith smiled like an ass.

"Bye Keith. Good luck out there." I started rollin' up the window and let my foot off the brake.

But the runt said "Wait, wait, wait" and knocked on the van like his bird was caught in the door. "Y'all from Nashville, right? Tennessee?"

We nodded.

"Well, I'm movin' up there pretty soon. Gonna try my luck up there, for real. You two inspired me. I'm gonna write a few more songs and I'm gone."

"How about that?" Ruby said. "Sounds like a plan. Well, when you decide to visit, give us a call and we'll show you around." She told him her cell number and he keyed it into his computer phone.

"Hell, you can stay with us once you get into town," Ruby said. "We got a nice place in the woods, about twenty-some minutes from the city. You can write all day, or fish, or whatever. And Reggie'll help you get some work." She turned to me. "That fine with you?"

Maybe it was the post-show buzz. Maybe it was the desert heat. Maybe it was the comfort of knowin' I had a case of Neptune sitting in the back of the van. But I cut the kid some slack. "Yeah, come on up," I said. "Be glad to have you." I knew he wouldn't actually show up at our front door, but I threw him a bone anyway.

"Oh thank you, thank you, thank you Mister Reggie, Miss Ruby." He shook both of our hands with a floppy fury, then our minivan rolled out of the Bible Baptist Church parking lot. We stopped at the red light next to the church, and I couldn't stop starin' at the rearview mirror. Keith was jumpin' and runnin' in circles, wavin' his cowboy hat and pumpin' his fists in the air.

"Light's green, hun." Ruby said.

We got movin'. "That kid's a nut," I said.

FIVE

RUBY AND I USED SOME OF THE OFFERING MONEY to cover lunch at a restaurant called Dos Tequilos off Interstate 10. Don't get me wrong, I loved eating beef dogs by campfires and sleepin' in the van for six days a week, but we both needed a proper meal and motel bed every so often and we were overdue. $229 was an especially lucrative haul for a church gig, so we got a big thing of queso dip with our burritos. That was good eatin'.

"I think I've changed my mind about youngins." I said starin' at the highway traffic. "We should get that birth control outta you and have a little boy and name him Spencer." I turned to her. "Then I'm going to do my best to make him cry every day."

She laughed. "That kid. Ugh. I weep for his mother." She gazed out the window and watched the shiny metal boxes rollin' down the highway.

I took her hand. "You were great today."

She picked up my hand and kissed each knuckle. "So were you, cutie."

I put our road atlas on the table and opened it to an overview of New Mexico. "Well, now that the last scheduled gig is done, we've got

18

some flex time if you still wanna keep with the original plan." I pointed to I-10 on the map. "We can head to Las Cruces tomorrow morning or drive on to Albuquerque."

She held my hands and squeezed. "Reggie...I am wore slam out. Just. Slam. Out. It hit me a minute ago." She leaned back into her seat and stared at the ceiling. "My fingertips are raw, my throat don't feel right and neither of us have earned a regular paycheck in almost three months. We've dipped into our savings hard. That's got me a tad nervous."

I knew our savings would have lasted us the rest of the trip, and I would've worked in a damn sewer to provide for Ruby, but that won't her point. We had planned on drivin' through Albuquerque, Denver, Cheyenne and Jefferson City before gettin' back to Nashville. That was gonna take another two weeks, easy. And my woman's face was tired.

Ruby got up and sat on my side of the booth and snuggled onto me. "I'm so thankful for you playin' and drivin' and takin' care of the bills and being so damn fun. And we're both ten times better performers than we were three months ago." She sighed into my arm. "But it's time to go home."

I closed the atlas and squeezed that woman tight. Even an orgasm stops being fun if you can't stop comin'.

❖   ❖   ❖

After lunch, we hit the road and got an hour east of Dallas before we parked at a campground outside of Caddo Mills, Texas. Truck stops and Wal-Mart parking lots were our usual venues whenever Ruby got tired of pissin' in the woods, but we needed to witness that big open sky one last time. The land around the campground didn't know whether it wanted to be forest or open plains, but that night sky was unblemished by light pollution. Once we ate dinner, we got in our sleepin' bags next to the campfire, polished off the last two cans of Neptune and stared upwards into the cosmos. Those stars were plentiful, bright, and surrounded by faint galactic colors no city dweller will ever know. Our hands clasped, and I pulled her close. She rubbed my chest underneath my shirt, and my britches got all crowded.

We were lucky, since most couples lost that primal way once they got married. But me and Ruby were hot from the start. Even though we met through church friends, Ruby never raised a qualm about our sinful premarital sex. I knew when she tugged me off in the back of my pickup after our second date that she was somethin' darlin'.

Thinkin' about our early years got me kinda hot, so I slipped off my jeans and tossed 'em out of my sleepin' bag.

"Mmmm?" Ruby moaned. She dragged her fingers across my neck and whispered little nothings into my ear. I unzipped her sleepin' bag and she gasped. My Ruby won't wearin' no britches and her legs were long and free and tight and strong.

I pressed my nose against hers, stared into her eyes, and grit my teeth. "You're so fine you make me mad," I said.

She unzipped my sleepin' bag and gave into her primal ways. And I ain't gonna go into any more detail, cause as I said earlier our lovemakin' ain't none of your damn business.

...Well, okay, I'll tell one part.

I was givin' her the Armadillo, and my Ruby was about to howl under the Texas stars. But she suddenly dug her teeth into my shoulder and groaned in celebration of our flesh. Her bite grew tighter and tighter until both of us exploded into the open air.

Phew.

I woke up an hour later, and Ruby was gently snorin' in her sex coma. I walked down to a little nearby pond and unzipped my britches. As I peed, the locusts sang their spring song, and the water rippled with a light breeze. I looked up to the stars, and found the Big Dipper and Orion's Belt, and I wondered where the Voyager satellites were and what they were seeing at that very moment.

I bet you're wonderin' how could a good ol' boy like Reggie know anything about some forty-year-old satellites? Like most things in life, I could blame it on sex.

✵   ✵   ✵

One of my earliest memories is of a preacher tellin' my parents' old congregation about the sin of premarital sex. I was only 4 or 5, but I immediately knew I won't going to obey that rule. Girls were pretty and tended to smell better than me, plus they were always down to have dirt clog fights. I never understood the whole 'cooties' thing either. I didn't know what sex was at the time, but I knew it involved getting nekkid with a girl, and that sounded all right to me, touchin' her toes and what not.

But then I got all twisted up as a teenager. Around the time I hit 15, my parents sat me down and told me I needed to get serious with God now that I was almost an adult. They signed me up for 'Leave Room for Jesus', an abstinence-only program held by my church youth group. Besides showin' medical pictures of advanced syphillis, I learned that God didn't want any consensual finger bangin', nor did he want me to pleasure myself.

The program left me in a goddamn bind. I had played with myself damn near every day since I became a teenager, and I had never subscribed to this 'no sex before marriage' rule anyway. But this fuckin' program warped my brain, and I convinced myself that God himself was testin' my resolve, and if I completely stopped beatin' off, God would reward me with enlightenment or suddenly inspire me to invent a fusion reactor. Plus, I wanted to make my folks proud. My momma wanted me to be a strong Christian boy, free from vice of any kind. I didn't want to let her down.

So I stopped beatin' off for 112 days. Almost four months of no masturbation whatsoever, all while my hormones were in their prime. I'd tick off another day on the calendar with each meatless day that passed, and I supposed that made the Lord happy. But I thought about touchin' my bird all the damn time. I read different translations of the Bible verses pertainin' to self-pleasure, hopin' I'd find one that would cut me some slack. Bottles of lotion taunted me. During our family trip to Wrightsville Beach, I had to keep a towel wrapped around my waist so all those bikini girls wouldn't call me 'boner boy'.

I truly believed that God would reward my vigilance by showing me a clear life path, and sure enough on Day 113, I suddenly decided I was going to become a urologist. I would dedicate myself to science, and I knew I had better get started soon if I was ever gonna be somebody. I found my old microscope set underneath my bed and took it to my bathroom. I set some blank glass slides on the counter and pulled down my britches.

"I'm gonna practice medicine, Lord," I said in a quick prayer. I squeezed some hair conditioner onto my hand and went to town on my hair-trigger. Hot damn, I tremored in absolute joy seconds later. With my legs all jelly, I loaded the wet glass slide onto the microscope stage, but the little light at the base was burnt out, so I couldn't see what my fluid looked like anyway. After that, I didn't give a fuck about science and went to town on myself again. Seconds later, I laid down on the bathroom floor and fell asleep, warm in blissful relief.

The next day, I doubled down on my virility and instituted Project Taste the Rainbow. The sole objective of this project was to have sex with a woman from every race and ethnicity in the world before I died. A noble, ambitious goal, I bought a box full of National Geographic magazines from a neighbor's yard sale and started lookin' for topless women. All the chicks I found seemed busy or tired or irritated at havin' their picture taken. I could understand that. If I had to carry a giant bucket of water on my head for three miles in the desert heat, I wouldn't want a stranger takin' pictures of my tits either.

I opened my last issue in a near-bored attempt to find a spank-worthy rack, and instead found a two page photo of outer space called 'Pale Blue Dot'. From millions of miles away, one of the Voyager satellites had looked back at Earth and taken its picture. Our planet was so damn tiny amongst the immensity of space and sun beams. Without the written description, I would have thought the Earth was just one of many faint stars. That picture knocked Project Taste the Rainbow outta my mind.

Ain't it crazy how forgotten memories can come back to you years down the line? I mean, there I was, peein' in a Texas lake, and I'm thinkin' about a picture I found fourteen years prior during a rubout session. Well, I never really forgot about the moment I found that picture, to be honest, since that one moment led to knowledge and questions that forever colored how I saw my world and my family.

Now I've never considered myself a smart man. I ain't good at arguin' for or against complicated matters, but I ain't trying to argue anyway. I truly believed the 'Pale Blue Dot' photo was a goddamn Rosetta Stone. If our giant Earth was just an anonymous pebble floatin' through the universe, then what did the people livin' on that pebble know about anything? That photo represented a truth I'd wondered about since I first disagreed with that preacher about premarital sex. A truth I had wanted to know ever since my daddy told me my momma had gone to a better place.

I was 17 when my momma passed, but it won't sudden by any means. Her passin' was a slow fade, recorded by years of countless doctor visits and therapies and various medical mess. On more than one occasion while sittin' by her bedside, I'd ask her why God let her sickness eat away at her, and she would usually respond by quotin' Matthew 5:45: He causes his sun to rise on the evil and the good, and sends rain on the righteous and the unrighteous. Then she'd talk about the mansion that was waitin' for her in heaven, and how our family would reunite in eternity. She said her faith in God's will gave her the last laugh over that cancer.

Now I loved my momma somethin' fierce, but I always thought those declarations were just wishful thinkin', and the Matthew 5:45 quote was the only biblical way to rationalize the fact that shit happens. God's will...God's will...whatever question I asked her or my preacher or anybody, the answer always came back to God's will, no matter how pointlessly cruel the world could be. God's will couldn't lose. But if God's will really was to torment my momma with years of pain and disabled utility, I began to wonder if God deserved to be worshipped. I did my best to keep that thought at bay, especially through her last few months, since I still considered myself to be a loyal Christian at the end of the day. Still, I felt like God was cuttin' us a raw deal.

I know what you're thinkin', that I was just angry about losin' my momma and I took it out on God. Ain't gonna lie, I was plenty upset after she passed on, but my spiritual doubts had already arrived while my momma was still relatively healthy, and they lingered even after the grief of her death had finally started to heal.

Over the years, I realized some people relied on God to cope with their powerlessness and the need to feel in control of their lives.

Some people want their lives to be part of a grander meaning, with God as the author of a master plan.

Some people just need to feel loved.

Some people just want to be with their family till the end of time, and they don't want their love to fade into oblivion.

This world is tough, and I didn't blame anyone for wantin' a little help and hopin' for the best. Sometimes it's the only card you got left to play.

But the more I lived my life, the more I wondered if people believed in God to protect themselves from the very real possibility that we might be on our own.

❄   ❄   ❄

While starin' up at the stars and standin' next to that pond with my britches zipped down, years of memories accelerated through my brain. The solar system and late night prayers and microscopes and youth group meetings and topless women in New Guinea and my momma's smile after my baptism and the whale that ate beach balls and my Ruby's hand in marriage, anything and everything collided inside my head as a single truth bubbled up from the oldest corners of my brain, whether I wanted to recognize it or not.

It was a truth I had always known but had always been too afraid to admit for fear of eternal damnation or disappointin' my parents. But it was my truth nonetheless.

Clarity overtook me, and that truth finally became words.

"I don't believe in God no more," I said.

I surprised myself after I said it. Part of me expected a lightnin' bolt to appear out of the clear night sky and smite my arrogance.

But the locusts kept singin'.

The breeze kept blowin'.

The world kept turnin'.

I did not believe in God anymore, and I felt fine.

I won't angry or sad or anything like what most preachers would have you believe about people that lose their faith. I was perfectly content with my thoughts, my view of the lake, my Ruby; hell, I was content with my life.

Recent news stories about death and sickness and disaster rushed through my head, and once I factored in the absence of God, the stories suddenly made a little more sense. Of course, I still didn't like that people murdered and cheated and got eaten by alligators, but I understood there won't no heavenly purpose behind every little thing, no cosmic intelligence manipulatin' the human species. God didn't kill my momma, the cancer did. That's it. We're just floatin' around in space, billions of people ridin' on a pale blue dot.

I zipped up my britches as I walked back up to campsite. I crawled back into my sleeping bag and spooned my Ruby, a living, snoring angel I could touch and see and love without need of a divine faith.

My newfound truth would be kept confidential between me and the Texas night sky, and I was more than fine with that arrangement as I fell into a deep sleep.

SIX

WE MADE GREAT TIME GETTIN' BACK to Nashville, and by 4PM we had already pulled onto the mile long dirt road that cut through the woods and led straight to our home on the east side of Marrowbone Lake.

"Oh, I've missed these trees," said Ruby.

"Mmm hmm," I mumbled. "Good to be back."

Ruby's phone rumbled. She took a look at it and said, "I just got a text from the phone company. It says 'Your service has terminated as of 12AM this morning. If you wish to resume phone service, please contact 1-800-ONETONE to settle any outstanding debts." She looked at me. "Reggie?"

"I paid off the car insurance until August, and I put the phone, lights, water, and rent on autopay through the debit card. I remember settin' it up cause it was giant pain in the ass."

She raised her eyebrows.

I laughed. "I'm serious! They got somethin' mixed up. You know I'm good with the bills and what not. Let's unpack the van, take a nap, then we'll head to the phone place before they close tonight."

Ruby stared down the road ahead. "All right."

I squeezed her knee. "We're good, darlin."

She braced herself on the dashboard and looked ahead. "Who's in the yard?" she asked.

Through the scattered trees, I saw unnatural colors down the road. Once we rounded the hill and reached the house, my stomach dropped. A bunch of pickup trucks were parked all over the front yard, a dump truck was in the driveway, and a bright yellow bulldozer sat chained to the flatbed of an 18-wheeler. People were haulin' furniture out the front door and onto the pickups.

"What in the piss?" Ruby said. She opened the door and jumped out of the van before I could stop. She walked through the yard, held up her arms and hollered at the workers carryin' our brown couch down the porch steps to a waitin' pickup. I couldn't hear her through the van glass, but those workers set that couch down in the yard and raised their hands in a 'don't shoot' gesture.

I parked the van and climbed up the porch steps just as Lonnie the landlord came out of the front door with his paunch leadin' the way.

"Reggie! Ruby! What are y'all doing here?" he said. "Figured y'all were gone for good." He took off his work gloves and scratched his gray moustache.

"What the hell is going on, Lonnie?" I asked with gruff in my voice.

"Well, we're gonna tear down the house tomorrow, then" -he waved to the trees surroundin' us- "the state is gonna carve out a highway that connects this part of the county with the rest of Nashville." He grinned and pointed to the ground. "They're gonna build an Automax right here."

"An Automax?" Ruby said. "There's one not ten minutes from here."

"Yeah, but it'll be convenient! said Lonnie. "I won't have to drive so far to get wiper fluid."

"How could you do this, Lonnie?" I almost hollered but kept my cool. "We've paid you on time and in full for over two years and now you're gonna-"

"You haven't paid me since January," he said.

Ruby cut her eyes at me, but turned back to Lonnie a moment later. We held a united front. For now.

"I tried to reach you last month," Lonnie said, "but I couldn't call because you refused to give me your phone number, Reggie. I remember you tellin' me it was 'none of my business'.

It won't none of his business.

"I set up automatic payments for the rent in mid February," I said. "A few days before we left."

"Never got 'em."

"Bullshit," I said. I knew he had to be lyin'.

"Now I never made y'all sign a rental contract," Lonnie continued, "cause I grew up with your momma, Reggie, and I knew she would have worried the shit outta me if I charged a deposit or tied y'all to a lease while you two were trying to start your life together. I owed her that much. But I didn't-"

"We're gonna get the sheriff involved, Lonnie." Ruby put her hands on her hips. "You gonna show your tail to the law?"

Lonnie huffed. "I haven't received any payment since January 30th, nor could I contact you. Those facts alone would've voided any normal rental contract even if you had had one, and the sheriff would respect that." He wiped sweat from his forearms. "Now I put your stuff in storage at the Easy Stow north of town. Paid for it outta my own pocket, thank you. And I let y'all rent most of the furniture, so I'm takin' all that for my new man-cave."

I sighed. "You're a grown man, Lonnie. Don't say man-cave."

The couch workers mumbled to one another and lifted up the couch again.

Ruby shot through her teeth, "Put. That. Down." Those worker boys did as they were told.

I rubbed my eyes, wonderin' if I was havin' some drunken fever dream. "Dammit, Lonnie, why didn't you call my daddy?" I asked. "He would've covered the rent or gotten in touch with me."

Lonnie's eyes bulged. "I didn't call your daddy cause I got tired of hearin' that old bastard's mouth, and I wasn't about to call him out of the blue, ask him for a couple thousand dollars, and have him threaten to shit down my throat again."

"If you never got the rent, then it's just sitting in our bank account. We can pay today and be done with all this. Lemme go to the bank and you can take your bulldozer elsewhere."

"Don't need your money no more." he said. "Three months' rent is little taters compared to what Automax is going to pay me for this land. I'll be sittin' pretty." He pat his belly a few times.

I pulled what remained of the offering money from my wallet and held it out to Lonnie. "This is for the storage unit and lettin' us sleep here for the night."

Lonnie sighed. "Reggie, you need to accept-"

"We've just driven from east Texas, and we are dog tired. We're stayin' the night in our home."

"I told you, Reggie, we have to finish loadin' the furniture."

I pressed the money against his tender belly. "Not tonight. We're gonna use it." He took the cash.

Lonnie counted my $97 and pocketed it. "The power company shut off the electricity weeks ago," he said, "and the water company is comin' tomorrow to do the same. And we still need to get all the furniture out so they can strip the wires and plumbin' in the mornin' for the bulldozer."

Ruby cocked her head back and laughed. "No. You're gonna get ALL of the furniture off the back of them pickups and you're gonna put all of it back in that house. Right now."

The workers stared at Ruby. None of them moved.

She raised her hands and hollered "Do I need to get ugly?"

The couch workers immediately lifted the couch back into the living room. The other workers hopped in various pickup beds and started haulin' dressers, tables and our bed back into the house.

Lonnie shook his head and spat on the porch. "We're back here at 9AM sharp. You two had better not be, or I'll call the sheriff on y'all for squattin'." He gave both of us the stink eye and walked down the porch steps.

After the workers returned the furniture and climbed back into their own pickups, Lonnie pulled his pickup by the side of the porch and rolled down his window.

"You're just like your daddy, you know that, Reggie?" he said.

I stomped to the end of that porch. "You're damn right I'm like my daddy cause if you don't get the fuck outta here I'm gonna shit down your throat."

Lonnie waved. "Have a blessed day!" He smirked and rolled out of our yard.

Ruby ran to the end of the porch, leaned over the rail and yelled, "No, YOU have a blessed day!"

Lonnie's pickup led the caravan of trucks back down the dirt road. The rumble of their diesels faded away, but I still had a dump truck and a bulldozer in my yard and a pissed off wife by my side.

We both stared at that dirt road for a time.

"Give me a minute," she said and went into the house.

Fair enough.

I walked down to the mailbox to give Ruby some space, and I found a bounty of unread mail. The goddamn post office didn't hold our mail like I had asked them to. Just another example why the government shouldn't run a business.

I flipped the various bills, newsletters, and pizza coupons until I found a firm envelope from our bank postmarked February 16th, the day after we began the tour. Inside was a brand new debit card, and according to the attached instructions, was sent to replace my expired card.

My expired card?

I pulled out my billfold and took out my debit card. Sure enough, it carried an expiration date of February 28, 2013. That particular day by the mailbox and the dump truck was May 1, 2013. No wonder the autopay didn't work. Double damn on me, how could I have let that slip by? Why didn't I check on the damn bank account every month like I had planned? Sweet hot damn. My carelessness had put Ruby in harm's way.

I went up the porch steps, ready for the chewin' out event of the century.

She was just sittin' in the middle of the living room, a space now crowded with a house's worth of furniture, but bare of any photo, memento or personal touch we had ever made in the past two years. My deerskull, my mini-fridge, Ruby's commemorative Johnny Cash memorial plate, the photos of her family and our weddin'. All of that now sat in a random storage unit.

"I shit the bed, darlin'. I'm so sorry." I could barely stand to look at her.

She stared at her fingers for a second. "This is a test," she said, and I knew what she was gonna say next. "This is a test from God." Her eyes glimmered. "Come 'ere," she said.

I sat next to her but I didn't touch. I didn't deserve to touch her right then.

"Everything happens for a reason," she said. "We were meant to return when we did. Lonnie would be tearin' down this house whether we had paid him or not, but if he had been able to call us last month, we would have cut our tour even shorter and raced back here to stop him. We wouldn't have played in Tulsa or Houston or El Paso. We wouldn't have played in that neat roadhouse in Morganton. You wouldn't have gotten locked in that rest stop bathroom."

I rolled my eyes and snorted.

"I want to be a musician, Reggie. I want to be a musician so bad." She placed her hands on my face. "I want the rush of performin' and the opportunity to create songs loved by total strangers, and I know you want all that too. I've always loved this little house in the woods, but we're comfortable here, and we could very easily fall back into old routines of treatin' music like a hobby or distraction. We've got to keep our pace. We've got to stay hungry for success. It don't come easy."

Ruby kissed me, slow and deep, like I provided the oxygen keepin' her alive. "Nevertheless," she said, "I'm still angry as shit that fatass Lonnie is gonna bulldoze our house, and I'm angry we can't do anything about it. So I'm going to go try and kill somethin'."

31

She got up and went to the slidin' glass back door. Her precious, precious ass gave me whiplash with her every pace. She opened the door and looked over her shoulder. "As long as the weapon stash is still in the backyard, I'm gonna go huntin' for a bit. When I get back, you're gonna make me laugh. Deal?"

"Yes ma'am." I said with a nod.

The glass door slid shut and I watched Ruby walk into the woods and open the steel trap door hidden in the ground. She pulled out a huntin' bow, a quiver full of arrows, a bottle of deer scent and a bright orange trucker cap. We weren't no "apocalypse" couple, but it was fun to pretend.

I sat in the livin' room, surrounded by furniture that wasn't mine anymore. Tomorrow we would be homeless. My Ruby wouldn't have a place to call her own.

I wanted a cold beer so bad, but I didn't even have electricity for my refrigerator.

SEVEN

I FOUND MY OLD FISHIN' POLE underneath the house and walked to Lake Marrowbone about a mile from the house. I untangled the line enough for a decent cast, baited the hook with some leftover hotdog and sat on an upturned plastic bucket by the lake's edge. The lure bobbed along with the calm waters of a Tennessee evenin'.

Fishin' always sorted shit out.

Tomorrow mornin', I would turn our cell phones back on, I'd call my friend Wild Bill about that drywall job at the local college, and I'd find a temporary place to stay while Ruby and I looked for a proper house. Hell yeah. Ain't a problem.

A breeze blew across the water and I thought of the night before, me standin' by that Texas pond and rejectin' God. I started to wonder if God was punishin' my blasphemy by taking away my home and threatenin' my Ruby, but I discarded the thought almost immediately. I had decided the previous night that God wasn't real, or at least He wasn't worth my time, and I couldn't blame my situation on a god I no longer took stock in. The present scenario was the result of my carelessness and Lonnie's greed. That's it. Shit happens.

And even if God really was punishin' me for no longer believin', would I really want to follow such a spiteful god anyway?

But another panic creeped into my gut, one more rooted in reality. My entire life had orbited around religion: family, friends, every damn thing. If my lack of faith got out…

I welcomed the distraction when I caught a nibble on the line. I reeled in a good-sized trout, about four or five pounds, and dropped it into a spare bucket full of lake water.

There won't nothin' to be afraid of. I'd keep my thoughts to myself and no one would know. And there won't no man in the sky ready to stick his finger up my butthole because I didn't believe anymore. I didn't need to pray for a meal cause I could catch my own fish.

❊   ❊   ❊

"Damn baby, you bit the fool outta me." I said, standin' topless before our bathroom mirror. A flashlight pointed its beam at the ceiling, illuminatin' the room with a faint glow. My mirror image told no lies; I had a deep purple bruise the size of a fist on my left shoulder.

Ruby poked her head from the shower curtain, her wet brown hair wrapped along her collarbone. "Mmm, that's what happens when you're cute. You get dealt with." She smirked and closed the curtain.

I rubbed the bruise and nodded in approval of her erotic handiwork. "We're gonna get all this mess sorted out tomorrow, darlin'. The phone, a job for me, a place to live, everything. I won't let you down again."

"We'd be losin' this house regardless of you paying the bills on time," she said from behind the curtain. "At least we didn't throw three months rent into Lonnie's pocket. Don't get me wrong, I'd rather be takin' a hot shower right now, but I'm past all that mess. Stalkin' around the woods today chilled me out. I saw an eight-point buck while I out there. Did you catch anything at the lake?"

"Yeah, a trout. Bout four or five pounds."

"Good. Show me later."

Her soapy hand rose above the curtain and her weddin' band glistened.

"It didn't matter how it happened, Ruby," I said. "I failed to provide for you."

She poked her head out again. "Reggie, I don't you need to provide for me. I ain't no helpless bird. We're in this together now. Things happen. We'll see it through."

"I know, darlin'. I'm just irritated that I got so careless."

She closed the curtain and returned to her shower. "You promised you'd make me laugh by the end of the night, and that frown of yours ain't helpin'."

A thought crossed my mind. "Let me get somethin' right quick."

I went to the van, got the fish bucket and returned to the bathroom. I lifted the bucket over the curtain and poured it into the shower.

"Fuck!" Ruby hollered. Her hands whipped against the curtain while the fish flopped around the shower floor. "It's a goddamn fish! Reggie DUNN!" She clambered through the back of the curtain with shavin' cream on her legs and punched my bruised shoulder with several sharp jabs.

"You scared me!" She yelled between laughter and punches. "I'm gonna get you, Reggie Dunn. So help me!"

I grabbed the floppin' fish and put it back in the water bucket. A slick Ruby leapt into my arms, her shavin' cream legs wrapped around my waist. "I'm gonna get you back," she whispered.

"Do your worst."

I took that woman to the livin' room couch and gave her somethin' to holler about.

I don't know why I keep bringin' up the sexy times cause they really ain't none of your business. And if I keep talkin' about our lovemakin' I'm gonna turn myself on and then I won't be able to think straight.

❁   ❁   ❁

Anything that helps get me laid deserves better than a hot skillet, so I drove back to the lake and tossed the fish back into the water. I know some of y'all were concerned about the damn fish, so there you go.

We moved some furniture around the livin' room so we could get in and out of the bed easily. Lonnie had apparently put the sheets in storage too, so we had to use our sleepin' bags and the Mexican blankets to keep us warm through the night.

Ruby asked me to pray with her before we went to sleep. We kneeled beside the bed and clasped hands.

"Dear Lord," she said, "thank you for gettin' us home after a long, delightful tour of your favorite nation. But now we're in a bind, and we are lookin' to you for guidance. Help us through this difficult time and put us where we're needed most."

She squeezed my hand tight, and I fought against the memory of a Texas campground. I couldn't lie to my Ruby. She deserved my truth, so I told it.

"Lord, I am forever indebted to you for hookin' me up with Ruby," I said. "She is a never-ending source of talent, laughter and love, and I'm a better man just for knowin' her name. She's the reason I get out of bed, sing songs or install drywall. Help me help her. That's all I want."

"In Jesus' name, amen." She said and kissed me fierce.

We climbed onto the bed and zipped one another into our sleeping bags. It took me forever to drift off, mainly cause I kept worryin' I'd accidentally admit heresy in my sleep.

❆　　❆　　❆

I had a dream where I floated off the bed, out of the house and up to the starry sky. At one point an asteroid hit me on the back of the head with a terrible hurt and I kinda woke up and asked if I was goin' into outer space, and outer space replied "Shhhhh."

So I got quiet and fell back to sleep and enjoyed the ride.

❋   ❋   ❋

That mornin', some terrible noise unleashed a deafenin' roar next to my head: "HRRRRRRRRRRRRRRRRRRRRRRRK!"

I shot up outta my sleep and immediately cracked my head against somethin' hard. I grabbed my forehead, and through the pain the only thing I could think to say was, "It's a screamin' whale!"

That whale screamed slam through my skull again: "HRRRRRRRRRRRRRRRRRRRRRRRRRRRRRRKKK!"

I opened my eyes, expectin' to see a bunch of whale teeth chompin' down on me. Instead, Ruby stood stradlin' over me, holdin' a damn truck horn over my head. I sat up in my sleepin' bag and looked around. I was outside in the middle of the yard, lyin' next to the cab of the 18-wheeler. I still had a right good bit of panic still flowin' through me, could taste my heart beatin' with every breath.

"Mornin', cutie pie!" hollered Ruby. She pulled the cord to the horn again and it roared another belch of noise. "I told you I'd get you!" She laughed and laughed.

"Har har har," I said as I dusted myself off. "I only shit my pants in terror, no big deal."

Ruby tossed the horn through the truck's open window and helped me get on my feet. "You almost woke up when I dropped your head on the porch steps. Otherwise I dragged you out here without a hitch." She did a little victory dance with her delicious hips swayin' to a silent beat.

I pinched her ass and kissed her. "Clever," I said. "I oughta throw you in the lake."

She grinned.

The early mornin' was dewy but still held a little bit of that crisp springtime air. Summer heat would obliterate that notion soon, and humidity would devour all.

"You ready to go?" I asked.

"I guess." She looked back at our first home.

"Don't seem right Lonnie just gets a free win out of this," I said.

"It's not fair."

A wonderful idea suddenly came to me. "You know, we've gotta air out all that furniture. Make sure there's no weird house smell when Lonnie takes it all for his man-cave."

Ruby turned back to me. "That's true! We owe him that much." She got a devious smile across her purdy face. The woman just couldn't stop turnin' me on.

We propped open the front door, and for the next hour we carried the couch, coffee table, dressers, love seat and bed deep into the woods behind the house. We placed every piece of furniture just as it been arranged before we had been evicted, except now the couch was wedged underneath a fallen tree. The beatniks might even have said our new setup had that Chinese energy.

"This ain't very Christian of us," she said as we put the mattress back on the bed frame.

"It won't Christian of him to kick us out, was it?"

"That's true. And we have to give the critters somewhere to sit," she said. "It's only right." She smiled somethin' devious and my oh my it made me wanna howl.

We packed up everything we owned and got into the minivan to leave. I drove to the end of the driveway so we could take one last look at our little house in the Tennessee woods.

"It was a great house," Ruby said from the passenger seat. "She deserves better than a bulldozer."

"Mmm hmm."

"You know, she needs a proper sendoff," I said.

I drove the minivan across the yard and parked right by the porch stairs. Ruby stepped out while I put a CD in the Discman connected to the van's tape deck and hit play on the appropriate track. Leadbelly's warm voice and old-timey sound provided our home's swan song with his waltz-time masterpiece *Goodnight Irene*.

Like some Cinderella story, Ruby took my hand as we walked up the stairs to the porch. We bowed to one another and then took each other close and swayed to that eighty-year old song. We danced for the memories, for the work we had put in the yard and for all the sex we'd had there. We danced for our future, cause the loss of a habitat would eventually lead to a fresh beginning elsewhere. It would never matter what kind of cabin or mansion or shanty we lived in, cause home for me would always be wherever Ruby laid her head.

I kissed my wife somethin' full, as Leadbelly sang out from the minivan speakers about how he'd rather die than live without his beloved.

That was for damn sure.

EIGHT

FUCK THE PHONE COMPANY, the water company, the power company, all of 'em. Just because I was almost three months delinquent they think they could charge late fees, credit holds, and all sorts of criminal bullshit. Okay, yes, I understood they had a point with the late charges, but I was still fuckin' mad about it. We couldn't afford utilities without wipin' out what remained of our savings, so I decided to hold off till we found some steady income and a permanent place to live.

I did catch a little break, though. Wild Bill called me back and asked if I was still interested in that drywall job for the local college, and I gave him the best "hell yeah" I could muster. He wanted me at work the next mornin'.

But we couldn't afford to rent a new place at the time, with the first and last month's rent and security deposits due upfront. Even though we had accidentally kept three months' worth of rent from Lonnie's grubby hands, it still wasn't enough to get us out of the hole. I asked Ruby if she'd be willin' to stay in the van for a few more weeks while we saved up a little more money, and she said she wouldn't play with my bird again until she had air conditionin'. I didn't blame her, though. I didn't like being touched when I was sweaty neither.

Only one person had the means to take us in while we saved up money. I figured Ruby might hate me for a while, but she'd be out of the heat, at least.

I called my daddy in the late afternoon and told him the situation.

He coughed into the phone. "Yeah, that's fine. But I ain't lettin' you sleep in the house. Then you'll get comfortable and refuse to leave. Your old room above the garage is dusty as hell, but y'all can stay there. There might be varmints livin' in the eaves, too. You've still got the key."

And he hung up.

❊   ❊   ❊

My old home was worn slam out. The one story house needed a fresh coat of paint, a new roof, and a few cats to hunt all the moles in the yard. The detached two-story garage needed a pressure washer some kind of awful. The trees by the long cracked driveway had grown over since I'd moved out some ten years prior, and the neighboring field out back hosted more weeds than soybeans. The blueberry orchard by the edge of the back woods looked healthy, though, and a few white beehives were still set up next to the half-burned down barn. I parked in front of the garage.

"I thought we were gettin' an apartment today or a hotel room. Not visitin' your daddy." Ruby said slowly.

I pat her on the knee. "I've got a job lined up tomorrow, and the money will start comin' in soon. But, uh, we can't afford a place right now."

She looked out her window and refused to respond to my touch.

"He'll behave, darlin'. I swear. This is only for a few days, and we're stayin' in the garage. We'll barely see him. Once the money rolls in, we're gone."

Ruby pointed at me. "If he gives me shit for what I eat, I'll kill him."

I smiled. "Fair enough."

41

We got out of the van and I accidentally stepped on the shattered hunks of an eight-ball. I unlocked the garage door after I gave the lock a solid kick. Besides my daddy's old blue Chevy pickup, that garage was full of half-finished projects, rusted tools, a barber's chair, and a torn-up pool table slashed by animal claws.

My parents had turned the space above the garage into a little apartment for me when I was 13. The only way in was through the wooden staircase inside the garage, though I had tried to sneak in and out with poorly made rope ladders a few times. And that squeaky garage door eliminated any chance for stealthy midnight escapes.

"Varmints!" A sharp voice shouted from the main house. Ludwell Dunn stood at his back door, a thin and powerful man in his early 60s, his skin weathered by work. He walked through the yard to the garage with two brooms in hand.

"Hey daddy," I said.

He grunted.

Ruby and Ludwell exchanged glances. "Ruby," he said.

"Ludwell," she replied.

He picked up a pool cue lyin' across the arms of the barber chair. "After you called I was gonna start cleanin' upstairs, but all I did was chase a bunch of raccoons off the pool table. They infested the damn garage. I broke the eight-ball when I threw it at 'em."

❉   ❉   ❉

Ludwell used to brag that he's weighed the same since high school, but in my youth I believed that man was a livin' titan. When I was 16, one of my high school buddies got me a pack of Camels, and I chain smoked those mother fuckers in the garage one night while listenin' to the country radio station. I wanted to up my tolerance so I could blow smoke rings and score some trim after the next high school football game.

I was on cigarette number seven when Ludwell suddenly opened the garage door and flicked on the light.

"What're you doin', boy?" he said.

42

An ashtray, a half-empty cigarette packet and a box of matches surrounded me. I had no excuse. "I'm smoking Camels, daddy."

"Camels!?" he said and closed the distance between us. "Boy, you know just as God made this earth green that this is a Marlboro house!" He took my lit cigarette, stubbed it out with his boot and grabbed the packet. I cried out once he shut the garage. I didn't know how else to land trim if I couldn't blow smoke rings.

❉   ❉   ❉

We squeezed past his Chevy and climbed the wooden stairs to the apartment. Hot damn it was stuffy. Aside from the little bathroom in the corner, there was my full-sized bed by the window facin' the driveway, a couple of couches, and a dial-operated microwave with a frayed power cord. It won't much.

Ludwell handed me a broom. "I come up here every few months to air out the room and make sure them trailer park kids haven't broken in again and huffed all my goddamn paint."

Ruby turned on the air conditioner window unit and sat on the bed. A poof of dust shot up through a sunbeam and made her cough.

"How are you, Ruby?" Ludwell asked. "What kind of crazy beatnik diet you on now?" He chuckled to himself.

"I am fine, Ludwell. Thank you." She stared out the window.

I started sweepin'. The room needed a damn good deal of care.

Ludwell set his broom down. "Reggie, come help me with the bees right quick. Gotta make sure this new queen is producin' enough brood."

"Right now?" I asked with a pile of dirt and dust at my feet.

"Come on," he said and went downstairs to the garage.

"Be right back, darlin'," I said to Ruby as I set the broom against the wall.

Ruby didn't respond.

"Are you okay?" I asked.

She turned back to me and gently slapped her legs. "Yeah, I'm okay. I'm just...this is a lot all at once, you know?" She shook her head.

"I know. I know." I struggled for some poetic lyric or insight to reinvigorate her faith in me, but I came up short. "Probably a pitcher of tea in the house."

She nodded and forced a sad smile.

"Reggie!" Ludwell yelled from the garage. "Get down here, boy!"

❈   ❈   ❈

Me and Ludwell put on bee veils and visited the hives. I stuck the nozzle of the smoker into the hive entrance and squeezed it a few times. He lifted one of the hive tops with a crow bar, and I gave the open hive another round of smoke to placate the bees for a spell.

"What've you been up to lately?" I asked.

Ludwell grunted. "Workin'. Eatin'. Sleepin'. Mess with these bees every now and then."

"You been spendin' time with anybody?"

"Naw. Ain't nobody worth seein'."

"What about the beekeeper meetings?"

"They kicked me out," Ludwell smirked.

"What the hell for?" I asked.

"You know how there's an emergency number for people to call if they've got a swarm on their property?"

"Yeah."

"It used to be Bill Skeeks' number. He'd get the call, then he'd assign somebody to take care of the problem. Well, I got the website guy to change the emergency contact to my number."

"That was enough to get you kicked out?" I asked as we started takin' out frames from the hive.

"About six months ago, I heard Lonnie Tew had called me a crazy hermit, so I started leavin' swarms of bees in that mailbox of his that's made out of a Civil War cannon. Then he'd call that number and he'd have no choice but to pay me $200 to remove my own bees. I did that three times before Bill Skeeks caught wind of it and gave me the boot."

Ludwell lifted another bee-covered frame from the hive and inspected the bees' handiwork. "Funny as hell watchin' him get mad whenever I pulled up his driveway. He hated givin' me those checks."

"I'm glad you got under his skin a little, cause all this is Lonnie's fault." I said.

"Lonnie is a goddamn snake, and I'd love to shit down his throat for five straight minutes, but he didn't fuck up your credit with a bunch of late payments. You did."

I watched the bees shuffle around the frames.

"Your momma would've scorched my ass if I blamed other people for my problems and refused to take control. Yes, it's a shit draw he evicted you like he did. But three years ago you vowed to look out for that woman and now she's sleepin' in the same room you grew up in. And it don't matter you don't have no money. Anybody can find or beg or steal enough money to get by. What does matter is that you're willin' to bleed and sweat for her and not compromise who you are because some idiot took advantage of you. Me and your momma taught you better than that."

I gave the hive another puff of smoke.

He set the top back on the hive. "Now get her out of that damn room tonight, and tomorrow mornin' you get yourself together."

When I finished with the bees, I went back to the garage, put the veil and smoker onto the pool table and found Ruby upstairs sprawled on the bed by the AC, starin' out the window.

"You wanna go get a drink at Saddles?" I asked her.

❊   ❊   ❊

Saddles was a great little honky-tonk about fifteen minutes outside of Nashville. The music was always top shelf, the taps were full of every flavor of Neptune ever invented, and the dance floor was the perfect place for hell raisin' due to the low ceilings and bad lightin'. If there won't somebody grabbin' asses or fightin' by the end of the night, then the place just won't as much fun.

Tuesday was always Open-Mic Night, and Ruby insisted on us playin' that night despite her voice being raw. "It'll give my sound more flavor," she told me on the drive there.

Once we parked the minivan amongst the dozens of pickup trucks, I started unloadin' the guitars when Ruby put her hand on my shoulder.

"Actually, I was thinkin' of goin' solo tonight, baby." Her other hand was on her guitar case. "Just wanna try somethin' different."

I said "Okay" and gave her the guitar case. I couldn't remember the last time she played alone.

"I'm gonna go sign up," she said and went into that neon honky-tonk, that knee-length skirt of hers hidin' the upper half of those long tanned legs.

I locked up the van and dropped my hand on the door. Holy hell, she might be slippin' away from me, I thought. But before I could utter a curse, my phone vibrated.

"Hey there, Reggie," said Wild Bill through the phone. "I got details about the job at the college tomorrow."

"Oh, thank fuck. Go ahead."

"Ain't happenin'."

"Okay, that's funny, Wild Bill."

"I'm serious."

I stared up at the night sky. It kept me calm.

"Yep, yep," he said. "A bunch of students are protestin' the Chinese drywall we'd be usin', cause it was manufactured through cheap labor. About fifty of 'em are sittin' in front of the work site, campin' out and playin' drums till the college buys more ethical buildin' products, so the damn school postponed everything until they figure out what to do. Ain't that some shit?"

It was hard to see the Big Dipper so close to the bright lights of the city.

Wild Bill coughed into the phone. "And of course those students organized the whole protest with their computer phones made in China by them suicidal roof jumpers. This is what happens when they don't charge enough for out of state tuition."

"Wild Bill, I need this job." I said and clonked my head against the van.

"That's just it, Reggie. I got you another gig. I got a seatbelt ticket a couple months ago but I forgot to go to court and they took my license for six months, so all next week I'll need you to drive me to and from a one-man job about forty-five minutes out of Nashville. I'll give you ten dollars and a pack of nabs."

I slapped my phone shut, and stomped the gravel parkin' lot five or six times. I needed to calm down before I vomited in rage.

I walked through the honky tonk door and emerged under the low ceilings of Saddles, eager to relax. With our funds low, I'd be drinkin' water all night.

It was a decent crowd for a Tuesday night. The young guitarist onstage sang some folksy tune about 'love is as common as the wheel', but nobody seemed to be listenin'. Amongst the riff raff, three guys I knew from various contract jobs named Nate, Robert and Johnny all stood by the bar, sippin' on tall boys. They each wore some variation of the flannel & boot combo over their prominent bellies, which had been built by countless work-day lunches at fast-food joints. Those three watched Ruby as she tuned her guitar beside the stage, but didn't seem to notice me standin' behind them.

"How about that? Ruby and Reggie must be back in town," Nate said after he sipped from his can.

"Damn, she is some kind of fine," Robert said with a low whistle. "Reggie must be earnin' somethin' big in to keep a woman like that around."

Johnny scoffed. "Bullshit. Yeah, she's a good lookin' woman, but she's mean as all hell. And Lonnie told me he evicted them just yesterday and she left Reggie right there. Apparently Reggie's credit has long since gone to hell, and she's put him in the poor house."

Nate and Robert shook their heads.

"And even if he wasn't in debt, he traded in their pickup for a damn wood grain minivan a few months back. What kind of woman could respect a man that don't drive a truck?"

Nate nodded. "That's true."

"I drive Lynette's van sometimes." said Robert.

"Well, you're a livin' joke, Robert." said Johnny. All three of them laughed. "But there's something else with Reggie. I bet he had that pickup truck just to make it look like he worked for a livin'. "

"At the end of one carpentry job, I remember Reggie sayin' he wished he could make a living out of playin' guitar and singin' country with Ruby." said Nate.

"Heard him say that too!" replied Robert. "And he always sang to himself around the job site. Once my wife brought me a thing of sweet tea from the house and I swear Reggie started singin' so he could serenade her away from me."

"See? There it is." said Johnny. "Makin' music is for Merle Haggard, George Jones, and the like. They had somethin' to say. Even somebody like Garth Brooks has his merits, even if he's about as country as a bagel. But Reggie? He don't know what it means to be country."

Johnny nodded to an oblivious Ruby across the room. "If you think about his wife, everything makes sense. She didn't take his name, she's always puttin' on airs, and she's always trying to pass off country as her genuine heritage."

Nate and Robert mumbled in agreement, and the three of 'em sipped their beer for a spell, lookin' at Ruby take the solitary stool on stage.

"I hear tell Reggie and Ruby went out west these past few weeks," said Nate.

"I'd believe it," said Robert. "Looks like Ruby got some of that desert sun on her pretty self."

"Mmm," mumbled Nate through his beer mug.

"I'll be right honest with y'all for a moment," said Johnny. "Ruby's legs look as juicy as a damn rotisserie chicken. I wanna gobble them things up."

Just as those idiots started to giggle, I spun Johnny around by the shoulders, picked him up by his cheap flannel shirt and shoved him against a wooden pillar. Nate and Robert stepped back. Johnny's weasel face grimaced until he recognized me.

48

"Well hey, Reggie!" Johnny strained out a laugh. "Didn't know you were back in town."

"Lookin' great, Reggie," said Nate. "That's a nice tan you got."

"Ruby looks healthy too." said Robert. "Uh, w-where've you and the wife been lately?"

"Been workin' out of state. It was right nice," I said without takin' my eyes off Johnny. "I coulda sworn I heard some fightin' words come out of you just now." Johnny tried to wiggle away from the pillar but I only tightened my grip. "Sounded like you compared my wife to a rotisserie chicken. Did I hear you right, Johnny?"

Johnny tried to grin. "Naw, Reggie, I ain't that cruel! I'd never compare Ruby to a rotisserie ch-"

I leaned my ear toward him and waited for him to finish.

Johnny swallowed. "A rotis...a ro..."

I looked into his beady eyes and smiled. "No, Johnny, go ahead. Say it a-goddamn-gain."

Johnny's eyes watered and he started movin' his jaw around like he was chewin' cud. Off to my right, I heard two guys laughin' like a bunch of hyenas. They were a couple of guys about my age, wearin' business suits and drinkin' blue cocktails, and they were filmin' us with their computer phones. I turned back to Johnny and let go of his shirt. His eyes were wide as a possum's when he ran out of Saddles, knockin' over a couple of tables in the process. Nate and Robert killed their beers mighty fast, nodded to me, and followed Johnny outside.

Ruby hadn't noticed the scuffle. She was smilin' and talkin' with a couple as she sat on the lone stool atop that tiny stage, her guitar across her leg. She started with one of her original songs, *Moonshine*, a fun number about a bootleggin' woman runnin' liquor in the Blue Ridge Parkway. Ruby snarled the lyrics and attacked that six-string with an aggression I'd never seen. I couldn't shake the thought that I was responsible for her change in delivery.

I heard those two business suit guys howl again. Whatever they were watchin' on their phones was killin' them with laughter. I went over to their table after one of 'em pounded their the table hard enough to make all the empty shot glasses dance.

"Excuse me, gentlemen, but did you record that conversation just now?" I asked.

The blonde guy looked away from the phone and almost shouted in joy. "Oh shit! You are the man!" He grabbed my hand and shook it. The other suit with the brown beatnik hair showed me the video of me tellin' Johnny what for.

To be fair, the recording captured Johnny's weasel qualities well, and I looked like some kind of tavern hero. I admit I grinned when I saw it.

"This is totally badass," the beatnik guy said as he took a drag off some plastic cigarette that lit up green. It smelled like strawberries.

"Here, have a drink, man." Blonde Suit said and handed me a half-drunk mug of beer. "You earned it."

I held up my hand and smiled. "Thank you fellars, but I'm on the clock. Have a good night."

"Thanks, man." said Beatnik Suit and both of 'em went to laughin' again. One of 'em yelled "FELLAR" just as I turned my back. I paused.

Now I ain't never had a problem with a person's origin. Everybody's from somewhere. And I understand how tourists might get tickled in a new land. Hell I'd probably giggle constantly if I ever went to Scotland. But I take umbrage at anyone that tours through another man's home and mocks it to his face.

I turned back to the suits. Their laughter stopped, and they both grabbed the edges of the table.

You can call it dumb luck, divine intervention, or a sudden case of lazy eye, but I glanced at the white name badge hangin' from the Beatnik's front coat pocket. I squeezed my eyes hard and leaned closer. Both of them leaned away, scared as squirrels.

Under his portrait, the Beatnik's badge read:

BEN HILLEMAN
STEAM RECORDS - NASHVILLE
ARTISTS & REPERTOIRE

I whistled and gave Ben Hilleman a slap on the shoulder.

"Glad we had a few laughs...fellers." I said. They finally breathed with a few nervous chuckles.

Why would they be at a rundown honky tonk like Saddles? It was common Nashville knowledge that all the record companies flocked to the Chickadee Cafe every Tuesday to scout for undiscovered performers and songwriters. That place usually got so crowded on Open-Mic nights you had to reserve a table a couple of weeks ahead of time.

Hilleman checked his phone. "Taxi's here." He looked to me and smirked. "You are funny, man." The Blonde Suit stood up just as Hilleman finished his beer and got to his feet.

"Are you gonna be here next Tuesday?" Hilleman asked.

"Uh, sure." I said.

Hilleman put his hand on my shoulder. "Cool, cause we're going to be back in town, and we're going to meet you here and we're going to party. You're going to take us all around this town, and we'll watch you get drunk and punch people."

I seized the opportunity. "Like at the Chickadee Cafe?"

Hilleman scoffed. "Naw, I have to go there every fucking time I come to Nashville. It's too damn crowded and everybody is so fucking serious."

I followed the two of 'em outside, and Hilleman looked around the parkin lot, gigglin' to himself. "This place," he said, "holy shit it's awesome. You've got all these big fucking pickup trucks and Jesus stickers everywhere. I always forget how fucking hilarious the South is."

"Well, do y'all wanna stick around here for a bit?" I asked. "The woman singin' right now is pretty good."

"She's hot, no doubt, man," said Hilleman as waved at the parked taxicab. "Maybe we can give her the Eiffel Tower next week." The blonde suit laughed.

If I had known what Hilleman had meant at the time, I would've kicked him in the head. "I'll buy y'all another round," I said. "Top shelf tequila. We'll have a big time."

"Next week, bud." Hilleman tipped an imaginary hat and they both climbed into the back of a Nashville taxi van. I read his record company name badge a dozen times as they got settled in their seats. "See, I told you we'd find somethin' fun!" Hilleman said to the Blonde Suit as he shut the taxi door.

Next Tuesday. Oh, next Tuesday was gonna be mighty fine.

I entered the bar just as Ruby strummed her final chord, and I whooped out a joyful holler over the spirited applause.

NINE

BY MY OWN NEGLIGENCE, I'd cast Ruby from her home to the dusty bed of my adolescence, and I had yet to come up with a new means of income. I had dropped the ball, but now I had a ghost of a chance to turn all that around.

Saddles was a genuine shit hole compared to the legendary Chickadee Cafe. That eighty-person venue is often standin' room only during Open-Mic Tuesday Nights, as country music executives frequently scout the place for undiscovered talent while everyone else wants to witness the birth of fame. Songwriters from all over America show up every week for the chance to play for their allotted four minutes, even if there's never enough time for everyone to perform. We had to visit three times before our names finally got drawn out of the ceremonial beer pitcher, and when we did get under that lone spotlight Ruby bout near clammed up. We had only committed to being musicians only a few weeks prior, and she gave a shy performance of *A Fantastic Color*. No one booed or talked ugly at the show, but she beat herself up for the longest time afterwards.

"I just forgot myself," she had said on the drive home. Her lapse in confidence inspired us to tour the hell out of America and gain experience.

But by the time I had met Ben Hilleman of Steam Records, Ruby and I had become seasoned performers, still fresh after ten weeks of non-stop playin'. We had developed the ability to charm a strange crowd, and Ruby's stage fright had vanished.

I saw no need to tell her about Steam Records' upcomin' return to Saddles, though. I didn't know if her stage fright would come rushin' back if she felt under pressure. Better to play it safe.

Back at our garage apartment, Ruby and I sat on the bed, a grin across her face. It was a damn relief to see her happy again, cause an unhappy Ruby is a heavy cross to bear. She bounced herself on the bed a few times.

"I'm glad we went out tonight," she said. "I needed it. And thanks for lettin' me play solo tonight. I just needed to prove to myself that I could do it."

I got under the covers of the bed and spooned my Ruby.

"You were a social butterfly tonight," she said. "Was that Johnny trippin' over the table when I started playin'?"

"Yeah, he had to go plug up the shit spillin' out of his mouth." I kissed her neck a few times. "Good work tonight. You were great."

She kissed my hand. "Thank you, hun. We'll play together next time."

The air conditioner in the window by the bed sputtered out and quit workin'. I hit it with my palm a couple times but it was KIA. "This damn thing is plain sorry." I opened the window beside the air conditioner and laid back down. The crickets and critters chirped through the humid night and the two of us listened to that sweet Southern night.

Ruby snuggled up to me. "You know, I was kinda upset earlier about havin' to move back in with Ludwell and this old room-"

"Oh, hadn't noticed."

She poked me with her elbow. "-but playing for those thirty-odd people tonight just got my mind right. Somethin' clicked. This air conditioner breaking down? Losin' our house? It's just a bunch of little obstacles, nothing more. We're in the Lord's hands, and there ain't no sense in worryin' about every setback, especially when there's music to make."

I stood up and pulled the chain for the ceiling fan. "I'll hold you to that tonight. No gettin' cranky when it gets hot in here."

"I'll do my best," she said as I turned out the light.

I laid awake for several minutes, unable to switch off. I got out of bed and flicked on my flashlight by the bed. I went over to the corner and opened one of those big plastic tubs in the back of the room and pulled out a bunch of relics from childhood: cassette tapes, toy tractors, and a few Ninja Turtles figures.

Yes, even a good ol' boy like me got caught up in the Turtles when I was 6 or 7. Some nights, I used to fantasize about one of the Turtles gettin' nekkid with their hot redheaded human friend April O'Neil while the rest of the Turtles grumbled on the other side of the sewer. I would writhe in bed for hours, all bothered up by my fantasies before I ever knew how to help myself out. You know, I never really thought about the turtle-on-chick action till now. Wow. April O'Neil was a goddamn freak.

Deeper inside the open plastic tub, I saw my illustrated Bible 4 Kidz, a colorful translation full of Biblical scenes and timelines detailing when and how various rulers died. The first page had been signed by my momma and daddy on Christmas Day of '94.

I had to tell Ruby I didn't believe anymore. The guilt of withholdin' important information from my best friend was eatin' holes in my stomach. I breathed deep and asked her, "Do you think people that don't believe in God are bad?"

"Not bad, no. More sad than anything. I have so many great memories of youth group trips and choir rehearsals and Easter get-togethers, so many wonderful things that wouldn't have happened if I didn't believe. And I can't imagine a world where we're just here, for no reason, and when we die we're just gone, and all of our love just disappears. Why would anyone choose to believe that?"

I cleared my throat. "Have you ever been friends with somebody that won't Christian?"

She sat up in the bed. "Preacher Hoffman says Catholics aren't Christian. But I used to work with some Catholics at the yogurt shop in high school, and they were nice. I never understood that really. I could have sworn Catholics came around long before Baptists."

"Could you be friends with someone who doesn't believe in God...at all?"

"I'd be nice, of course. But there wouldn't be much we could relate to, especially if they're always makin' fun of my faith. And if they're not willin' to consider God and Jesus, well then I don't see how a true friendship could work. A non-believer would only hurt my relationship with God, and I'm not about to put any friend before the Lord." She paused. "Why do you ask?"

Maybe I should've come clean and spilled my change of heart and saved myself from a year's worth of pain and tears and glory. Maybe I should've been honest and let Ruby find a mate worthy of her spiritual ambitions. It would have only taken a few brief declarations, and she would've left me to stew in my blasphemy forever. But the idea of not sleepin' next to her for the rest of my life made me wanna cry.

"Oh, I was just wonderin' if Johnny was saved," I said. "The thought of him roastin' in brimstone..." I suppressed a smile just as Ruby got out of bed and crawled over to me in the corner.

"That's sweet, lookin' out for him and all. And if he truly wants to be saved, he'll realize what a good man you are and come to the Lord by his own desire. I wish that's what missionaries would do, and not strong arm people into faith. But if Johnny won't respect the fact that you and I worship God, then I don't want much else to do with him, honestly."

I nodded and my stomach twisted up with every second my lie went unchallenged.

Ruby's phone vibrated on the night stand. Ruby got up and looked at her phone.

56

"Who is this?" she asked. "I don't recognize this number." She hit a button on her phone to let the call go to voicemail. She had just sat down next to me again when the phone started vibratin' again.

Ruby shot up and answered the call. "Who in the damn hell do you think you are callin' somebody in the middle of the night?" She got quiet for a second until she said, "Keith Neck? From El Paso?"

"Keith Neck? Why's he callin' so damn late?" I asked with a knit brow. Made me wish I hadn't paid off the phone company.

Ruby listened to Keith's blather. "Wait, you're in Nashville? Right now? Where are you goin'?" Ruby covered the mouthpiece on her phone and said, "He wants to stay with us."

"Huh? No way. It's too late. Tell him to go get a motel and we'll meet up tomorrow."

Ruby listened to the phone again. "Keith, how about we…You can't afford a motel?"

"Ah shit," I muttered under my breath. I knew where this was goin'. Ruby won't gonna leave Keith out in the wild in a strange town. Her heart was too big.

"Well…look," she said. "Come stay with us. We're livin' next to Reggie's daddy at the moment. The road here is swarmin' with deer. Do you have a GPS?"

She gave him Ludwell's address and hung up. "He said he'd be here in less than twenty minutes."

"He must've been jokin' about being in Nashville at 12:30 in the morning," I said. "Had to be."

"Sounded serious to me." She said. "I'm gonna get the flashlight from the van and wait by the end of the driveway." Ruby got out of bed and put on her clothes. She stopped at the top of the stairs. "Before we greet our guest, were you done talkin' about Johnny?"

I stood up and stretched. "Yeah, yeah, just tryin' to help out the poor son of a bitch."

"Well, if there is anything I'm certain of, it's that Jesus loves you, and so do I." Ruby smiled and went down the stairs.

We stood by the road for ten minutes in the thick country darkness, waitin' for a little weiner named Keith Neck. He called Ruby again when he got close, and once we saw headlights far down the road Ruby flicked on the flashlight and waved it in the air. Sure enough, Keith pulled his Toyota sedan onto the gravel driveway and put it in park with the engine still runnin' and the lights shinin' onto the garage.

The moment Keith stepped out of the car, I let him have it. "How are you gonna drive over a thousand miles without money for a motel, you dumb bastard? And why did you not confirm we were in town first? We told you in El Paso that we'd be on the road for another two weeks, and yet here you are."

Keith laughed. "Well, I knew the Lord would provide somehow, and yet here we all are. Everything worked out, didn't it?"

"Well, good job on findin' this place in the middle of the night," said Ruby. "I'm glad you're safe." Keith walked up to Ruby and hugged her tighter than expected for someone we had only met once before.

After he let go of her, he walked up to me and held out his hand for a handshake. "Hey Mister Reggie, good to see you again in the land of country music."

Yellin' at him about his stupid road trip clearly wasn't goin' to get through to him, so eased off. "So you're gonna make country music while drivin' a Toyota four-door?" I asked and shook his hand.

Keith chuckled. "Yeah, but I'll do whatever it takes, even if I have to drive a foreign car. When I get done with the world nobody's gonna care what I drove in the early days." Ruby asked him more questions about the trip: how long it took, and so on.

I could've sworn I heard a metallic click from the direction of Ludwell's house. Amongst the black shadow of the front porch there was a tiny red ember floatin' in the air. I reckoned it was a lightnin' bug when a terrific burst of fire and thunder erupted from the house and echoed across the country dark. I stood over a hunched down Ruby and pressed us both against the front of the Keith's car. Keith jumped back into his car and crammed himself into the bottom of the passenger seat.

"Best go on, now!" Ludwell hollered from the dark porch, that red ember still burnin' from the tip of his cigarette. "I've engraved my name and address on everything I own, so there ain't nothin' here worth stealin'!" He fired his shotgun into the air again, and the muzzle flash lit up his face.

I stood and held up my hands to the house. "Whoa! Whoa!" I yelled. "Daddy! It's us! Reggie Dunn!"

"Reggie, huh? Prove it! Years ago, I found you with a microscope. What had you been doing with it?" The cigarette's red ember danced as he shouted across the yard.

"Daddy, I ain't saying that in front-"

Ludwell cycled his pump action shotgun with a fresh round. That noise was unmistakable.

I threw up my hands and hollered, "Beatin' off! I was beatin' off on the microscope slides! In my bathroom!" I shouted.

Ludwell walked across the front yard to Keith's car, the shotgun barrel was hinged open and restin' on his shoulder. He spat his cigarette onto the driveway and stomped it out with his slipper. "The hell y'all doin' out here?"

"We've got a visitor," said Ruby. "Keith? It's fine now."

Keith opened the passenger door and climbed out of the Toyota. He made a little wave to Ludwell.

"How y'all gonna invite somebody to my house when you ain't run it by me? Ludwell asked quietly.

"He's an unexpected visitor," replied Ruby.

"Hmm." Ludwell looked Keith over. "Unexpected sounds mighty close to unwelcome."

"He drove straight from El Paso, Ludwell, and I'm sure he's wore slam out," said Ruby. "He caught us by surprise, too. He's here to break into the country music business."

Keith held out his hand, still shakin' from the gun blasts. "Keith Neck."

Ludwell stared at him. "You huff paint, Keith?"

Keith put his hand down. "No sir, I'm a Christian."

"Huh." Ludwell walked back to the house. "He can sleep with y'all," he said without lookin' back. "And you're gonna pay me back for wasting two shotgun shells, Keith Neck. It ain't wise to call on people in the middle of the night." He opened the front door and yelled "Welcome to Nashville" just as the door slammed behind him.

TEN

NOT TWENTY MINUTES AFTER ALL the ruckus in the driveway, Keith collapsed onto the big couch in the garage apartment and fell into a deep sleep. I was prepared to tell him not to walk around that tiny place only wearin' his boxer briefs, but he conked out fully-dressed.

Me and Ruby laid in bed, only a few feet from our guest. "That boy pushed himself hard to get here," Ruby said in the darkness.

I had to give him that. He may have had a dumbass plan, but he was hungry to achieve somethin', and he drove for a solid day to try his luck in a new town where he only knew a couple of people he'd met once. Before he fell asleep, Keith mentioned he was so jazzed up after the Sunday performance in El Paso, he spent the next day and a half writin' song after song. And you know what? With the whole heartthrob look he had, I wondered if he might actually get somewhere. His music might even be pretty good, for all I knew.

"Yeah," I said. "He's all right."

✻   ✻   ✻

I woke up early and met Ludwell in the garage as he was leavin' for work. He shook his head when I told him about Wild Bill's disappearin' job and his failure to appear in court. "Wild Bill is just plain sorry," he said.

Ludwell stopped before he climbed into his truck. "We had a temp worker quit a few days ago. Come on if you wanna earn your livin'."

My next eight hours were spent rippin' up old carpets for a massive computer lab on the southern side of Nashville, over near Murfreesboro. I pried and slashed and tore and earned my $70, while Ruby took Keith to get our belongings out of Lonnie's storage unit. The work went by quickly, but a thought flashed across my mind when I was rollin' up a few yards of worn out carpet: The memory of Keith huggin' Ruby for a little bit longer and little bit tighter than a new friend should. The thought made me chuckle, because I knew Ruby wasn't attracted to adult-sized children.

With the sweat of a Tennessee work day dried against my skin, I climbed into the truck with Ludwell. That brief moment when you climb into your truck and survey the work completed at the end of a long day was usually a blissful moment, but Ludwell hadn't rolled down the windows or turned on the air conditioner by the time I buckled up. That sharp heat bout near ate me up.

"Can we get some AC?" I said as he pulled out of the parkin' lot.

"Broke," said Ludwell.

He pulled a cigarette out of his shirt pocket and lit it with both hands, his left knee the only contact with the steering wheel while we merged onto Interstate 24. I tried to roll my window down but the handle wouldn't lower the glass. "Your window don't work," he said while he thumped cigarette ashes into one of the air vents.

"No wonder the AC don't work." I pointed to the air vent he just used as an ashtray.

"Ashtrays spill in here."

"Then I'll get you a cup with a lid."

'You see any cup holders?"

He took a drag from his cigarette and slowed the truck amongst the thick rush hour traffic.

"I don't hear you complainin' about that crack in the windshield or my broken seat belt." he said.

"Ain't my business if you torpedo through that windshield," I replied.

Ludwell scoffed. "Seat belts. Buncha liberal bullshit. My daddy never wore a seatbelt a day in his life and he lived to be ninety-five." He tapped more ashes into the air vent and suddenly honked the horn when the car in front of us refused to speed up. "Get on, now!" he yelled at a gray Honda through windshield.

"We're in the slow lane, daddy ."

Soon all traffic crept to a halt. Ludwell laid on the horn for a good five seconds before he took another deep drag from his cigarette.

"So you and Ruby toured the country, playin' music?" he asked.

"Yeah. It was pretty fun. Wish we could've kept doing it. That's how we met Keith, in El Paso."

"Huh. Thought y'all moved to Canada."

I turned to him, and waited for him to run his mouth.

"I thought y'all went up to Canada," he continued, "to have some secret baby so it would get free health care for life."

I faced back to the highway and smiled. "That sounds like me. Always lookin' for hand outs."

"But seriously, remember when your old youth pastor did that? Karl whatshisname? He took his horse-face wife and birthed some ugly kid up there. They took that country for suckers. I remember that one night them two were supposed to have dinner with us, and your momma spent a couple of hours makin' beef egg rolls, and they stood us up with nary a phone call or apology. Oh, this traffic." He rubbed the steering wheel as the cars up ahead finally started movin'.

As soon as he gained the room, Ludwell ran that truck wide open. The speedometer hit 80, 85, 90, and his old truck rattled and buzzed down the busy highway. He barely missed rammin' into the back of an 18-wheeler with a bumper sticker that read I HAUL FOR JESUS. I had little desire to have that sticker or my kneecaps rammed through my mouth.

"Damn, daddy, why are you goin' so fast?" I yelled with my hand gripped on the bar above the window. He swerved around a dump truck and caught the exit ramp off the highway.

"I wanna get home so I can relax!" he hollered. We rocketed down several more miles of road, dodgin' vehicles at unreasonable speeds until we got away from the urban sprawl and neared his house.

Once he zoomed into the garage, I expected him to bolt out of the truck and run for the commode, but he climbed out with nary a hurry or a word. He strolled across the yard like he was livin' in a postcard, unlocked the lock bolt on the back door of his house and went inside.

By the time I followed him inside the house, he'd already propped up his feet in his blue recliner and cut on the TV.

The screen door slammed behind me. "You did 90 down I-24 in rush hour traffic so you could watch the news?"

"You're welcome," He said with remote in hand.

My daddy was a piece of work. Trying to argue with him or call him out on somethin' was like fightin' a greasy goat. You couldn't ever pin him down.

I laughed to myself and sat on the couch. I hadn't been inside the main house for a few years, and most of the livin' room hadn't changed. The brown carpet, the wood panelin', the china cabinet full of lobster-themed dishes from our family vacation to Maine in '93, all of it was in its right place. In the kitchen that new microwave was still sittin' on top of the broken one, eight years later. The only additions were a flat screen TV opposite his recliner, and a new restin' place for his old acoustic guitar. That mahogany beauty hung from the wall next to my end of the couch, and I ran my fingers across the strings. Still in tune. The tone was somethin' wonderful.

"When was the last time you played?" I asked.

Ludwell muted the TV. "Been a while. Few years, I guess. I just take it down every now and then. Dust it, keep it tuned up. Your momma always liked to listen."

❖　　　❖　　　❖

My momma was a good woman and a fine mother. She loved me strong and often but she kept me in line. She would've made me eat those cigarettes if she had caught me smokin' that one night instead of Ludwell. Momma first got sick when I was eight, and she fought that disease for another decade before she passed. Doctors told her any pregnancy during cancer would be considered high-risk, so she and Ludwell decided I didn't need any siblings.

The last time I heard Ludwell play his guitar was on one of the last nights before Momma died. He strummed all her favorite songs for her, like *Get Rhythm*, *Forever and Ever Amen*, and *The River*, with both he and I sittin' on chairs by her bedside and singin' our hearts out. I held her hand throughout our performance, and the three of us had a big time.

Despite all the chemicals and radiation her body had been dragged through, Momma kept her spirits up. When Ludwell offered to drive her to the hospital after several songs, she replied, "I've been good to the Lord for my fifty years, so he'll forgive my tongue, but I ain't dyin' in no goddamn hospital."

Her last request was for *Jesus Loves Me*, and she sang as much as her strength allowed. She made Ludwell play it four times in a row, and each time I sang loud and clear.

❆   ❆   ❆

I took the guitar off the wall and held it out for Ludwell. "Give it a pick, daddy. Mock Alan Jackson like you used to."

He raised his left hand at the elbow and rubbed his fingertips with his thumb. "Naw...these've long since gone tender."

"Well let's drag them fingers across a cheese grater, get 'em tough again."

He cleared his throat with a thick bray. "I'm gonna see your momma again one day, and when I do, I'm gonna play and sing and dance with her for the next half of eternity. And I'll get as a good as Chet Atkins, cause he's gonna teach me. But till then there just ain't much worth playin'."

I brought the guitar to my lap and put my nose near the sound hole. That mahogany smelled of the sweetest lumber. "Could I play it for a while?"

Ludwell gazed at me, stern and silent.

I pressed down one last E chord and hung the guitar back on the wall hook. "I think I heard Ruby pull up." Ludwell unmuted the TV and returned his attention to the news. I walked to the back door and paused, distracted by the framed Bible verse hangin' above the light switch. In thick blue letters hand-stitched by my momma, it quoted Joshua 24:15 -

AS FOR ME AND MY HOUSE, WE WILL SERVE THE LORD.

Momma's initials and 1998 were sewn into the corner.

That one moment was the most I'd heard Ludwell talk about my momma since she had passed eleven years prior. A little part of me wanted him to interrupt my leavin' and tell me to sit back down so he could talk about Momma some more. But he started snorin', and I left him to his recliner.

ELEVEN

KEITH JOINED LUDWELL AND I on that carpet replacement job at the Murfreesboro computer lab for the rest of the week. There won't no money to be had for him, but he accepted the job as his payment for stayin' in Ludwell's garage. Keith was our gofer those days, takin' scrap to the dumpster, grabbin' tools or goin' to the store to buy Ludwell more cigarettes. At first I imagined the kid would start whinin' by 10:30, but when we needed trash removed or the crow bar from the truck, Keith would sprint to the task. His work ethic happily surprised me.

All that speedin' around just about cost him though. I had bought a new staple gun to use for the carpet paddin', and Keith wanted to contribute more to the project. He pulled the staple gun out of its plastic packagin' and examined it like he was checkin' it for ticks. "Do they pre-load these at the factory?" he asked as he looked down the business end of the staple gun.

I held out my hand and hollered "Don't point that at your fa-"

Keith squeezed the grip on the gun and an inch long staple bolted past Keith's face and launched itself into the ceiling ten feet above his head. He stared at that staple for the longest time, overcome by the act of almost blindin' himself. My first instinct was to scold his recklessness, but his obvious shock proved he had already learned why he should respect his tools.

I went over to him and said, "Yes, some of them do ship preloaded with staples. You all right?"

He nodded slowly and gave me the staple gun. "I'll just carry the carpets for a while."

I pat him on the shoulder. "I did stupid shit at 21 too. Don't worry about it."

Keith kept workin' hard after that, but he froze up after Ludwell slapped that same staple gun in his hand and told him to start gettin' the carpet paddin' down. I saw him barely holdin' that staple gun, afraid to even grip it properly. But once Ludwell went into another room, Keith came over to me and asked "Could you show me how to staple the paddin'?" He wanted back on that horse.

I taught him how to put that paddin' down and I'll be damned if he did a right good job.

❈   ❈   ❈

Ludwell's dinner table hadn't hosted a party of four in several years, and Ludwell himself was excited for the takeout meal Ruby and I had picked up, but he quickly became concerned after we prayed over the meal.

"Where's the bread?" Ludwell asked as Ruby pulled the Chinese takeout from the plastic bags.

"You don't need bread with Chinese food." Ruby said. "Rice will be your carbohydrate."

"Don't give me that beatnik talk." He said as he looked into all the plastic bags. "How's a nation of a billion people feed everybody without biscuits? Or rolls?"

Ruby, Keith and I focused on dumpin' our food cartons onto our plates. Ludwell sat there, his own carton unopened.

"What am I supposed to do with this butter, then?" He pointed to the ice cube sized hunk on his plate he had carved out for himself.

"Just put it back in the fridge." Ruby said and got to work on her General Tso's chicken.

Ludwell gruffed and poured his sesame chicken and fried rice onto his plate. He mixed a thick slice of butter into the rice and took a bite. He paused to chew, then mumbled somethin' right before he started shovelin' heaps of food into his mouth."You did a helluva job today, Keith." Ludwell said through a mouthful of fried rice. "Pretty good work."

I nodded in agreement. "Right good work, Keith."

"Thank you," said Keith. He did do a good job that day, after I taught him how to apply the right kind of force to the staple gun. He was a quick study, no doubt. Maybe there really was more to this kid.

After a minute of silent communal eatin', Ludwell asked Keith, "So you've come up to play country, huh?"

Keith nodded as he chewed.

"What makes you better than all the other wannabes in this town? Are you really that good?" Ludwell shoved more chicken down his gullet.

Keith smirked and ran his hand through his hair. "Mister Ludwell, I really am that good. And you know why? Because I merge a classic country sound with modern lyrics for today's world." Keith set his fork down and laced his fingers together, obviously delighted somebody had asked him this very question. "But besides my unique take on country, Mister Ludwell, I've played alongside my church choir on many occasions, and I've even played by myself during services. People have told me countless times how my voice filled their spirits and inspired them to follow the Lord's plan. And I've heard the recordings from those services, Mister Ludwell, and I bout near moved myself to tears my voice carried so well in the sanctuary. I've got the proof right here."

He pulled out a bunch of red plastic strips from his pocket and set them on the table. "These are flashdrives, and they've got my recordings, bio, contact info, head shots, everything. When I meet some big shot record guy, I'll have these puppies ready."

Ruby and I glanced at each other, and she rolled her eyes. The kid didn't long for confidence.

"I believe the Lord led me here to Nashville to become a musical success," Keith continued, "and ain't none of Satan's obstacles gonna stop me neither. Even some of my church friends expressed reservations about my musical ambitions. I'm gonna prove 'em all wrong, and make 'em feel stupid for never believin' in me."

"Everyone seemed to love you in El Paso," said Ruby. "I bet you've got more hometown supporters than you realize."

Keith gave a light shrug. "Some people thought I was really comin' up here to become a model."

I snickered.

"But I'm gonna prove 'em wrong," continued Keith, "with my guitar and a load of killer songs. I'm gonna hold sway over the hearts of millions or I'm gonna die tryin'. And besides the Lord's call for me to pursue music, I've quickly realized ladies love musicians. The girls at my church fight over me all the time."

Ruby smiled. "That's quite true. I'm always smitten by clever, handsome musicians." She squeezed my bicep and kissed my cheek. "That's how this one nabbed me."

"Oh, how did y'all meet?" Keith asked.

"Uuuuggggggghhh," Ludwell groaned.

Ruby flicked a grain of rice Ludwell and it landed on his shirt. He plucked it off and ate it without any fuss.

Ruby grinned like she always did when she reminisced. "Reggie and I met when a church friend of mine took me to this little midnight party in a strip mall parkin' lot, the kind of gatherin' with the lawn chairs and drinkin' and talkin' on the back of pickups. Now amongst all them people, there was one guy playin' his guitar and knockin' back Neptunes like a cow at a trough, and once I heard him lead a singalong of *Midnight Special*, I knew I needed to know more about him. He and I talked in that parkin' lot long after everyone else had left, and he gave me a quick peck at my front door just as the sun started risin'. He played it cool and drove me crazy."

I held her hand and said, "I knew what I was doin'."

Keith laughed.

She whispered in my ear, "Yeah, that next night you went down on me like a damn badger."

"You are correct," I said and smiled.

"How different in age are y'all?" Keith asked.

"Almost ten months," we both said.

"Ruby's older," I said. She pinched my nipple through my shirt.

"Oh, okay, so you like the older women?" Keith asked smilin' ear to ear.

"Heh heh, yeah, I suppose I do," I said and squeezed my darlin' person. "A ten month difference makes our relationship hot."

"Yeah, you've got that youthful zest," Ruby replied.

Keith snapped his fingers and said, "Well Ruby, if you think ten months is hot, then the eight years between you and me would be a damn volcano."

Ludwell started to laugh but coughed up a mouthful of chicken. I held a stern gaze on Keith. "Whatcha mean by that, Keith?"

Keith's smile sunk into worry. "Wait...I mean..." he stammered. "If, you know...if, uh...Ruby and I, uh...ever...dated..."

"You know, I could have sworn I was married," Ruby said and put her hand on her cheek as if she were bothered by some tough problem. "Reggie, now ain't I married?" The both of us exchanged inquisitive looks.

Keith froze like a deer caught in a two million candle power spotlight. He didn't take his eyes off me.

I suddenly laughed and Ruby laughed and Keith eased up.

Ludwell ate his coughed up food again and said, "If you're lookin' to date, Keith, I just passed 61. I'd blow your goddamn mind."

Ruby and I had a good belly laugh while Ludwell smirked to himself and Keith kept his eyes on his plate. And it was funny, you know? Keith and Ruby, together, sharin' dates and romance. The very notion was silly. Farfetched. A dadgum joke.

TWELVE

PER HIS PREDICTION, OUR CHURCH ate Keith up. He tagged along with me and Ruby throughout his first Sunday morning in Nashville, and you'd think he was a TV star. The Sunday School loved him whenever he spoke, the seniors were charmed when he called them all "sir" or "ma'am", and all the young women damn near killed over whenever he looked in their direction. I know Keith mentioned there were some in his El Paso church that wanted him to fail or somethin', but I couldn't see where that claim could have any truth, cause he had our congregation at his command.

I had to hear his little story about him being a travelin' musician about fifty times, and his face exploded with grins every time somebody praised him for his bravery or hoped to hear his music on the radio one day. Can't tell you how many grown men pat me on the shoulder and told me "That Keith Neck is a nice boy!" like I had raised him off my own tits. And Keith had those people charmed without ever playin' a note of his music. In fact, he hadn't played his music in front of me, either.

I hoped Preacher Hoffman would go off on one of his "news story" sermons where he takes some random current event and ties it back to

Jesus, no matter the subject. My personal favorite was the time he brought up a city budget debate and claimed, "If more people trusted in God, then we wouldn't NEED traffic lights! Jesus would lead the way!" The congregation loved that one. They responded to that with numerous amens and praises.

I was countin' on Preacher Hoffman to head for one of his classic detours and avoid heavier topics, but of course, Preacher Hoffman spoke about Jesus eatin' with the tax collectors and prostitutes, which led to a message focused on relationships between Christians and non-Christians. He fired off, "Only Christ was strong to venture into a dark place full of sinners and pagans and emerge unblemished!"

He quoted 2 Corinthians 6:14 and my gut turned: "Do not be yoked together with unbelievers."

My throat tightened up as he spat 2 John 1:10 and 11 with venom: "If anyone comes to you and does not bring the teaching of Christ, do not receive him into your house, and do not greet him, for the one who gives him a greeting participates in his evil deeds."

Preacher held out an open hand and shouted, "If the non-believer rejects your place as God's witness to them, what use is that friendship? Your eternal salvation shouldn't be threatened because you enjoy the company of a non-believer! Just as Matthew 18:9 tells us, it is better to gouge out your evil eye than throw your entire being into the fires of hell."

My mouth got dry, my palms started sweatin'. I hoped Ruby wouldn't have some epiphany between the sermon and my clammy left hand, but she just gently stroked my knuckles as the preacher rambled on with a growin' fury. I wondered if the preacher's topic was more than coincidence, if the universe was tellin' me somethin'. But if the universe really was talkin' to me, that means there had to be a being behind the talkin' and why wouldn't that Being call itself God if it could direct the actions of a small-time Tennessee preacher, but couldn't all that just be a convenient explanation for all of the things I'll never understand or the coincidences I can't control? I was moments away from havin' a conniption.

Meanwhile, Keith sat to my right, and some young woman passed him a note scribbled on an empty offering envelope. He wrote on the envelope and passed it back, smilin' like a loon as the Preacher warned us about the fires of an inescapable hell.

❈   ❈   ❈

On the night before the next Open Mic night at Saddles, Ruby, Keith and I gathered in Ludwell's backyard for a little music circle. Sittin' on lawn chairs with a cooler full of Neptune between us, we played our acoustic guitars by the skeeter-repellin' torches, singin' our hearts out over renditions of *The Bottle Let Me Down* and *Nine to Five*. I even taught Keith how to play *Let Your Light Shine On Me* like Blind Willie Johnson. I tried to imitate Blind Willie's gravelly vocals, but my attempt only made everyone think I was about to start coughin' blood.

All night long, those crickets chirped and the air was warm.

My world was good.

"Thank you for helpin' us out this week, Keith," I said after Ruby and I finished playin' *Are You Sure Hank Done It This Way*. "The computer lab job, runnin' errands with Ruby, everything. Appreciate it."

"You got it, Mister Reggie. Glad to help y'all for helpin' me."

"You ever hear back from any of them girls at church?" Ruby asked. "They were all about some Keith."

"Ha, well, Miss Ruby, yeah, one of them texted me a couple of pictures."

"Oh yeah? What cup size were they?" I said and Ruby smacked my shoulder. Keith made an open D chord on his guitar and shot me a shit-eatin' grin.

I gave him a thumbs-up and strummed a quick piece of *Whiskey River* before I stopped and said, "You know, Keith...you've been here almost a week and we've yet to hear one of your songs."

Keith's head snapped like a squirrel's. "Really? You wanna hear some? No one's heard my new ones yet."

"Shit, sure," I said. "Gotta try 'em out."

74

Keith leapt up, ran into the garage and came out a few seconds later with a three-ring binder in hand. "You think Mister Ludwell would want to hear? I can knock on the door again."

I looked towards the house, and the livin' room light was on beyond the closed blinds. "Naw, that's fine," I said. "He's probably eatin' his raisin bran and 'nilla ice cream about now. Best let him be."

Keith sat in his chair and set the binder out in front of him. He flipped back and forth through the pages, stoppin' every few seconds and singin' little melodies to himself before going to another page. "Okay...okay...okay..." He stared at a page for a long while. "Okay...this is called *I Am The Mountain*."

"I am the mountain!" I said. "Sounds like a song about someone that's reliable through the bullshit."

Keith strummed a downbeat number with four verses and no chorus. One verse he sang:

Innocence bred to consume
Only see the spirit of the times
Wrap them up, protect the womb
I am the mountain

Giving to fools I'll never defend
Home is never quite home again
Drilling through the earth to find my friend
I am the mountain

Ruby and I clapped once he finished. The pain was over, thankfully. Damn dreadful, that song was.

"I like..." Ruby paused and said "...your style. Never heard anything like that before." Keith looked to me for my verdict.

"Yep, yep," I said, "...I like how it...uh...how it probably sounds like what all that internet music sounds like." I expected Keith to question my meaningless bullshit, but he couldn't stop grinnin' from all the attention.

"Yeah, it's supposed to be about whatever you want." Keith almost shouted he was so excited.

"Have you ever played your songs for anyone, or been taught songwritin'?" Ruby asked.

"Nope! I'm a self taught songwriter. Here's another one called *Free Pour*. It's about a bartender and the people he serves."

"All right, this sounds more like it, now!" I said.

Ruby gave a little "Woo!"

Free Pour was another downtempo number that must've lasted over five minutes.

Good natured souls all want to be
wherever they are not
To get out of town
Or return home for good
But everyone wants out
from the den of thieves
Before their heart scabs over

Once you find the glass within the ice
Don't stop until you've escaped

I mean, goddamn.

As Keith bored the shit outta me, a shadow walked from the house and came up to the circle. Ludwell stood between Ruby and I, and he listened as Keith finished up his tune about a terminally depressed bartender.

The noise wears you down.
The noise wears you down.

Ruby and I again clapped once Keith finished, but Ludwell gave Keith the stink eye.

"Lemme get this straight," Ludwell said. "This song is about a bartender that don't like being a bartender...because?"

"Because he's sad to be workin', cause he's wearin' his body and heart out," Keith said. "I imagined what it must be like to work for-"

"Sad to be workin'? He's SAD to be workin'?" Ludwell's voice went up like someone told him to go shit in a suitcase. "If he ain't wearin' out his body every day then he ain't workin' hard enough. And what would this bartender be doin' if he weren't workin' then? Sittin' at home, watchin' TV and waitin' on a handout to reach the mailbox?"

"He's just writin' what he knows," said Ruby.

"Well, what he knows is stupid," replied Ludwell.

"He didn't write that song for you, Ludwell," she hissed back.

"He said he wants to make country music." Ludwell turned to Keith and said, "Now I ain't tryin' to be an asshole, but that song just ain't country. A man either takes pride in his work or he does somethin' about it. And goddamn, son, you're what, 16?"

"21, Mister Ludwell."

"The hell you writin' dirges for? Where's the fun? Where's the hellraisin'?"

"Well, I-"

Ludwell interrupted him. "Why do you want to make country music? Beyond the whole God's call thing."

"Because I enjoy it and I believe it's where my personal image will be best represented."

Ludwell raised his arms like a referee signalin' a touchdown, "Who gives a piss-shittin' fuck about image? Only when you're responsible for a good song will anybody even start to give a damn about your image, and it takes more than an accent and a steel guitar solo to call a song country."

Ruby rolled her eyes at Ludwell and looked to Keith. "The main thing about songwritin' is honesty," she said. "Your songs don't have to be factual, but they always need to reflect the truth as you see it. You follow?"

Keith nodded.

"That last song is about a bartender, but you never describe why's he's still workin' in a place he hates," I said. "Why does he hate it? Is he workin' to provide for his family, or is he just savin' up for video games? If you never explain where you're comin' from, how can we start to appreciate your song? I know all that internet music loves double meanings and difficult lyrics, but in country you just gotta come out and say what you mean, straight up."

Ruby leaned forward, fired up by the shop talk. "And you don't always need to involve complicated chords if your melody and message are strong. One of my favorite songs is built solely around G, A minor, and D."

Keith nodded his head every time one of us said somethin', and his focus never broke. Ruby and I fired off songwritin' tips left and right: Keep it simple; work on ideas as soon as you get them; write everything down whether it's good or bad; play in front of people as often as you can.

Ludwell looked me over. "All right, all right, I'll give Ruby credit for her advice, cause I've heard plenty of her tunes, but you're actin' like Randy Travis over here. Now Keith may have made some bullshit music, but at least he had the nuggets to play it. What do you got?"

"I've got a few songs of my own." I said.

"Yeah?"

"Yeah."

"All right, then." Ludwell crossed his arms.

I adjusted my guitar and flipped through my mind till I found my fingers in a 7th fret B chord. "One day, I wanted to write a fun drinkin' song for layabouts. It's called *Paddy Wagon*."

Before Ludwell could make some comment about me writin' a song about myself, I banged out a quick three chord bastard of the blues:

I can never drink too much
Because my liver
It knows no fear
And I will never work too much
Cause it's not worth it except for
sex and beer

But I can't understand

78

why you can't let me be
or why you never let me sleep

We're all goin' on the paddy wagon!
We're all goin' on the paddy wagon!

And in a near-monotone melody, I spat:

Make me smile
fold back my ears
And I will live a thousand years
Got no bed?
Then sleep right here!
We're all goin in the paddy wagon!

Ruby and Keith cheered once I finished, and even Ludwell gave a few claps. "Thank you, thank you," I said. "It would be fun to have a little fiddle in there, mixin' things up."

"Damn, that was pretty good, Reggie!" said Ruby. "You got any more surprises?"

I got down right bashful from my own wife and turned away for a second. "Yeah, I've got a few. Most of 'em aren't worth hearin' since they're how I cut my songwritin' teeth, simple two-chord nothings, really. A few more are worth a listen, though. One night I was listenin' to the old blues men, scarred men carved out of stone that needed the music to pull them through the bullshit. I wanted to write a folk song like they did, so I wrote this. Called *Tramping Ground*."

I quietly strummed a waltz-time tune and dragged my vocal from a mumble to a full-throated boast.

There's a man who can help me
at the trampin' ground
There's a clever beast that'll hear my plea
at the trampin' ground

I can earn my share of silver
at the trampin' ground
For the price of my lover
at the trampin' ground

I sang and wailed about a devil's deal gone sour, and I earned another round of clappin' once my Leadbelly knockoff finished.

"It ain't Robert Johnson, but you ain't half bad," Ludwell said. I thought he was about to reach out his hand for a pat on my shoulder, but he clenched his fist and crushed a skeeter on his forehead instead.

"Well, I need to talk with Reggie for a minute," said Ruby. "I think you dropped your wallet in the soybeans this afternoon." She got up, set my guitar against my chair, and led me by the hand down to the old soybean field. I checked my right front pocket with my free hand, and confirmed my wallet was right where I left it.

Ludwell got close to Keith as we left the circle. "I'm gonna get you to workin' with the bees," Ludwell said, "get you wearin' that full cotton beekeeper suit in the grand heat of the day, and I shit you not that you will find somethin' worth singin' about."

Ruby and I walked through several neglected rows of soybeans until the torch circle in the backyard was a hundred yards away. She stopped me and held my hands. "How long you been squirrellin' away songs like that? When were you gonna play them for me?"

"Been writin' about a year, maybe a little longer. And I don't have that many winners, darlin'. I've only come up with a few hours' worth of meaningless shit, songs that just ain't ready for primetime. You, on the other hand, have been makin' songs since you were 15 and it shows in every new one you write. I'm just havin' fun."

Snippets of Ludwell's rant hollered across the dark field. "...my daddy handled pesticide with his bare hands for years, and he outlived every liberal that tried to outlaw... "

Ruby slipped her hands to my rump, and her eyes shined in the Tennessee moonlight. "Well, you need to keep writin' songs, then. So we can write a song together."

I pulled her in close and lifted her up. "We've already written a box set of music together, darlin', and that box set is called 'An Anthology of Fuckin'.

She threw herself back as she laughed. "Gimme that shirt, you big bear." I set her on her feet and took off my tee-shirt. She gasped.

"What? What? Do I got a deer tick on me?" I got all concerned.

"No," she said with a breathy drama. "That bruise I gave you last week is bout near healed up. We can't leave your shoulder without a bruise. Gotta freshen that thing up!"

She tackled me at the legs and I went down like a dummy at football practice. She undid both our britches and threw 'em somewhere into the soybeans.

"You know the things about these old fields?" I asked as she laid down on top of me and sucked on my earlobe.

"Huh?"

"You gotta watch out for snakes."

A snake found her, sure enough. I did my part and she did hers. She bit my left shoulder so damn hard my hand almost went numb.

We rustled down in the plants and gave the soybeans somethin' to talk about, even if it won't none of their damn business.

THIRTEEN

ON THE DRIVE DOWN TO SADDLES that next night, Ruby thumped a quick rhythm out on the armrest and said, "A few days ago I realized it's a little silly to pursue a music career without havin' a backup plan. So I thought of going to school for music therapy. It'll take a few years, but I can use music to help people, pull them through their problems, and make a steady paycheck. What do you think?"

"Oh yeah, absolutely," I said. "Somethin' like that is worth the aggravation of school. And you know what, I'll look into trade school and study weldin' or plumbin' or somethin'. Plumbin' is a good trade, from what I hear." I wanted to add "but we might not have worry about money after tonight," but there were too many movin' parts to tease that kind of success, too many things out of my control. But I could still imagine her delight after we earned a record contract. She would dance and shout for days.

"How about you Keith?" I asked. "What's your backup plan?"

Since all the rear seats had long been taken out of the van, Keith sat cross-legged on the floor next to his and Ruby's guitar cases. "You mean if music don't work out?" he asked.

"Yeah."

"There ain't no question," he said. "Music is gonna work out for me. Never thought about anything else. People have always told me I'm handsome and I have a good voice, so I've always known I'll be somebody one day. "

"You got no other interests?" Ruby asked.

"Naw. I went to community college in El Paso until this past January, but all those general study classes felt like high school part two. And I was workin' in that car insurance place up until last week. Other than that, I don't have any experience in much else. Don't need any, no how."

I involuntarily grit my teeth as his awful songs fluttered across my brain, but we had just pulled into the Saddles parkin' lot, so I let it go. He was just bein' a kid, I thought. That ego would get popped on its own.

Before I stopped the van, I said to Ruby, "I don't wanna make a habit out of this, but I want you to play on your own again tonight."

"Really?" she asked, confused. "I thought we could try out one of your songs."

"Yeah, just one last solo show. I'll be back next time."

"Okay. You better not get lazy, though."

"That is the last thing I would do, darlin'," I said and squeezed her leg.

Once we stopped, Ruby hopped out, grabbed her guitar out from the slidin' door and took off to the front entrance. "See y'all in there," she said as she walked across the dirt lot.

"Guess I'd better see who the competition is, too." Keith said and stepped out of the van with guitar case in hand. I waited until Ruby had gone inside Saddles before I caught up to Keith between a couple of SUVs.

"Hey, wait one second," I said as he turned back toward me. "Don't play tonight."

"What?" Keith said with a single flared nostril.

"Don't play tonight. Say your throat's sore or somethin'."

"Why? I wrote a song called *Everybody Everywhere* after y'all went lookin' for your wallet in the soybean field and I wanted to test it out on an audience like you told me to do."

I scanned the parkin' lot for any sign of Ruby or a well dressed record company man. "Look, Ruby needs the stage to herself for as long as possible because there might be a guy from Steam Records here tonight."

"STEAM RECORDS!" Keith hollered.

I held out my hands in a 'whoa there' posture.

"How do you know that?" he asked quietly.

I told him about my previous meeting with Ben Hilleman, and how he told me he'd would return for a night of hellraisin'.

"Hot shit!" he shouted. "I'm on this!" His smile ran from ear to ear and he tried to march toward the front door of Saddles, but I grabbed his shoulder and pulled him back.

"Hey, tonight ain't for you." I said. "You just hopped on this music train. You and I are gonna do whatever is necessary to get them to focus on Ruby. I'm gonna keep him here as long as I can, and hopefully when this guy leaves he won't be able to imagine a world without the music of Ruby and Reggie. Besides, I'd bet he'd rather look at an attractive woman over a man like yourself."

I pointed to him when I said 'man'. He grinned when I did that. I wasn't even tempted to call him a little weiner, either.

He chewed my offer over, stared at the dirt on his sneakers for a moment and said, "You're right. I'm gonna help you and Miss Ruby get your feet in the door. She's a lot prettier than me, anyway."

Keith and I walked toward the Saddles entrance and slapped him on the shoulder. "I don't know. Those girls at church might contest that notion."

Waylon Jennings sang through the house speakers of Saddles, and the stink of dried sweat and booze foreshadowed another fine Tuesday night in my favorite little honky tonk. The regulars haunted their usual tables and perches, and Ruby sat with the other musicians waitin' their turn for ten minutes on the open-mic stage. I didn't spot Hilleman.

Keith asked, "You see him?"

I shook my head. "Give him time. Eight o'clock might be early."

Keith sat down with Ruby, and I leaned against the same pillar where I'd scared Johnny the week prior. I looked around the honky tonk and through the windows facin' the parking lot, beggin' to see our chance at glory stroll through the door. My stomach leaped for a second when a hand fell on my shoulder, and I turned to meet Mister Opportunity. It was Wild Bill instead.

"Hey there, Reggie," he said with a beer mug in hand. His thick salt and pepper beard was uneven, his trucker cap dirty, and the legs of his coveralls were torn all to hell.

"Hey, Wild Bill, lookin' good," I said as we shook hands. "Hey, if you can't drive, how'd you get here?"

"Walked."

"Damn, your house is eight miles from here."

"Yeah. A dog chased me for a couple miles. Bit me five or six times. It wouldn't have happened if I'd had a ride." Wild Bill huffed through his nose.

"Sorry to hear that," I kept watchin' the parking lot windows as Wild Bill scratched his neck.

"That's okay, you can make it up to me," he said. "I was thinkin' we could drive back towards my house tonight and go pick up that dog. I kinda wanna keep it. Can you take me?"

"We, uh, just cleaned out the van, Wild Bill."

"Oh, that's okay. Dog might not like bein' trapped in a van if we could get him. He'd probably shit all over my house, too. But have you ever seen-"

Wild Bill rambled on for a spell, but I stopped listenin' when I saw a taxi cab pull into the parkin' lot and drop off four well-dressed men. Ruby had just finished the final song of her ten-minute set, and another guy was already takin' her place on the open-mic stool.

Long haired Hilleman and his blonde buddy (I'll call him Blonde) came through the front entrance, flanked by a couple other fellars. All of 'em looked fancy in button shirts and slacks, except for one of the new guys was wearin' a big foam cowboy hat, like one you'd find at a carnival game. Hilleman saw me across the honky tonk and yelled a bunch of nonsense. The four of them came over to Wild Bill and me.

Hilleman introduced me to his new friends, but I couldn't remember their names, so I'll just call the short black haired one Slick and the goofy lookin', hat-wearin' one Cowboy. "These two are friends of ours," Hilleman said. "They're dentists from New Jersey, and they're visiting Nashville for a few days."

Slick looked around and said, "You made us come down here for this?"

Cowboy also checked out the happenings of Saddles and grimaced. 'This place doesn't look that crazy, Hilleman. It's just a bunch of hicks standing around, drinking and singing."

In any other instance, I would've shoved that cowboy hat onto that man's face and punched 'em straight in his bleached teeth. But I heard Ruby's laugh from the other side of the honky tonk, and I steered my energy to more productive areas. I had to be the happy host.

"Gentlemen, meet Wild Bill." I pat him on the back.

Wild Bill just stared at the tourists and drank from his mug.

"Why do they call you Wild Bill?" Blonde asked.

"Cause I once stabbed this guy in the cheek when he wouldn't pay up after a game of cards."

Their smiles vanished, and they all stared at Wild Bill, mouths open.

Then he said, "And sometimes I don't pay my water bill so I have to shit in the woods."

Those four howled in laughter and high fived each other.

"Let's drink!" shouted Cowboy, and the other three hollered 'YEAH!"

Blonde pointed at me as his posse leaned against the bar. "You're buying the first round, right?" He formed a gun with his thumb and pointer finger and made a "BSSH!" noise through his teeth.

"Yeah, I've got this one." I waved to the bartender, pointed at those four bozos, then gave myself the thumb. The bartender nodded and took their orders. "Be right back." I said to Hilleman.

I walked over to the musician's table by the stage and pulled Keith out of a heated discussion over the merits of boot-cut jeans. We stepped away from the pryin' ears of the waitin' musicians, but Ruby watched us from across the room. I gave her a wink before I spoke to Keith. "How many are playin' tonight?"

"Five," He said. "Ruby said it's the biggest turnout the place has had in a while. She doesn't get to play for another hour."

"All right, okay." I took $50 out of my billfold and gave the cash to Keith. "Get the lead performer to swap places with Ruby, then give each of 'em ten bucks if they'll let her play for the next hour. Tell 'em her family is in town and she wants to show off for 'em. I'll distract Ruby for a second."

Keith took the money and went back to the musician's table. I gave Ruby the 'come here' gesture with my hand, and she walked across Saddles, that body curvin' all the live long day.

"Damn darlin', you are lookin' saucy tonight," I said with a whistle. "You could wear a burlap sack and still drive a man crazy."

Ruby smiled. "Thank you, handsome. What'd you need?"

I kissed her good, then said "That's all."

She cut her eyes at me. "You up to somethin'?"

"No ma'am. I'm clean. Oh, and you sounded great just now."

She cut her eyes at me and went back to her seat. Damn her skirt gripped that ass so good.

Keith gave me a covert thumbs-up just as a foam cowboy hat flew into my face.

"Come on! Let's do shots!" Cowboy shouted.

Soon after I finished a shot of tequila with Hilleman and his lackies, Ruby took to the stage amongst the cheers of the musician's table.

"Thank y'all for lettin' me play so soon," She said into the mic. "I ain't got too much family here tonight, but I'll sing for the cutie that brought me here."

For the next hour, Ruby tore through a solo version of the setlist that she and I had honed during our tour across the US. Her vocals were a fire, a great fire, and her pickin' proved to be a deliberate joy.

Hilleman and his boys drank hard; the beer and the shots and the cocktails never stopped. After my complimentary round, Hilleman pulled out a credit card and told the bartender to keep the drinks comin'. I babysat my second beer to keep my head on straight, but it didn't make much difference. They all got toasted drunk so damn fast, my praise for Ruby got ignored, and they never shut up long enough to appreciate a lick of her music.

"Yeah, this guy is on probation with Steam Records," Blonde said as he pointed at Hilleman, "so he was assigned to Nashville to get him out of the New York scene. And before you ask, he put too many strippers on the company card."

"I also haven't landed any decent talent in the past year," Hilleman said. "But that isn't my fault. Ever since I got here, the Chickadee Cafe has always been too damn crowded with industry people to have any fun there. I mean, shit, I discovered The Yoga Mats two years ago, and made Steam a metric shit-ton of cash in the process."

"Steam needs to cut you a break," Cowboy said.

"And I don't even want to think about Nashville Broadway, rife with hacks playing in every damn bar on a Monday afternoon. Jesus, that street is so fucking desperate."

Before more drunken ramblin' could commence, I changed the subject. "How do y'all like the music here?"

"Eh, it's all right," Hilleman said without even lookin' at Ruby. "So I bet you're a Republican. Tell me about that."

"Nope," I said with a forced grin, tryin' to make light of his assumption. "That ain't me at all. I don't care for political labels, myself. So long as people ain't hurtin' or threatenin' one another, then their business is their business." I chuckled and added, "I can even appreciate a lot of-"

Those four fellars cheered over my talkin' right when a waitress brought over another tray of shots and beers, and they sloshed down it all down hard. None of them asked me to continue, nor did I attempt to do so.

Seconds later, they all started askin' me stupid questions. I put on a brave face for my woman, and I played the good sport as they laughed harder and harder.

"Hey! How many people here actually finished high school?"

"Are you still upset about the War of Northern Aggression?"

"How can you live on fifteen dollars an hour?"

"Why can't Southern people drive in the snow? There's a quarter inch of snow on the road and you all turn into idiots."

I ignored that last part and said, "Almost everyone drives on summer tires cause it only snows like that every few-"

Hilleman stood up and said, "We should just hack the South off of the rest of the country so we don't have to deal with them anymore. And then they can take all their backwards, religious shit down to Cuba."

His friends laughed and highfived each other as Hilleman mimed a handsaw cuttin' through the table. "ERK! ERK! ERK! ERK!" Hilleman made his own sound effects.

I let a lot of shit slide that night, and I passed it off like it was all a laugh. By that point, Ruby had played for nearly an hour, and none of them had said word one about her. I felt like a pushover and a goddamn slimeball.

Wild Bill had fallen asleep at the table beside ours, his face pressed against the sticky table top. Hilleman leaned toward him and asked, "Is he dead?"

Slick neared Wild Bill and poked him in the ribs a few times. Wild Bill didn't budge.

Slick yelled "I think he's dead!"

Goddamn those four laughed and laughed. Cowboy banged his table with a fist and made all the glasses jump.

I shook Wild Bill's shoulder until he snapped up and shouted "Whotheytryintobe?" in a hot sweat.

Of course them boys exploded into more hysterics. Drunken spittle flew out of Hilleman's mouth onto the table.

Ruby began *A Fantastic Color*, the song that typically ended our set. She had four more minutes to land an impression on Hilleman.

They finally calmed down once Wild Bill went to the can. Blonde flicked his tongue in and out of his mouth like a lizard as he tamed his laughter. I wiped my mouth with a napkin and set my hands on the table top, but I had no laughter to tame. My patience was runnin' low.

Hilleman looked at me with glossy eyes. "So...I bet you like NASCAR."

With all the stone cold in my bones, I looked him in the eyes and replied, "Fuck you."

They melted down into laughter so hard that Hilleman shoved Slick off his seat, and that fool kept on laughin' after he cracked against the scuffed wood floor.

Record company or no, I was sick of their shit. I stood up, ready to flip that damn table. Just cause you're drunk don't give you permission to be an asshole.

Not three seconds before I was gonna drag Hilleman by the collar over to the stage, Keith sat in Wild Bill's former seat and slapped Hilleman on the back.

"Say fellas, y'all are havin' a big time over here." Keith said in an exaggerated Southern twang.

Slick shouted a "Woo!" in reply.

"Well, if y'all were tryin' add more to your evenin'," Keith continued, "may I suggest the gal on stage."

They watched Ruby knock out the second verse of her tune, her eyes closed and lost in truth. While the suits watched her, Keith waved to the bartender, who brought over a tray of whiskey shots for the four of them.

"Yeah, I remember her," said Hilleman. "She's pretty hot. What about her?"

"That's Miss Ruby Naris, some of the local talent."

"And my wife," I said.

Hilleman's face twisted like he'd just smelled pig hocky. "Eh, ew, no. We're trying to clown around tonight."

Keith put his arm around Hilleman. "Oh, that ain't no worry. I bet if you talked sweet to her, I bet Mister Reggie wouldn't mind swappin' her with you for a bit."

My blood turned into nuclear waste. My fists clenched. Visions of terrible, unhinged violence passed through me. But Keith looked at me and mouthed 'sorry' as Hilleman and his gang oogled my wife. High octane rushed through my body, but Keith had succeeded in one minute where I had failed for an hour.

"You know how you can get her to like you?" Keith asked. "Tell her you're with Steam Records, show her your work ID, then tell her you'll need a private audition to see if she's worth recordin'."

Hilleman shook his head and slurred, "I've tried that, doesn't work as well as you'd think."

"Give it a try on this one," Keith said. "You never know."

And in a moment of fateful timing, Ruby stopped strummin' her guitar and sang the final chorus of *A Fantastic Color* acapella. Her voice swelled and dipped and lent that soggy honky tonk a beauty reserved for more precious atmospheres. Hilleman listened with his mouth open, as if Ruby had discovered a long-lost chord.

"Holy shit," Cowboy said as Saddles erupted into applause after Ruby finished. The foursome all clapped along.

Hilleman nodded. "I have to bang her."

"Me too," said Blonde.

I shot up and felt like slammin' their faces with a slidin' glass door, but I walked behind Keith as he put his arms around Hilleman and brought him to meet Ruby by the side of the stage. I stood by Ruby's side, a buffer to any more interference. Keith introduced Hilleman to Ruby, and they shook hands. The silence provided by the changing of open-mic performers let me hear every drunken slop of Hilleman's tongue.

Hilleman eyed her over without any attempt at stealth. "You have a great voice, and...uh...great calf structure," Hilleman said as he swayed in place.

"Thank you very much!" Ruby said.

"Tell me Ruby, do you have a recording contract?" Hilleman asked.

"No, I don't," she said.

"Do you want one?" He pulled his work ID away from the clip on his jacket and held it to Ruby's eyes.

Her face sparkled. "You're from Steam Records?"

Hilleman let the drawstring pull his ID back to his belt clip. "Yes," he replied. "Ben Hilleman, A&R extraordinaire."

She beamed at me for a split second, but quickly contained her energy and played it like a sexy sexy sexy sexy professional. "Okay, that sounds great, yes."

"All right, I will need you for an audition tonight so we-"

"Tomorrow," I said loud and clear.

"I'm busy tomorrow," Hilleman said, "so it's now or never. An audition tonight would determine-"

"You'll have the audition tomorrow morning," I said. "Downtown, at the Steam Records office."

Ruby looked puzzled. "I just played for an hour, Mister Hilleman. Why do I need to play again tonight?"

"The acoustics in this place are spotty, so we need to hear you somewhere small and isolated from this crowd." Hilleman replied. "So yeah, let's audition tonight and sign the papers tomorrow."

Keith leaned between Ruby and Hilleman. "You should call your receptionist, Mister Hilleman, and let her make that appointment."

With the back of his head to Ruby, Keith winked at Hilleman, and Hilleman's intoxicated brain took a few extra seconds to grasp the ruse.

"Ah, yes! I need to call Meghan and tell her to schedule an appointment." Hilleman pulled out a computer phone from his coat pocket and started mashin' the screen. "All right, one sec, okay it's ringing." He put the phone to his ear, but Keith took it from him and looked at the screen.

"Okay, we're not tryin' to call Google Maps," Keith said as he messed with the phone. Hilleman snatched for his phone but Keith turned away from his hand and said "Nope. I'm tryin' to help you land some talent, remember? You just keep havin' a good time."

Hilleman adjusted his jacket and winked at Ruby with both of his eyes. His head drooped, his body swayed, and his skin was all sweaty, but to his credit he kept tryin' to put out the vibe.

Keith announced "Here we go, I'm callin' your receptionist Meghan." He held out the phone between the suit and Ruby, and gave a light swat to Hilleman's chest. They both snickered.

And I'll be damned if Keith didn't call somebody. The screen read:

NASHVILLE

STEAM RECEPTION

(MEGHAN)

CONNECTED

I barely heard the beep used at the start of voicemail recordings, then Keith pointed at our guest. Hilleman suddenly yelled, "Hey Meghan, you fucking fox! This is Ben Hilleman! I've got some game-changing talent coming in tomorrow, and I need you to-" Hilleman giggled "-cancel that 9AM appointment with Randolph Suggs!" Hilleman swung his arms like an umpire signalin' 'safe'. "Did you write that down? Cancel Suggs! Fuck his comeback! We've got talent to acquire, and we're gonna give her a pearl necklace!" He nearly killed over laughin' after that one. "We're going to have, uh..." Hilleman pointed at Ruby.

"Ruby Naris!" she said.

"And Keith Neck!" Keith yelled.

"And Reggie Dunn!" I hollered.

"Yeah!" Hilleman said. "The whole gang will be there. Loads of new talent tomorrow at 9AM. We're gonna get the pussy, then we're gonna talk to the pussy. You got all that, Meghan? You long-legged fuck demon?"

Keith ended the call and slapped the phone into Hilleman's hand. "All done. Thank you, sir!"

Ruby shook Hilleman's hand with vigor. "Thank you so much for this opportunity, Mister Hilleman! I'll be there tomorrow, 9AM sharp!" Ruby was glee incarnate.

Hilleman smirked at Ruby. "Yes, of course, of course, everyone will know you after tomorrow. But right now, you and I need to find a corner and-"

I stepped between the two of them. "You and your boys need a taxi so you can hit the next drinkin' hole, don't you? Keith, could you call them a ride, please? The taxi number is above the cash register at the bar."

Keith nodded and walked to the bar to fetch the taxi info. Hilleman tried to step around me toward Ruby but tumbled and collapsed onto an empty table.

"Ain't no time for nappin'." I said as I lifted Hilleman by the collar of his jacket and got him back on his feet. "You've got plenty world-shakin' to do before tonight is over. Come on, follow me." Hilleman reached over my shoulder and tried to stroke Ruby's hair, but I shoved his hand into his jacket pocket instead.

I led the suit and his buddies to the bar, where they settled their tabs with drunken scrawls. By the time I had convinced them to tip forty dollars apiece, the taxi had pulled up outside. Keith, Ruby and I escorted them out of Saddles and into the back of the taxi van.

"Guy in the gray suit is payin'," I told the driver. "Take 'em some place nice downtown." Hilleman reached for Ruby from inside the van and said, "Can I suck on your-" but I shut the slidin' door before he could finish, and seconds later that taxi was down the highway.

The three of us hooted and hollered joyful nonsense into the night. Ruby leapt into my arms and kissed me time and time and time again. "Did you know they'd be here tonight?" Ruby asked.

I nodded.

She threw her head back and sighed. "Oh, I'm SO glad you didn't tell me. I would've been a nervous wreck."

I set Ruby down and shook Keith's hand. "Great job, Keith. That was some smooth shit with the phone. Just don't offer to swap my wife anymore, aight?"

His eyes teared up as he smiled. "You got it."

*　　*　　*

And before you ask, yes, we drove Wild Bill home, and no, we didn't go lookin' for that dog.

FOURTEEN

STEAM RECORDS OCCUPIED THE TOP FLOOR of a nine-story office building in downtown Nashville, and from the moment I stepped off the elevator I bout near wanted to giggle. All sorts of framed posters and gold records and flyers from legendary country concerts were scattered all over the walls of the reception area, with a big steel version of Steam's logo - A profile of music notes ridin' up a conveyor belt - hangin' behind the wooden reception desk.

"Hello, can I help you?" asked the redheaded receptionist.

"Yes, you can," said Ruby as we approached the desk with guitar cases in hand. "You're Meghan, right?"

Meghan the receptionist nodded.

"Hi Meghan, I'm Ruby Naris, and this is my husband Reggie Dunn and our friend Keith Neck, and we have a 9AM audition with Mister Hilleman."

Meghan chuckled. "Oh, so you're the talent today! He hasn't come in yet, so please have a seat until he arrives."

We had just turned to sit down when a guy in sunglasses stepped out of an elevator and walked through the fancy glass doors of the

Steam Records lobby. His suit was terribly stained, as if he had slept in a grease pit all night.

"Meghan, I know I'm late for Suggs. I'll be in there in ten minutes." Hilleman said with his head low, walkin' towards a hallway beyond reception.

"Good morning to you as well, Ben," Meghan said. "Your 9 o'clock is here."

"I know, he's in the conference room, waiting for his geriatric comeback," Hilleman grumbled. "Do me a favor and ask him not to kill himself before the meeting."

"No," said Meghan. "Your new 9 o' clock is standing right here."

He looked at the three of us and froze. "Oh shit," Hilleman said. "Oh shit on me." He approached the reception desk and took off his sunglasses. "You're...actually...here." He looked me up and down with bloodshot eyes.

"Yes sir, Mister Hilleman! 9AM sharp, like you said," Ruby replied.

Hilleman leaned over the desk and whispered to Meghan, "Call the security guy downstairs and get them out of here."

Meghan pushed his face away with her pointer finger and said, "I am not kicking out your 9 o' clock appointment. And you had a lot of other people sitting in on that meeting."

"You cancelled our meeting with Suggs?" asked a strong voice from the hallway. A short, older man in a navy suit stepped next to Hilleman. He looked like a bossman if I had ever seen one: stocky and a little gruff. "I'm sure our dedicated, hardworking Ben Hilleman has a great reason for canceling a meeting with the nearest thing this company has to a guaranteed win," the Bossman said.

"Don't worry, sir, we've been scheduled to meet with Suggs for weeks," Hilleman replied. "Meghan, please consult my schedule and tell Mister Riddle that the meeting with Suggs is still on for 9AM today." Hilleman looked to Bossman Riddle and said, "He simply hasn't arrived yet."

Meghan read her computer screen. "The schedule reads: 9AM, Ruby Naris, Keith Neck, Reggie Dunn, talent acquisition. Your original appointment with Suggs was cancelled by your voicemail request."

"I didn't request that," Hilleman scoffed.

Meghan activated her speaker phone and replayed the voicemail from the night before. She rolled her eyes after she was called 'a fucking fox', and Hilleman buried his face into his hands when he heard himself tell Meghan to cancel the appointment with Suggs. Ruby and I exchanged a little high five when we heard our recorded selves. Meghan cackled when Hilleman's drunken self christened her a 'long-legged sex-demon'.

"You wish," she said.

Bossman Riddle faked a smile and turned to us. "Excuse us, folks." He tapped Hilleman's shoulder and pointed him to the closest door off the main hallway. Hilleman obeyed, and the two of them entered that room. Once inside, Bossman slammed the door.

The door must've been pretty thin, as I barely heard Bossman say, "Start talking."

Silence, then Hilleman said somethin' about "a bar last night."

"Actually, you know what? Shut up," said Bossman. "I'm tired of giving your horseshit the time of day. You were already this close to being blacklisted from what's left of this industry, and now you've thrown away a meeting with a platinum-selling artist for some local roughnecks. Who are they, anyway?"

Hilleman mumbled.

"Have they sent us demos?" Bossman asked.

Silence.

"Do they have some buzz going around?"

More silence.

"Any buzz at all?" Bossman's tone turned sharp. "Did you meet them last night?"

Hilleman mumbled again.

Bossman laughed. "We're still going to have that meeting with those people, and do you know why?

Hilleman paused, then said "Because maybe they'll say something racist and it'll be funny?"

98

"Fucking Christ," Bossman replied. "You scheduled a meeting, and we're going to have one. You're going to lead it, and you're going to provide constructive feedback. By the time you are finished wasting everyone's morning, Meghan will hopefully have convinced Suggs to come in later if he hasn't already jumped off the Shelby Street Bridge! You haven't done any decent work in many fucking moons, Hilleman, and you better pray that you found a diamond last night in that pile of shit you call a career, or you're fired. Today!"

Bossman stepped out of the room with a warm smile. "So which of you folks came here to play for us, huh?"

❊   ❊   ❊

Ruby paced across the small empty office. "Tell me I'm good."

"You're great," I said.

"Tell me I'm confident."

"You're a natural."

"Tell me something funny."

"I'm diggin' these open-toe boots of yours. Pretty sure I want to make love to your feet."

Ruby laughed and wiped away a tear.

"That's not a joke," I said.

Ruby and I were across the hall from the conference room where we'd have our audition. She had told Bossman Riddle we needed to tune our guitars before we played. Not true.

"Darlin', this won't be no different than all the other times we've played for people."

"This one counts, Reggie. The future could hinge on one wrong note. You heard them out there, they expect us to fail like we're some backwater fools."

I held her shoulders. "Lemme tell you somethin'. Tomorrow, that sun is gonna rise, with or without our names on some fancy contract. Besides, we're ahead of the curve, anyway. We haven't recorded a damn thing yet and already we're about to play for Steam Records. Steam titty-fucking Records, Ruby. I've already run out of ways to say

99

hot damn. Worst case scenario is they don't sign us. If so, we learn from our mistakes and we carry on."

I gently rubbed my thumbs under eyes and wiped the tears from her cheeks.

She grabbed my hand, pressed her forehead against mine and closed her eyes. "Dear Lord, this is it. Please be with me and Reggie as we play for the generous people of Steam Records. Lord, you know what lies in our hearts. This might sound like pride or vanity, but I want this, Lord, and I know Reggie does too. We want to showcase the talent you've given us and share it with the world, and we promise with our eternal souls that we will glorify you every step of the way. But if that ain't your plan, we'll accept that and praise you for all our days. In Jesus' name, amen."

"Amen," I whispered as I kissed her. "Now let's go get ours."

❋   ❋   ❋

Sunlight filled that ninth story conference room with a mornin' glow, and I felt humbled to stand within the Nashville skyline. Hilleman didn't share my wonder, since he was more concerned about loadin' up his electronic cigarette with the green light at the end. He and the three other Steam representatives sat at the end of a long conference table next to a small open space at the front of the room. Aside from Hilleman, there was Bossman Riddle, and a right purdy business woman with long black hair, and a plaid wearin' fellar in his 30s that resembled a heavy-set Willie Nelson, as if smokin' all that cheeba finally made him binge on a truckload of cheese doodles. Keith sat close to Bossman, the two of them havin' a quiet conversation. Keith handed him one of his red flash drives, and asked him to "check out my modern country sound." Bossman grinned and pocketed it.

Ruby and I walked to the open space before the table, guitars strapped round our necks and at the ready.

Bossman stood up once he noticed Ruby and I. "Come in, come in. Well, everyone, Randolph Suggs will definitely be in later today, but in the meantime, Hilleman has arranged a special presentation of new

100

talent that simply cannot wait." Bossman sat down and looked to Hilleman as he muttered, "Turn off that damn e-cigarette. It smells like a farmer's market."

Hilleman sighed as he put his plastic cigarette in his coat pocket and looked up to the overweight, plaid wearin' Willie Nelson guy. "This is Hoover Uzzell, creative consultant. He produces a lot of our albums. Most of them have gone platinum."

Hoover made a quick wave to Ruby and I.

Hilleman squeezed his forehead. "And that's Erin Villeda. She's another A&R rep."

All seventy-two inches of Erin Villeda stood up in her fancy suit jacket and pencil skirt getup, her eyes level with mine. "I'm pleased to meet you all," she said, "even if my valuable time would be better utilized elsewhere." She shot Hilleman the bird and sat down. Hilleman half-assed a jerkin' off motion.

Now I'm a dedicated husband, but as I stood in that conference room I suddenly imagined Ruby and Villeda sharin' carnal pleasures in a barn full of hay. I don't know why a barn full of hay. Maybe they had been balin' for winter and they needed a break so they wondered how fast they could finger each other and then one started gushin' and other just had to keep from gettin' the hay wet so they both face dived into-

"Let's get started." Bossman's words cut through my wonderful thought. "Miss Naris, the floor is yours." He gestured to the open space at the front of the room. I felt ready to rumble, but Ruby looked tense, her smile miles away. Villeda pulled out a computer phone and pointed the lens at Ruby. "Introduce yourself, please." Villeda said.

Ruby rubbed her forehead. "I'm Ruby Naris. From Nashville...born in, uh, North Carolina...I like to sing, cook, and hunt."

Hilleman snickered after she said 'hunt', and said "HUUUHHHH-NNNNNNNT" in a drawn out Southern accent. In any other circumstance, Ruby would've tried to sock him in the mouth for laughin' at her, but she just clammed up like she was at the Chickadee Cafe again. Her eyes watered, and she swallowed a few times, and she squeezed the strings against the fret board with all her might. My Ruby won't right. She had to loosen up immediately.

Hilleman groaned and said "Let's get this goose chase started, please. We need to discuss my severance."

I laughed and pointed at Hilleman. "Have any of y'all actually ever chased a goose? They're crafty. One time my daddy got it in his head that we were gonna have a Christmas goose for our holiday supper. He went to Lake Marrowbone and cornered one of 'em, but the rest of the flock snuck up behind my daddy and goosed his ass over and over like he was on an assembly line."

Everyone turned to me while Hoover laughed. I gave Ruby a wink, and she smiled while the staff considered me the fool.

Ruby took a deep breath and held her head high. "I know y'all think we're a joke," she said. "I know you're only giving us this time because Mister Hilleman messed up some big meeting and you want him to look stupid. But we're the real deal, and you're gonna love us."

I picked off the opening licks of *A Fantastic Color* as Ruby strummed the rhythm, but Bossman stood up and shouted over the music before she ever started singin'. "Whoa, whoa whoa, hold on," he said. "You're a duet?"

Ruby and I both nodded.

Bossman Riddle turned to Hilleman. "Okay, granted, I was pretty tanked last night, but she played solo," Hilleman said. "I'm fairly sure she was pretty good on her own."

Bossman closed his eyes, took a deep breath, then looked back to me and said, "Mister Dunn, could you have a seat please?"

I chuckled again. "Thanks, but I sing best on my feet."

"Please, Mister Dunn," he insisted. "If our rep recommended a solo artist, then we need to hear Miss Naris on her own. We need to make sure his scouting skills are up to snuff." Bossman turned to Hilleman and gave him the stink eye.

Ruby looked like she might get upset enough to say somethin', but I nodded to her and gave her a thumbs up.

"Bet they just wanna hear us one at a time to start off," I whispered as I walked toward an open seat. I propped my guitar's neck against the table and sat down next to Hoover, who held one of Keith's red flashdrives in his hand. Keith shot me a brief smile from the other side of the table, then turned back to Ruby.

My turn will come up, I told myself. I had to let Ruby get her foot in the door. Then I could come in and do some hellraisin' of my own.

Ruby put her fingers back on her guitar and closed her eyes as her music overtook the room. There never had nor will there ever be a stronger rendition of *A Fantastic Color* than the one Ruby performed for those record people. She landed every note and delivered that final, acapella chorus with everything she knew.

They loved her.

Bossman stood and clapped.

Villeda cheered.

Hoover nodded with his applause.

Even Hilleman smiled once he saw everyone's reaction.

Bossman left the room and yelled "Meghan! Come in here. You need to hear this!" Meghan entered the conference room and Ruby played another original song by Bossman's request. Ruby almost couldn't hit the high notes of *Moonshine* since she couldn't stop smilin'. Bossman slapped Hilleman on the back after she finished.

Those record people praised my Ruby with the glory she deserved, and she stood at the end of that conference table, her smilin' lips wet with tears, her guitar glintin' in the morning sun.

"Stupendous, Miss Naris!" yelled Bossman.

"Did you write those songs?" asked Villeda.

"Yes, I did," Ruby replied.

"And the biggest crowd you've performed for?" asked Bossman.

"A congregation of around two hundred."

Bossman and Villeda leaned toward the center of the table for a second and conspired while Hilleman giggled to himself like a loon. Hoover wrote in a notebook on the table.

"She's beautiful and talented. She could be a late 20s Taylor Swift," Villeda said to Bossman.

"Or a country Adele," he replied. "She's definitely something."

Bossman got up and walked to the front of the room. "Ruby, it wasn't dumb luck that brought you here today, nor was it due to the flagging work ethic of Mister Hilleman. Rather, something greater has delivered you to our attention. You are a good performer, Ruby, but we can make you great." He held out his hand. "Will you become a Steam recording artist?"

Ruby squeaked and shook Bossman's hand as the applause restarted.

"Well, that was unexpected," Bossman said to Hilleman. "Good job."

Hilleman pumped his fist in the air and walked over to Ruby to shake her hand.

"Ruby," Bossman said, "I'd like you to follow me so we can sign a few documents and brainstorm on how to best present your personal story. I'll see everyone else at the meeting with Suggs. 11AM, right, Meghan?"

"Yes sir," Meghan replied as she and Villeda followed Bossman towards the exit.

"Whoa, whoa, hold on," I said out loud. "You ain't heard me yet."

Bossman paused by the door. "Mister, uh..."

"Dunn," I said.

"Mister Dunn, we will be spending what's left of our small discretionary budget on developing the artistic brand of your wife. I'd say this serendipitous meeting has already gone exceedingly well for you and yours."

I got to my feet. "I'm Ruby's guitarist, and I'm a songwriter myself. Me and her make honest music together. We're a package deal."

"Well, we need to build Ruby's new career one step at a time." Bossman looked at his watch. "If you'll have a seat in the lobby, we'll be finished in about half an hour. Thank you for coming along."

I grabbed my guitar and immediately bust into *Paddy Wagon*, poundin' the barre chords as hard as I could.

Hilleman threw his hands up and yelled "Stop! Stop!" before I'd finished singin' the first line. I stopped playing and he said "Please stop. You were a hilarious drinking buddy last night, and thank you for driving Ruby here, but even you've got to recognize that you don't fit any kind of image we promote for our country artists."

Bossman nodded. "That's true. You're on the beefy side, Mister Dunn."

"Beefy?" I said. "I might have a little pooch in the middle, but these calloused hands were forged out of workin' for most of my 29 years, and there ain't nothin' more country than hard work."

"I agree, Mister Dunn." said Bossman. "Country music prides itself on certain virtues, and you certainly embody many of those virtues. You are the very type of person we aim to entertain."

"Exactly. That's why you need authentic stock like me in your stable. I know how it is for workin' folks, and I have a unique perspective y'all can't get from nine stories up. Anything else would result in fake, plastic music, and nobody's gonna buy that shit."

Hilleman rolled his tongue around the inside of a smirk and took slow, careful steps toward me. "Do you like pickup trucks?" he asked.

"Of course," I said.

"Is America the greatest nation on the Earth?"

"Never seen proof statin' otherwise."

"And why's that?" Hilleman asked.

"Cause I'm free to be who I want to be," I replied.

"I know you like telling stories about the good ol' days."

"Heh heh, I guess I do."

"And I know you like workin' hard."

"Damn right."

"And do you love Jesus?"

The air slipped out of my throat, but I didn't dare look to Ruby. Even a microsecond of delay would've planted a terrible seed.

"Yes." I swallowed hard.

Hilleman leaned on the chair closed to me. "We know all of that already. We've known it for decades. The Southern man, how can I put this... has a more limited range of interests and beliefs, and thus can easily be appealed to. He's a simple man."

I squeezed the guitar neck white knuckle tight, tryin' my best to ignore his offense and get on with this audition.

"In fact," he continued, "very few of Steam's country songwriters have ever performed full-time blue collar work. You know the song *It's About Time For a Kick in The Mouth*?"

"Hell yeah," I said. "That one sounds appropriate right now."

Hilleman smirked. "The four guys who wrote it used to work in banking in Delaware. They all moved down here years ago when they discovered how easy it is to fart out a pop song, add some steel guitar twang and call it country music. The singer of that song, Charlie Chestnut, is one of the quietest, gentlest people I've ever met, but he looks like a half-drunk hick ready to fistfight over a parking spot. He didn't write that song, but Charlie Chestnut performs it like he did, and that's why it sold over a million copies last year. And we've released hundreds of songs just like that over the years. Understanding the target audience is a valuable thing."

Hilleman looked me dead in the eyes. "The overwhelming majority of modern country stars are simply attractive people that know how to sing. They don't write their own music. There are teams of songwriters that tell them to sing about high school love or drinking in a bar or being a proud American. Because we choose the right image, country fans eat up every redneck cliché we throw at them, over and over and over again.

"You are a well-researched demographic and nothing more. I will never need to know you in order to sell to you. You've been gleefully devouring so-called plastic music all your life, Reggie. The sad thing is you never noticed."

We stared into one another. A lesser man would've gone toe-to-toe, but my own talent needed to shine this fool down. I adjusted my guitar and banged out the chords to *Paddy Wagon* again and sang that second verse straight into his face. But I didn't even make it to the pre-chorus because a hand came from beside me and mashed itself against the fret board. My chords thudded into a mess.

"Reggie," Ruby whispered into my ear. Her hand stayed on the fret board.

I stopped playin'.

"We've done so well today," she said.

"I don't sing plastic music, Ruby." I kept my eyes on Hilleman. "And I ain't no simple man."

She leaned in closer. "Please don't do this." She took her fingers off the fret board and stroked my cheek.

I turned to my smiling darlin', and I wanted to keep her tears away with all of my heart. "I'm better than that bullshit," I whispered to her. "You know it."

"Please, Reggie," she whispered back.

I looked away from her and took my hands off the guitar.

Bossman clapped a couple times. "All right Ruby. Follow me and we'll get a rough battle plan drawn up. Your songwriting skills are obvious, so we'll have a talk with the creative team and see what we can do." Villeda followed Bossman out of the room.

"Everybody got a flashdrive, right?" Keith said as he followed everyone else out of the room. "Let me know if you need another one for a friend."

I watched Hilleman saunter out of the room, delighted he had saved his career and made me look like an idiot in a single meeting.

"I'll be out in a few minutes," said Ruby. "Thank you for supportin' me." She gave me a brief hug and ran off to follow her contract.

I admired the Nashville skyline through the window again, the sky blue in full bloom. The guitar hung round my neck from the strap.

"I'd like to hear the rest of your song, Mister Dunn," Hoover said from behind me. "If you've got the time."

"Thank you for the offer, but I ain't got it in me right now." I said as I packed up the guitars. "You're a busy man, anyway. You don't need to waste your time listenin' to more plastic."

FIFTEEN

WE WENT TO GET SOME FOOD right after we left Steam Record Headquarters, but Ruby barely ate her fried chicken sandwich due to all her laughter and talk about her upcomin' albums, shows, and television appearances. She kept gettin' in and out of our plastic booth and doin' little dances in the aisle. The joy overcame her numerous times during that lunch. After a few seconds of calmin' herself down and chewin' her sandwich, she'd rev herself back up again without warnin'.

Keith laughed along with Ruby and danced with her during a few of her ecstatic outbursts, but he otherwise ate his chicken tenders with a little grin glued to his face. I knew he had grand designs on his own music career, but he didn't harbor a lick of spite or envy in his eyes. The kid seemed genuinely excited for Ruby. Maybe he really thought Bossman Riddle would listen to that flashdrive and give him a chance.

As for me, I swear with all of my heart that I was incredibly proud of my Ruby that day. I swear I was. But my stomach twisted in pain whenever she mentioned her dreams and royalties and how we'd never have to worry about money again. Sure, my jumbo-sized chicken combo meal and three cups of sweet tea probably didn't help, but that stomachache went beyond grease and Sweet N' Low.

Our duo had died not an hour prior, and Ruby couldn't stop smilin'.

❆   ❆   ❆

Me and Keith sat in Ludwell's backyard that night, the chairs and guitars and skeeter torches out again. Ruby had gone out with her girlfriends to celebrate, and Ludwell refused to get out of his recliner and come outside. When I had told him about Ruby signin' a record contract, he just cleared his throat and said, "Oh, that's nice. Right nice. Can you run to the gas station and get me a pack of nabs?"

I briefly saw his cigarette fire floatin' by the backdoor as Keith and I sat in the yard. He never came to visit us though. I figured he was just obeyin' one of Momma's biggest rules: no smokin' in the house.

Keith and I didn't do as much song-playin as we'd had a few nights prior. I mainly strummed random chord shapes and stared up at the stars, wonderin' if I was lookin' at some important constellation or planetary body.

Keith sang under his breath and made up little melodies as he cobbled chords together, but he never could settle on a good idea. After twenty minutes of driftless sounds, Keith spoke up. "I'm kinda glad I didn't play today. They probably would've called my songs awful."

I stopped strummin'. "We really weren't tryin' to be ugly the other night, promise. But your songs... they just ain't there yet."

He looked at his fingers and silently changed shapes against the strings.

"I mean, shit, you're still learnin', Keith. So am I. At least you had nuggets to play those songs for us. I'm proud of you for being willin' to improve."

"Thanks." Keith took a deep breath. "I'll try and learn from those songwriters on the Steam payroll. I'm sure Ruby will cross paths with them at some point. Just gotta be there and stake my own claim."

109

I sucked through my teeth. "I don't know if I'd trust those professional songwriters, to tell the truth."

"Why not? You heard Mister Hilleman. They've probably written a bunch of songs we've liked. They're professionals for a reason."

"Yeah, but Hilleman also broke country music down into some sort of formula for appealin' to folk like us. Like we're too stupid to want anything different. I get the reasons, yes, they wanna make money, but music is greater than that. Music is the most versatile tool known to humankind. Music can fire you up, calm you down, stir up lovemakin', soothe your pain, let you daydream, and so on. You can sing wherever and whenever you need. If you've got a heartbeat, you've got music." I sat up on my chair and readjusted my guitar. "Hell, if Hilleman thinks it's so damn easy to write a country song, then I'll make one right now."

I imagined a target audience of people like Johnny and Lonnie Tew, people with the base intelligence of a sack of peanuts. I started thunkin' on a couple of basic chords and sang:

I'm like you
I work hard
I go to church
I drive a truck
got mud all down the sides

Keith laughed and pumped his fist in the air. He leaned forward and set his guitar on the ground as if he wanted to hear more. So I chewed up some more thinkin' for a second and spouted out nonsense based off Hilleman's country song checklist. Keith chuckled at nearly every line I sang, and I got a few solid laughs out of him when I made a crazy lyric about Old Glory. For the bridge, I just banged on a C chord and listed more great things about America:

Hot dogs
Fireworks
Doin' all the fat girls

110

Gasoline
Front yard
Everybody workin' hard

Blue sky
Big tits
Beatin' off a limp dick

I could barely play by that point cause we were laughin' so hard, but I carried on. After a couple of false starts and dud lyrics, I finished my work inspired by the Hilleman music formula. I called it *Thought About America.*

I was right pleased with myself. "It would be somethin' if on that big G chord at the end of the chorus, I could get a three piece horn section to really add some bam. Buncha trumpets and trombones to blast it wide open."

" Hilleman said you gotta have a steel guitar, otherwise no one will like it." added Keith. "Besides, I don't think there's much brass in country."

"True, but if it would make a song better, then people would go crazy for a barkin' hound dog."

"I suppose," he said. "Can I hear it again, all the way through?"

So I played *Thought About America* in its completed form to Keith, and he watched my hands for the chords. By the end of the second verse, he had picked up his guitar and was strummin' right along with me.

I'm gonna sing y'all the original version. Probably go in the audiobook version or somethin'.

THOUGHT ABOUT AMERICA

I'm like you
I work hard
I go to church

111

I drive a truck
got mud all down the sides

And I live in a nation
where we like havin' a good time
And where puttin' in an honest day's sweat
never hurt no one

You can tell those bleedin' hearts
that all those chemicals in my chicken
taste mighty fine to me.

And the Lord will look the other way
if I crack the skulls
of some fools
disrespectin' Old Glory

Hand over my heart
Fate in the stars
May the Union never part
Well I thought about America
Brought a teardrop to my eye
But only children cry
and I'm a patriot until I die!

Hot dogs
Fireworks
Doin' all the fat girls

Gasoline
Front yard
Everybody workin' hard

Blue sky
Big tits

Beatin' off a limp dick

Ain't nowhere in the world gonna top that!
Now you just repeat after me!

Hand over my heart
Fate in the stars
May the Union never part
Well I thought about America
Brought a teardrop to my eye
But only liberals cry
and I'm a patriot until I die!

Keith stood and clapped when I finished. "Damn, well done! That is a song!" he cried.

"Heh, thank you. We should call up ol' Hilleman and see what he thinks."

"He'd probably think you kidnapped one of his songwriters."

I laughed. "The words are a bit on the nose, ain't they? I like the melody though. Might use parts of it in other songs of mine, though. Cannibalize 'em."

Ludwell's back screen door slammed and I saw Ludwell's shadow cross the yard to the garage.

"Hey," I called out. "Come sit with us."

"Aaaaagggggh," Ludwell replied. He climbed into his truck and drove onto the dark highway, that engine gradually rattlin' its way out of earshot.

"Has Mister Ludwell always been so..." Keith trailed off.

"Fussy? Naw. He's all right most of the time, even fun every now and then. But he tends to think that if you've got time to smile, you've got time to work."

"Hmm." Keith went back to random, gentle strums as we both looked toward the old soybean field.

You know, with all the time I spent with Keith Neck those days, I started to admire the guy. I really did. And out of sheer curiosity, I said "You mind if I ask you somethin'?"

He nodded.

"Why did you really come up here to Nashville?" I asked. "And why now instead of next month or next year?"

Keith thought for a second. "Well, I've always wanted to go on this big adventure to go chase down my dream, and when you and Miss Ruby came to El Paso, I knew it was time to stop thinkin' about it and go do it. I quit my job and drove here before I lost the nerve."

"I can understand that."

"Plus I kinda want to prove everybody back home that they're wrong about me. They all think I don't have what it takes to be a professional musician."

"Who all said that to you?"

He got quiet. "I mean, nobody's said any of that to my face, but I can see in their eyes that they want me to fail. They don't want to admit I'm destined to be a famous songwriter."

"Wait," I said, "so no one has actually said any of these things?"

"Again, not to my face, but-"

I held up my hand. "You see? There you go. Granted, I don't know your hometown friends, but you're a charismatic guy with a lot of potential, and I have a feeling all of that is in your head. You're a likeable person. If you constantly worry people won't like you because you're honest to yourself, your brains will eventually turn into charred slag, and you-"

I stopped myself before I could spout anymore hypocrisy. I couldn't even follow my own advice when it came to losin' my religion. I had no right to instruct him how to think.

"You'll be fine," I said.

In that same moment, I realized I needed to atone for how I treated him when we met. Keith had been nothin' but helpful and kind ever since Ruby and I met him, and I was in the wrong.

"Also," I said, "I was not nice to you the first time we met, nor was I kind when you first got to Nashville. I don't have a good reason for callin' you names and I don't want to you to think I'm against you or your dream or your talent or whatever. You've been mighty helpful to Ruby and me over the past week. You're a good man and a hard worker, and I apologize for showin' my tail."

The torchlight bounced off my guitar, the stars shined on, and I anticipated his response.

"I never thought you were against me," he said. "Just thought you were hard to please. To be fair, I didn't plan this trip very well. It was kind of reckless." He laughed to himself.

"Either way, I'm sorry I acted like that. I've got your back."

He smiled. "Thanks, Mister Reggie. That means a lot."

"Call me Reggie. I'm not that much older than you."

"Thanks Reggie."

"And as for those hometown folks that may or may not be rootin' against you, pay 'em no mind."

"I try not to," he said. "I mainly get that feelin' from people at my church, anyway, so I don't have to see them too often."

When Keith said that, I suddenly recalled all times people from my church told me that my momma was in a better place or makin' the Lord smile, and a bolt of irritation shot through me.

"Let me tell you," I said, "I've met plenty of Christians that are just plain rotten. They cherry pick passages out of a made up book they don't half understand, and they use it to rationalize their shitty behavior."

Fuck my dumbass mouth. I sat there for a second before I fully realized what I had just said.

"Hang on, hang on," I said. "I meant to say that people act like the Bible is a made up book. That's what I meant."

Keith leaned up in his seat. "No, it's okay. I get what you're sayin'. Besides, we should be free to discuss faith like adults."

I nodded.

"Did you actually say what you meant when you said Christians pick passages out of a made up book?"

"I really did misspeak," I said. "That's all."

115

"You can trust me. If you're havin' questions, or you're thinkin' about becomin' Presbyterian or hell, even Lutheran, you can confide in me."

I hadn't shared my atheism with anyone since I had realized it, and up until then I was cool with keepin' it to myself. But I was hurtin' that day. Ruby had cut me deep at Steam Records, and I was in a rare state. I wasn't at full strength.

Keith had proven himself as a damn fine friend, even when I wasn't kind to him. If there was anybody I could trust besides Ruby, it was him.

I let the crickets and torches noise off for a moment. "It's been a slow realization. When I was young, I figured that turnin' the other cheek and prayin' would always get Jesus on my side. But what I've learned about astronomy and science and history and life itself...all that painted a more objective picture."

My momma's sickly hands flashed over my mind right then.

"Don't get me wrong, I wish, in the deepest corners of my being, that my love and my loved ones could be preserved forever. The idea of heaven minimizes the pain and fear of death. But heaven and faith and God's will...they all make us feel like we have control when we really don't got a lick of it. When I was a teenager, after my momma passed, I wondered if God had some vendetta against me or my family, or if he wanted to see the world burn. Or maybe he didn't even possess the power to affect our lives, or maybe he didn't care. But I finally realized it makes more sense if there ain't no one up there at all."

I exhaled and stared across the soybean field. "I don't believe in God anymore, Keith," I said.

I strummed a soft progression for a long while, and listened to the crickets chirp.

He coughed a little and squirmed around the chair before he said, "Wow...I don't know what to say. When did you realize this?"

"Recently," I said while my nerves collected themselves. "The day after Ruby and I left El Paso. I realized it at a campground in east Texas. I don't feel no different, mind you. I'm still a little overweight, still got debt. But the world makes a little more sense."

116

"But you ain't no scientist. How can you believe all that evolution and space stuff is true? So you believe in continental drift?"

That last question was silly enough to give me pause, but I continued. "That's true, I ain't no scientist. And I can't disprove a divine creator any more than a preacher can prove him. But even if God is real, life has shown to me that God is frequently unwillin' or unable to protect mankind from the terror and injustice of this world. That ain't a god worth my worship."

"So when we die, you believe that we just fade away into nothin'?"

I pondered for a moment. "Yeah, I suppose I do. I don't want it to be true, but with all the bullshit in the world, it's the only answer that makes sense to me."

We listened to the night for a long while until Keith whistled and asked, "Does Ruby know all this?"

"Naw. Not gonna tell her, either. No good can come of it."

"What about Ludwell?"

"He don't need to know either. Nobody does, really."

"So you're just gonna keep fakin' your faith and church for the rest of your life?"

I nodded. "My perspective ain't nobody's concern. People write off Southern folk often enough just for bein' Southern. I don't need the Southern folk to write me off, too."

"But you're not being honest," Keith's voice got louder. "That's you just told me to do: be honest. Y'all got married as a Christian couple and now you are somethin' different. You aren't holdin' up your end of the bargain anymore. Doesn't Ruby deserve to be with someone who shares her faith?"

That question twisted my stomach harder than a gallon of sweet tea ever could. "I've asked myself that many times since last week. But Ruby and I are a pair. I love sharin' a yoke with her. My affection for her will never yield to a belief that ain't botherin' nobody but me. She is the absolute best thing in my life and I would rather get stabbed in the head a thousand times before I cause that gorgeous woman to doubt her faith."

We sat there for a minute, and let the mid-spring night sing its song.

"That's tough to hear," he finally said. "Ain't gonna lie. It's real tough. But I see where you're comin' from. I actually think it's cool you have the guts to ask questions. And I appreciate your trust in me."

"Bear in mind, I'm still processin' all of this myself," I said. "This is between you and me. All right?"

He stood up with guitar in hand. "You've got my back, I've got yours. Thanks for another night of music, Reggie."

"Good night."

I played *Always On My Mind* as Keith walked back to the garage. I breathed a big sigh, relived Keith didn't turn into somethin' vile on me. I felt better after sharin' all that with him. Bein' honest always felt good.

A few minutes later, the headlights of Ludwell's old truck pulled into the driveway. Seconds after that rumblin' engine shut off, Ludwell walked up with a plastic bag in hand.

"Hey daddy, where'd you go?" I asked.

He pulled a longneck Neptune out of the bag and handed it to me. "Y'all didn't have no beer. Ain't right."

I twisted off the bottle top and took a swallow as Ludwell took Keith's old chair. "That song about America. Heard you makin' it up as you went. Sounded good. A little stupid, but good." He opened his own bottle and drank.

"Thank you," I said. "Just some little goof I made up. Makin' fun of bad country music. That record company thinks they've got us figured out. I think they're half full of shit."

"Good. Glad you ain't seein' Ruby's deal as some end all, be all. All them record people know how to do is make money. That's it. They can manufacture all the polished, patronizin' crap they want, but they'll never cram genuine heart into a formula."

I said "Well, now that she's got a contract, Ruby is gonna start makin' all kinds of money-"

"Her contract don't guarantee a damn thing. Not a damn thing. She may very well fall flat on her face. And if that happens, you'll be there for her. That's who you are and who I raised you to be." He lit a cigarette. "Now gimme that guitar, boy."

I handed the guitar over, and he cracked his knuckles before he took hold of the instrument. He played various chord shapes across the neck as a warm up, but his dexterity already shined through.

"You need to keep writin' songs," he said. "You should try writin' more stuff that ain't so goofy. More like that deal with the devil tune, I suppose. As long as you're true to yourself, people'll recognize that, even if they don't understand at first. They eventually figure it out."

I didn't know how to respond, as my daddy hadn't shown much of an interest in my life for the past several years, and now he was rainin' me with praise and sage advice. I took another drink from my Neptune. "Play me a strong one, daddy. Show me what you're talkin' about."

He played *On A Monday*, his voice weathered by time and Marlboros and the long-ago departure of his own darlin' person. I sang along with my daddy, unable to keep the music contained. He played for another hour, coverin' Johnny Paycheck and Merle Haggard several times over, and by the time we got up to quit, I could've sworn I saw Ludwell Dunn smile.

SIXTEEN

THE RECORD COMPANY WAS HOSTIN' a big photo op for their quarterly shareholders' report, and Ruby was invited to come down for her first promotional duty as a Steam artist. They told her to bring a few different sets of beat up clothes, cause she was gonna get messy for her debut music video, and she wanted me to drive so she could review a new contract the company had mailed her that mornin'. Keith rode along in the seatless back of the van, convinced he'd get more face time with upper management.

My more cautious side wished I hadn't been caught in the moment by the bonfire and told Keith about my spiritual about-face. A tiny germ of worry tried to take over my mind in the hours and days followin' our discussion, but every time it popped up, I reminded myself that Keith had a good heart, and he had no incentive to rat me out. My secret was not compromised. I had plenty else to worry about, anyway.

During the ride out of Nashville, I flicked on the country station, not thinkin' much of Charlie Chestnut as he sang *No Streetlights*. It was a song I'd sung along with numerous times over the years, and I had never questioned its authenticity. I started brakin' on the offramp of the highway just as Chestnut sang the bit about "lovin' his family and his land of the free".

And like a recent moment at an east Texas campground, several ideas suddenly clicked in my brain.

I stopped singin' along and chewed that line over as we waited at the stoplight. "Lovin' his family and his land of the free." It won't much different from countless other country songs I knew. In fact I could've named you a dozen country songs right there that mentioned how much the singer loved his family or his nation or how he earned his daily pay. And that was precisely the problem.

"Hey Keith, you got one of them computer phones, right?" I asked.

Keith nodded in the rearview mirror.

"Could you look up this song and see who wrote it, produced it, and what not?"

Keith pulled out his phone and started thumbin' his way across the screen. When I pulled up to a stoplight a few seconds later, he handed me his phone on some encyclopedia page for Charlie Chestnut's *No Streetlights*. I found the credits and couldn't believe my damn eyes. Six songwriters, and none of 'em Charlie Chestnut. It took six damn people to write this three minute song. And the recording itself was produced by four other people, includin' somebody named X-Ray. I looked X-Ray up and saw they were based out of the Lower East Side of Manhattan and had dozens of songwritin' credits on a bunch of familiar country songs, along with several other tunes I'd never heard of before. I didn't care how many songs he or she had sold, anybody who called themselves X-Ray is an asshole.

Above all that, Charlie Chestnut proudly sang:

I'll take the country dark any day
And you can keep your city slicker mess
Where you worry about your nine to five

Cause I'm livin' free on my own land
And there aren't no streetlights
Blockin' my view of the Lord's Heaven in the sky

Hilleman was absolutely completely one hundred percent correct.

It was fake. Plastic. A joke.

I was bein' appealed to, plus I was fairly certain Charlie Chestnut thought I was stupid.

"Light's green," said Keith.

I handed his phone back to him and got back to drivin'.

I startin' runnin' through discographies in my head, comparin' my favorite songs against my epiphany. I started doubtin' the heart and spirit of almost my entire music collection. The more I thought about it, the more likely modern country was infested with plastic X-Ray music, full of patronizin' scenarios that would've fit perfectly in my *Thought About America* tune.

Now don't get me wrong. I ain't got no quarrel with somebody coverin' somebody else's material. I knew for a damn fact the Man in Black himself played many a song written by other people, but he definitely didn't pass them off as if he wrote 'em. Hell, I've covered plenty of songs in my time. Years before, when I was tryin' to get Ruby to play with my bird, I must've sung her every country song I knew. Singin' a song written by somebody else won't the problem.

My problem was that Charlie Chestnut championed himself as some lonesome maverick that didn't rely on nobody. His debut album was called *I Pull My Own Bootstraps, Dammit*. And the shit thing was that I knew in my heart of hearts that Charlie Chestnut probably won't the only singer guilty of projectin' this public lie. Given enough time with that computer phone, I knew I'd find a laundry list of musical heartbreak.

My heart puttered for a minute and I figured my left arm might start tinglin' any second, and I almost asked Ruby to take the wheel, but I somehow didn't go into cardiac arrest, even as I questioned the very music that had been the soundtrack of my life. So many songs I had loved suddenly seemed as fake as margarine.

I pointed at the radio and said "Ruby, you hearin' this? Hilleman was right about stupid country lyrics and how they-."

"I'm sorry, but lemme get through this first, please, hun." She didn't look up from the contract in her lap.

I was about to bring this up to Keith, but he was singin' along at full force, and I didn't wanna piss in his punch bowl.

I tried to forget about it and just enjoy the music. I really did try.

✻   ✻   ✻

Thirty minutes later, we pulled onto an access road adjacent to an open field. A great white tent on the edge of that field protected a slew of business people and film crews from the Tennessee sun, while a couple of guys walked around the field with a firehose and sprayed it with water from an 18-wheeler tanker truck parked further down the road, turnin' that field into a muddy paradise. Cameras, tripods and lighting rigs were scattered throughout the grounds.

My twelve-year old self would've went into hysterics if he could've seen the fantastic spread of four-wheelers, pickup trucks and massive 4x4s parked alongside that access road. All of the four-wheelers had keys restin' in their ignitions, just waitin' to get cranked wide open. Hot damn, I almost committed grand theft auto right there.

Bossman Riddle and Villeda the A&R rep came up to meet us before I got to play with the vehicles, both of 'em wearin' fancy flannel shirts and rubber boots.

"Ready to get messy?" Villeda asked Ruby, and my previous girl-on-girl hay bale daydream fluttered across my brain. Oh, that one request got me so excited I probably looked like I was carryin' a .357 in my $20 jeans.

✻   ✻   ✻

"All right, so we're going to rehearse, then we'll film it for real," Villeda said. She told Ruby to stand at the edge of the great mud field and not look directly at the camera during recordin'.

"Do I need to move?" I asked Villeda. I was standin' right behind Ruby.

"No, this is just a rehearsal," Villeda replied. "Now Ruby, this video is a proof of concept type of thing, and if it turns out well then we'll turn it into your first music video."

Ruby gave her a thumbs up, then turned to me and said, "Do I look nervous?" This woman was in short shorts, a green tank top and knee high boots. She exceeded the conventional maximum on the fuckability scale.

"Hell naw. Look down right smokin'. Now is your time to shine, darlin'. Ain't no reason to be nervous."

"Okay, good. Stay here for the rehearsal?"

I kissed her hand. "Absolutely."

Ruby turned back to the camera and conversed with Villeda about her life's trivia: who she was, what her background was, all that mess. I figured Keith would be goofin' around by the four-wheelers but I couldn't see him there. Instead, I saw him under the great white tent, talkin' with Bossman Riddle.

Villeda made me leave once they finished the rehearsal, so I walked over to the great white tent to fetch some drinks for me and Ruby. I overheard Keith and Bossman's conversation as I ate a couple of donuts, so I listened in as I waited for Ruby to finish.

"The other day wasn't some karaoke free-for-all Mister Neck," Bossman said with his back to me. "It was a talent acquisition for Ruby and Ruby alone. As I told your beefy friend, I have no desire to hear you or your songs unless they've been submitted for review by one of our A&R people."

"But Mister Riddle, I've got a passion for country-"

"Yes, yes, you have a passion for country music and you want to share that unique passion with the world, blah, blah, blah, and you can make me lots of money. Fascinating, Mister Neck. Now, if you'll excuse me."

Bossman tried to walk away but Keith sidestepped him and said, "But you just said I had the look of a future star."

Bossman paused. "Yes, Mister Neck, but I said that only-"

"And we talked about the industry for several minutes after Ruby's signin', didn't we?"

"Yes, yes, we did," Bossman replied. "Now, will you-"

Keith snapped his fingers. "The free concert that Ruby's playin' next Friday in Centennial Park."

"What about it?"

"Who's playin' before her?"

"No one. She's opening for Randolph Suggs."

"Can I play before Ruby?"

Bossman didn't respond, but he didn't try to leave either.

"You listened to the songs I gave you on that flashdrive, right?"

"Believe it or not, I gave your music a generous thirty seconds to impress me, and I had to pass. You have a decent voice, but you are not yet a songwriter. Excuse me, Mister Neck."

Bossman tried to walk away but Keith stepped in front of him again.

"LET ME PLAY!" Keith hollered with a hint of anger in his voice. Everybody under the big tent looked over to Bossman and waited for that stocky old timer to plant Keith in the ground.

Keith took a deep breath and quietly said, "I didn't mean to holler. Please gimme ten minutes. Three songs. That's it. You'd be playing recorded music anyway."

Bossman stared at Keith for a second, then finally asked, "Do you want money?"

Keith shook his head.

"Will you change or disrupt the gear onstage, even in the slightest?"

"Not at all. I'll use what's there. Swear." Keith held up his palm. "Mister Riddle, this is my destiny and I will not let you down."

Bossman huffed. "Fine. You get ten minutes. As long as you don't whip anything out I really don't care. Don't speak to me again." He walked off toward Ruby, his face buried in his computer phone.

Keith spotted me and walked over with a big ass smile. "You hear that?"

"Yep," I said as I finished my last donut.

"I'm gonna play for an audience, Reggie. A live audience."

"Sounds good. You and that guitar will warm 'em up for Ruby."

"Naw, I ain't goin' solo. I'm gettin' a band together. Bass, drums, second guitar. Gonna knock it out."

I scoffed. "You got a band already?"

"No." He looked around the tent for a second. "But I'll hire one. I'll get the money one way or another. I got a question for you, though."

I started to grin as I awaited his request. I knew he'd ask me if I'd play guitar for him while he danced around for his ten minutes in the spotlight. I waited for him to ask if I could get my musician friends to help out too. But instead he asked, "Can I play one of your songs?"

"Huh?"

"Can I play that song you wrote a few nights ago? That fun one about America and the record company?"

"You mean that *Thought About America* song? Keith, that was a joke. I was tryin' to make you laugh."

"Yeah, but that song was really good. This is my chance, Reggie. Who knows? I could be the next Conway Twitty or Myles Butterworth."

"I don't think Myles Butterworth ever wrote a song about limp dicks."

"I can change the words. That song could win a crowd."

"I'm glad you like the song, but you need to pull your own wagon and stand above all the plastic out there. If you wanna make music for real and become an artist that means somethin' to people, then you'll sing your own song next Friday."

He grimaced. "Please?"

"No," I said and looked him dead in the eyes. Part of me wondered if he was gonna holler at me too.

Instead, Keith took stock and smiled. "You're right. Myles Butterworth would go out with his own material. Thanks Reggie." He slapped me on the shoulder just as his eye drifted to the muddy field. "Is that Miss Ruby?"

Out in the mud, a jacked up 4x4 was pullin' a black inner tube through the mud on a long stretch of rope. Ruby sat on top of that inner tube, wearin' a bicycle helmet. A golfcart could've outrun that 4x4.

126

"Oh, that's a bottle of piss," I said to myself and ran out into the mud. When that truck drove by me, it didn't splash a lick of mud, and Ruby looked bored as hell when her tube slid by me. Camera people were shootin' the scene all over, but those pictures had to be turnin' out shitty. I threw up my arms, got out several yards in front of the truck and waved for the driver to stop. From what I could see from the ground, the driver was a middle-aged good ol' boy with a dull expression to rival Ruby's inner tube boredom.

Seconds after the truck braked, a pony-tailed Hilleman stomped across the mud field with a green bandana across his neck and pleather chaps coverin' his jeans.

"Well, hawdy, partner!" he yelled over the truck's idlin' engine. After he paused to listen to his headset, Hilleman got closer to me and shouted in a cornpone accent, ""You ruined the shot, you dumb hick, huh HA!"

"You kiddin'?" I hollered over the noise. "I bet those photos y'all took look dull as hell, with this slow ass drivin'."

"We've got liability issues, all right? Can't go ass wild with this thing. We're finished with it anyway." Hilleman walked around the back of the truck, disconnected Ruby's inner tube tether from the truck's hitch, then climbed up to the driver and told him to park by the fleet of vehicles on the side of the field.

"Seriously?" I hollered as soon as Hilleman had hopped down off the truck. "This 4x4 is a work of art and you're gonna put it on the bench?"

"This isn't some hayseed barbeque. We're professionals." Hilleman said as he stared walkin' to the big white tent, his pleather chaps far too clean for my likin'. Before he was out of earshot, he looked back over his shoulder and shouted, "Now get out of the shot!"

I stepped away from the 4x4 and watched it drive out of the mud. No sooner did I look over at Ruby in her inner tube did I realize that drastic action had to be taken. Yeah, I was still hurtin' from what she did to me at Steam Records, but I had to give her the benefit of the doubt. She made a mistake, and we would work that out in time. This video shoot, however, was a once in a lifetime opportunity, and my darlin' person wasn't gonna be let down by some half-assed muddin'.

Ruby started to climb out of her inner tube, but I hollered "Wait one second!" and ran over to the fleet of vehicles by the access road. I picked the biggest four-wheeler on that field, hopped on, confirmed the key was still in the ignition, and fired that bad boy up. It purred up mighty fine.

My heart had been close to shatterin' in two after my Charlie Chestnut moment. Every impulse told me to let that four-wheeler go wide open.

"STOP! STOP!" Villeda yelled as she ran up to me from the tent. I gave her a minute while I found all the handlebar controls.

"You are not insured to drive this vehicle, especially not around our artist," she said once she reached me.

"That artist is my wife. I know what she can handle on a tube." I chuckled at my own joke.

"That doesn't matter," she said. "Please get off the vehicle."

"Look, muddin' is all about speed and hollerin' and bein' stupid. Y'all need more stupid."

I thumbed the gas and took off into the mud. I stopped by the end of Ruby's rope and hooked it to the back of the four-wheeler. "Toss that helmet away, darlin'!" I yelled over the idlin' engine. "Your hair's simply too fabulous!"

She tossed that helmet into the air and suddenly it was our third date all over again. Once I saw the camera crews were payin' attention, I whipped that four-wheeler all through the field and got mud flyin' high. Ruby's tube dragged across the mess and I could hear her laughin' after every slide. Of course I spun tires in front of Hilleman just to douse him in wet earth. He started shoutin' and I spun more mud straight into his face. It was delicious.

I whipped Ruby around the field one last time for the camera people and parked the four-wheeler dead center in the mud patch. I stepped off the vehicle, ready to pounce Ruby with a few thousand kisses, but she was immediately surrounded by photographers and record company people in rubber boots. I couldn't even see where she was.

"She's fine, everybody, promise. We used to do this kinda shit all the time," I said as I walked up to the scene. "Now move, I'm huggin' my wife." I pushed through a few cameramen to find my Ruby lying on her side in the mud by the inner tube. "Damn, baby, are you hurt?"

"No, Reggie, we're takin' pictures." She said without taking her eyes off the camera in front of her. Looked like she was in the middle of gettin' nekkid.

"Well, why you layin' in the mud with your shirt half off and your legs all nice and wide like I've been turnin' you on?"

"They wanted to try somethin' different," she said. "Something a little more flirty."

"Flirty? Only fourteen year old girls use the word flirty."

Villeda spoke into her headset. "Okay, let's get one of the male models over here. Let's try some fun romp pictures."

I kneeled in the mud and got ready to snuggle my Ruby in the mud, but Villeda shouted, "No no no no. Not you."

I looked at her and said, "You want some boytoy to romp all up on my-"

Some young fellar in a red flannel cutoff shirt came over from the tent and started talkin' to one of the photographers. He was a handsome son of a bitch, couldn't argue, if you like your men tall and pretty. Probably smelled good too.

Okay, this whole affair was just gettin' out of hand.

Out of nowhere, Keith slid between two photographers and kicked a heap of mud onto a couple of record company suits. "Here I am," Keith said. "Let's go." He crawled over to Ruby and leaned against her in the mud.

"You're not one of the models," Villeda said to Keith. "Move."

"With this face, does it matter?" Keith traced a semi-circle around his head with his hand.

"Hey Keith!" Ruby said. "You know what, Miss Villeda? Let Keith in for a few shots."

"We've got the model right here, ready to go."

"Oh, it'll be fun," Ruby replied and pat Keith on the shoulder. "Just a few pictures, then we'll get all the models you want in here."

"Yeah," Keith smirked. "We're natural together. The camera will pick that up."

Villeda shrugged. "Whatever. You're cute enough. Okay, let's get a few shots of Ruby and this guy tosslin' round. Family friendly with a touch of sexy, of course."

Keith got behind Ruby, wrapped his arm around her stomach and laughed. I stepped around Keith and leaned close to her as the photographers grumbled about me bein' in the shot. "You don't have to do this, darlin'," I said. "You're a singer, not some hillbilly hussy pretendin' to be a damn hog."

I barely heard her say through her teeth, "I'm workin', Reggie." She kept her eyes on the cameras or Keith or Villeda. She looked at everyone but me.

Keith held Ruby's cheek as if they had been kissin' and they both laughed while the cameras flicked and flashed some more. Nobody asked Keith to do that move. I mean, it looked convincin'. Really convincin'.

I stepped back and let the camera people do their thing while Ruby and Keith splashed mud on each other and posed around the inner tube. I tried to sit on the four-wheeler, but Villeda yelled at me and told me to get out of the shot.

My stomach lurched somethin' awful, so I went over to the giant white tent so I couldn't hear Ruby havin' the time of her life.

SEVENTEEN

THE FOLLOWIN' SUNDAY MORNIN', we pulled into our church's parkin' lot with little discussion takin' place in that minivan. Right before I threw the van into park, Ruby quietly said, "Keith, you can go on ahead. We'll be right behind you."

Keith got out, and Ruby and I sat in silence, watchin' various members of the congregation as they walked up to the Sunday School building. Me and her hadn't been doing so hot since the muddin' photo shoot a few days prior. We still shared the bed above the garage, sure, but we had barely talked except when she needed me to take her downtown for more meetings with the record people. Plus I hadn't seen them titties in three days, which may have well as been forever. And she was lookin' mighty fine in her light blue flower dress, though she was minus her usual smile.

Ruby huffed through her nose. "I'm sorry I was short with you at the mud thing." She stared at the van's Discman, still velcroed to the dashboard. "I know you didn't want them paradin' me like some hillbilly idiot, takin' advantage of my body and what not." She took my hand and rubbed my knuckles. "But I'm a big girl. They ain't gonna do anything I don't approve first, and honey, you've got to realize that all

131

these pictures and meetings and legal jargon is our ticket to a better life. And I've gotta get my foot in the door before I can start demandin' changes. This whole setup is hangin' off gossamer thread, as it is."

She didn't mention anything about her not havin' my back at the record company meetin', when those suits shut me down before I could sing my damn piece. But she was tryin' to make amends, and we had to start somewhere.

"And you know Keith just touched me for show, right? You can't even see his face in the pictures."

I shrugged.

Finally she smiled. I reached over and hugged her neck. "Is there anything you'd like to say?" she asked.

I was confused as hell. "Huh?"

Ruby cleared her throat and scanned over my shirt buttons. "Is there anything you would li-"

I snapped my fingers. "Oh! Right, right, you're right. There is."

She wanted an apology on my part. A good apology, free of bullshit. I had been so caught up by her offenses I didn't even stop to consider my own.

I sputtered out "I...am...sorry...that..."

The anticipation on her face was thick as road tar. I combed my memory for emergency procedures. What made her short with me in the first place? Me telling her what to do. When did the cold shoulder begin? During the sexy poses of the photo shoot.

Wait! Got it! I almost chuckled when the answer slapped my brain in the fanny.

"I'm sorry I gave you a bunch of static during the shoot. I should have trusted you to make the right decision for yourself. Those pictures just brought my blood to a boil. Sorry."

That grin of hers flew wide open. "Thank you, honey. I appreciate your trust." She kissed my lips and a devilish look came across her. "You know, we ain't been...intimate in a while."

"No ma'am," I said between kisses. "We have not."

Ruby checked out the windshield then licked my ear. I shot into the back of the minivan and started takin' off my Sunday britches. "Come on back, baby. Keep that dress on, too."

Somebody knocked on the passenger window before Ruby could join me. Ruby opened the door and started talkin' with ol' Miss Ramsey about church happenings.

"Oh, what are you doing back there, Reggie?" asked Miss Ramsey.

"Ruby and I were about to study the Song of Songs, Miss Ramsey."

She gasped and stepped away from the van.

"Oh, he's messin'," Ruby said. "He's just gettin' changed."

Ruby shot me a wink and left the van, my hand deep in my underblossoms.

❊   ❊   ❊

At the end of his sermon about Biblical genealogy, Preacher Hoffman suddenly got all smiley behind the pulpit. "We have a final announcement before we close this morning. Miss Ruby, would you join me by the podium?"

Ruby braced herself for bad news. "Who's died this time?" she muttered as she stood out of the pew. Preacher Hoffman took her hand as she climbed the steps of the stage and turned her toward the congregation.

"Miss Ruby, on behalf of the church, I would like to congratulate you on your recent signing with Steam Records of Nashville."

I'll be damned if that church didn't start clappin'.

Clappin'.

In a Baptist church.

On a Sunday mornin'.

For almost ten seconds.

You'd have thought Christ himself had come down out of the choir loft.

Ruby beamed and mouthed 'thank you' to the congregation. I yelled a quick "Yeah!" at the height of the fanfare.

133

"Now Ruby, in celebration of your achievement, we are hosting a lunch buffet immediately following the service, and everyone is invited for food and fellowship."

Preacher led the closing prayer with Ruby by his side. He asked for the Lord to "guide Ruby, and allow her music and love for the church to strengthen the hearts of your faithful, and let her prove to the world that she follows the one living God."

A few old-timers and Keith immediately replied with a loud and clear "Amen".

❊   ❊   ❊

The congregation herded down to the picnic shelter at the back of the church property for a lunch that was somethin' else. Fresh creamed corn, chicken pastry, collards, butter rolls, naner puddin', all the classics were accounted for. People sat on steel foldin' chairs, on brick walls, in the grassy space beside the shelter. Chatter echoed between the wooden ceiling and the concrete slab, with laughs sprinkled here and there. Everyone was havin' a big time.

I stood with a few friends and ate the hell out of some bite-size bacon-sausage ball concoction. "I'm gonna have to get a few more of these little bastards," I quietly said to the group and got a good laugh. As I was scoopin' more sausage balls onto my plate, I realized I'd lose everyone and everything surroundin' me if my atheism ever got out. I didn't buy the God part no more, but I still loved the community aspect of church, despite the bad seeds within the congregation.

Bradley Bass crossed my path just as I finished at the buffet table.

"Congratulations, Reggie," he said with plastic cup in hand. "All that tourin' paid off for Ruby."

"Oh yeah, sure did. I'm proud of her." I took a swallow of my sweet tea.

"Good luck with the future." Bass started to leave but paused and said. "And if you ever need to talk about doubtin' your faith, you can always come to me."

I choked on the tea and tried to say "What?" between coughs. When I could breathe again, I asked, "Why do you say that?"

"Heard you'd been havin' questions and problems, some stemmin' from your momma's passing years ago, rest her soul."

My voice clinched.

"I hope you work it all out, Reggie. I do. Just don't give up on Jesus. He'll never give up on you." He patted my shoulder and walked out into the sunshine.

I had never really needed to deal with raw panic before that moment, but if I had to describe it, it was like my brain had to pee and there was no way to piss it out. I threw my plate and cup into one of the garbage cans and scanned the shelter area for Keith Neck. Miss Edna, an old goat of a woman, bumped into me by the dessert table.

"Reggie Dunn, Reggie Dunn," she said as she shook her cane at me. This might sound hateful, but I swear Miss Edna didn't need that cane like she claimed, since she used it more to point than walk.

"Hey Miss Edna, have you seen my friend-"

"Let me tell you somethin'," she said in a sharp tone. "There will be a day of judgment, mark my words, and all the arrogance of the world won't save you from the eternal fire."

"Don't know what you're on about, Miss Edna. But have you see-"

"And I won't feel any sympathy for you that day, either, Reggie Dunn! Turnin' your back on God. The shame!"

My only option was to walk away before I started pluckin' her fuzzy upper lip. I didn't make it five steps before the very round Ricky Brown slapped me on the back. I greeted him and asked if he'd seen Keith.

"Yeah, saw him somewhere around here, gettin' another bowl of pastry. Funny I should run into you, Reggie, cause I heard the strangest thing about you a minute ago."

I scanned the assembled again without even lookin' Ricky in the eyes. "Try me."

"Nancy Cannon said you weren't Christian no more, that you were atheist now. I told Nancy 'Hold on now, Reggie's a good man. He wouldn't do that. He's got more sense than to throw his life and soul away. The church has been good to him.' That's what I told her."

The back of Keith's head caught my eye, not five feet away, so I said, "Excuse me" before I went over to Keith and poked his elbow. He faced me with a huge grin, his social circle of young ladies swoonin' over his every move.

"Hey big man!" he said. "Glad you're here. I want you to meet the foundin' members of my fan club. Problem is that these girls don't believe I'm playin' at the Centennial Park show before Ruby next Friday. Tell 'em how good I am, Reggie." He turned to a few of the girls and did a little dance before he said, "Oh, by the way, I'm gonna leave here in a minute with..." He pointed to the short blonde girl.

"Larissa," replied the blonde.

"Right! I'm gonna leave with Larissa and the rest of these ladies to go swimmin' in some old quarry. I forgot my bathin' suit, ladies, so I might have to resort to desperate measures.

A few girls laughed. Others just smiled in blank adoration. Keith ate that shit up.

"A word, Keith." I started pullin' on the back of his arm, but he stayed put.

"Oh, just one second, big man."

This couldn't wait. I got close to his ear. "Hey, did you tell anyone about that talk we had last week? The important one I told you in confidence?

"Oh naw. Not a soul. I was talkin' to Miss Cannon about different interpretations of faith, and...wait, well, I guess I brought up how you had some theories about God and faith...oh man, she must have taken that the wrong way." Keith grew a concerned look on his face. "I didn't mean to."

Damn damn damn. I kept my cool as best I could. "Keith, please be more careful what you say. This congregation knows how to gossip."

Out of nowhere, Ruby stepped beside me and asked "Can you help me carry some food to the car?"

Keith slinked back into his fan club and I followed Ruby over to the bread table.

"They want us to take home as much as we want," she said. Can you grab the mashed taters and some of the rolls and bring them to the van?"

"That's all you need me for?" I asked.

"Yep," she said as she stacked plastic containers of corn.

Miss Edna approached the other side of the table and whispered to Ruby, despite the fact I could easily hear her. "We need to talk, Ruby. There is an unbeliever here today, breakin' bread with us in the shadow of the Lord's house." Miss Edna cut her eyes at me somethin' hard.

"That's nice, Miss Edna, but I'm too busy to hear your mouth right now." Ruby grabbed the container full of corn and walked towards our minivan.

Miss Edna was taken aback by the snub. I picked up the mashed taters and smiled as I said, "Well, Miss Edna, I'm fairly certain God would want you to mind your own damn business. Have a good evenin'." I shot her a wink and followed Ruby to the minivan.

I put the dishes under the van passenger seat. "You have a good time?" I asked.

"Great time," she said. "So generous of everybody. I did have a couple people try to pass some stupid rumors off on me."

"Yeah?"

"Yeah," She said as she shut the slidin' door. "One was about you not bein' Christian anymore. Another was about you bein' Catholic. Miss Edna figured that was the same thing."

"Huh. I'm not surprised Miss Edna ain't never read a history book. Might make her brain melt down."

"Typical bullshit from the usual suspects. A select few think they're above sin while they're gossipin' about nonsense. And wouldn't they think that we would've discussed somethin' as important as that already?"

I managed to nod. "Of course."

"Cause I know you're a Christian." She turned to me, those brown eyes perfect.

"Absolutely," I said without hesitation.

"Oh, you've got some gravy on your beard, there." She leaned in and licked the gravy off my cheek. "If I weren't around you'd be a grown mess, wouldn't you?"

Goddamn, was she right.

EIGHTEEN

KEITH VANISHED AFTER the church lunch. By the time we got back with the casserole dishes in hand, Keith's car and belongings were long gone, even though he'd ridden with Ruby and I that same mornin'. He probably got one of them fan club girls to drop him off right after I tried to speak with him. I tried callin' him five times that day, but my calls kept endin' before I could reach his voicemail. If he had talked about our conversation by honest accident, he sure won't too concerned about my feelings on the matter, and if he was textin' Ruby, she wasn't sharin' it with me.

Later that week I finally received a single text from him:

SORRY, I LOST YOUR NUMBER
REALLY BUSY RIGHT NOW
HOPE YOU'RE WELL

How anybody could lose a single phone number on a cell phone, I'm not sure, but I'm positive it involved about twenty pounds of horseshit. I let it go, though. He was a twenty-one year old kid. He was still allowed a few more years of not usin' his noggin. He was probably havin' a big time with them girls.

But even with Keith out of the garage apartment, things didn't return to normal.

Wish I could tell you everything was gravy between me and Ruby after that church lunch. Wish I could say we spooned for the remainder of the calendar year. Life would've been a lot simpler. But great music is seldom made out of happy times, as if Johnny Cash hadn't proven it enough.

There had always been an extremely sensitive balance between Ruby and I. If somethin' was eatin' at one of us, the other would know it just from a shorter than usual hug or an odd glance. She wouldn't come out and ask, but she always knew somethin' was off with me, and I worried that the church gossip had sparked up lingerin' speculation.

Now the next bit sure as hell ain't any of your business, but it provides what some call context, so I'll allow you a few details.

Not even humpin' the hell outta each other mended the tension between us. The night after the church lunch, we were goin' at it in the missionary position, a.k.a. Ol' Reliable. Mid-thrust, Ruby stopped and proposed a new position: reverse cowgirl. If you ain't familiar with it or you ain't near any pornography, you've got your flagpole on bottom, your v-hole on top, and your lady's back to your face while she rides your twisted thing like a bronc. We had trouble gettin' started when her back was already to me, so she faced me and suggested I get inside her first, then she would slowly spin around into reverse cowgirl and we'd go to town.

But whenever she tried to turn around with my junk in her thang, I kept gettin' visions of my junk gettin' ripped off my pelvis cause she moved wrong or slipped during the rotation. Never in our sexual history had I ever thought like that or doubted Ruby's physical ability. She couldn't turn past halfway before I'd grab her, tell her to wait, then get her to readjust for another try. Normally we would've had a good belly laugh over our sexual fumbles and carry on with a more conventional union, but after three tries she got fed up and laid down on the bed beside me.

I've always been down for new ways to bang her, no matter how goofy or dangerous. I knew that she knew the absence of my appetite was the symptom of a bigger problem, but she didn't say anything. The rumors, Keith's photogenic hands where they didn't belong, the snub at the audition. All those things led me to doubtin' her trust, and she could tell somethin' was amiss.

Afraid of openin' myself to questions I wasn't prepared to answer, I didn't say anything either. We just stared at the ceiling until I heard her gentle snores.

Like a damn fool, I didn't say anything.

❖   ❖   ❖

Ruby and her band spent that week rehearsin' with a Steam Records appointed band that had been playing together for the past two years. I got to hear them in their rehearsal space and hot damn they were already tight, what with a good lookin' woman on lead guitar, a heavyset young guy on standup bass, a bald fellar on the drums and another good lookin' woman on the keyboards. And Vanessa, her new guitarist, played a mean six-string. This woman could play licks that I hadn't even thought about while still doin' backup vocals. She was just killer. It was tough to see Vanessa takin' my place at Ruby's side on stage, but my darlin' person sounded all the better for it.

The band rehearsed seven uptempo country-pop songs for their thirty-minute Centennial Park set on Friday, and all but one of those songs had been composed by various writers on the Steam Records payroll. Ruby never seemed to mind, though. She could never stop smilin' the whole time she was behind the microphone, and that warmed my insides. Thankfully, the Ruby Naris Band rehearsed *A Fantastic Color* and retrofitted it for a bigger crowd by adding a modest drum beat and some keyboard fills. It wasn't as wonderful as Ruby's usual acoustic renditions, naturally, but it would win over new listeners.

141

With Ruby rehearsin' her cute ass off, and Keith becomin' a phantom, I was left to my own devices. My carpet replacement gig with Ludwell had ended, so my income slowed to $0. I needed to get me and Ruby out of Ludwell's guesthouse before it made things between me and her even worse. Seein' as how Ruby's contract signin' with the record company had been an impulse buy, I reckoned Ruby wouldn't get paid more than $500 for her upcomin' performance, and who knew when she'd actually have that check in hand. Plus we had to plan for the possibility that Ruby's career with Steam Records could be over as soon as her show ended. We needed more reliable income.

That Tuesday mornin', Ruby and I were startled awake by powerful bangs comin' from the garage underneath. I went down the stairs and found Ludwell standin' by his workbench, hammerin' bent nails back straight and puttin' them in empty peanut butter jars.

"Mornin'," he said. When Ruby came downstairs, he banged a sheet of plywood as hard as he could just for the sake of noise. He smirked when Ruby and I grimaced at the terrible volume of the hammer strike. "Come on, I'm driving y'all today."

We piled into the old truck to take Ruby to her 8AM call time, and aside from the knockin' engine that ride was borderline silent. Ludwell even attempted to make genuine small talk with Ruby once he switched on the country station, asking "Do y'all sound like that? What about that?" Ruby slept on the middle seat with her head on my shoulder throughout the twenty-five minute drive, unaware of Ludwell's efforts to communicate.

I nudged her awake in the rehearsal studio parkin' lot and received a half-awake kiss as payment. She even gave Ludwell a muted "thank you" as she climbed out of the truck. "We're playin' late tonight, so don't worry about pickin' me up. Vanessa will take me back. Have a good day, Ludwell."

Ludwell grunted his farewell.

❖　　❖　　❖

142

At twenty over the speed limit, he drove me all around Nashville that mornin', takin' me to every job center and temp agency he could recall. After the third stop, I asked him, "Why ain't you ever comin' into these centers with me? You don't have a job either."

"I've got a job lined up next week, clearin' out beaver dams behind Tom Honeycutt's land. I can afford to take a break."

"So drivin' me around all day is a break for you? I can drive myself."

"Eh, got nothin' better to do today. Gotta keep you in line, anyway." He sparked another cigarette.

After four hours of job searchin' and a few double sausage biscuits, I finally got a job at the Fat Bargain department store as a temporary contractor to help dismantle the store for its going out of business sale. I'd start the next day.

"Well done," he said after I got back in the truck. After he took a drag from his cigarette, he squeezed my shoulder for a few moments in a gesture that could've been mistaken for parental compassion. My brain almost melted down from sheer shock, especially when I saw there was no gun pointed at his head.

"Well, you wanna get somethin' to eat?" He asked as he threw the truck into gear. "We got time to kill before supper."

Spendin' time with my daddy was usually an exercise in patience. He didn't have much fun outside of eatin' and smokin', even when I was little kid. But the new job and mild heat of that day put me in a more daring mood.

"You wanna go hit some golf balls instead?" I asked.

❊ ❊ ❊

We weren't at the driving range for five minutes before Ludwell started gruntin' at his golf club. Between every swing he'd hiss somethin' foul, until the soundtrack of my visit was the whiff of clubs, the music of songbirds, and the hushed rhythm of "god...god...goddammit...dammit...dammit..." Every missed swing or bad shot warranted color commentary from the patriarch of the Dunn

143

family. Finally he hit a ball that barely passed the twenty yard mark, so he hollered "AAAAARRGGHH!" and threw his golf club across the green. It thwacked against the golf ball picker at the fifty yard range and scared the hell out of the driver.

Ludwell tossed his hands up. "Yeah! How about that!"

There was no sense in gettin' embarrassed. If I asked him to quit, he would've made a bigger fuss and turned his rage onto me, turnin' me into the fool. So I played it smooth. "It's about time you passed fifty yards, daddy. Ready to go?"

I gave the remainin' bucket of balls to a father and daughter a few booths away, a little envious of their peaceful time together.

"Them balls were defective, boy," Ludwell said as we idled at a stoplight. "I'm tellin' you. I can drive a damn golf ball. And that rubber tee was floppin' around, couldn't hold my ball up for shit." He thumped more cigarette ashes into the leftmost air vent. "Poor manufacture. I'm tellin' you."

I couldn't help but smile. "It's a nice day, not too hot, we're about to get dinner, and we just hit a load of golf balls, but you still got a temper."

"Bet your ass. I don't tolerate bullshit."

"Daddy, why don't you make like the cool kids and chill out."

I flicked the air conditioner lever from OFF to MAX, and a cloud of gray dust burst from the leftmost air vent and blasted Ludwell in the face with several years' worth of cigarette ashes. He sat there, still, quiet, and the top half of his body coated in dark gray dust.

I suppressed my coughin' long enough to say "Well shit on me, daddy, the AC's workin' again." Then I laughed and laughed and laughed between a fury of dusty coughs. I could barely breathe through the dust until I opened my door, but Ludwell only wiped his eyes clean and hocked a mouthful of ash onto the dash. Any second now, Ludwell would explode into thunderous profanity, more dust would fill the truck as he raged, and I'd probably kill over from the giggles.

But he laughed.

Ludwell Dunn, the most closed off man I'd ever known, was now covered in the remnants of his favorite pastime, and bonafide laughter was rollin' out of his slim belly.

Our stoplight had turned green, but Ludwell had yet to move the truck. The driver behind us yelled through his windshield and honked his horn over and over. Ludwell rolled down his window and stuck half of his ash-smothered body out. "Shat up! SHAAAAAAAT UP!" he hollered back at the driver.

Fuck knows that driver didn't expect to see a goddamn ghost yellin' out of a beat-up old truck at a stoplight, but he sure as hell quit honkin' and waited for us to go on our own time. Ludwell got back in the truck and hit the gas. "I'm talkin' with my boy, dammit," he said.

❈   ❈   ❈

Ludwell fired up some burgers when we got back to his house. Even after he showered he still had some ashes in his thick gray hair.

As I sat on the couch, starin' at the old family photos on the wall, I found the nuggets to reach out to the man I called my daddy.

"Where all the home movies at?" I yelled across the living room.

For the longest time, the only sound was the fryin' of beef patties on a hot griddle. Finally I heard him say, "Closet at the end of the hall."

I fumbled through that closet, pulling out boxes, bed sheets and a few broken vacuum cleaners before I discovered the plastic container of videotapes, film reels and a Super 8 projector. I took a few picture frames off one of the livin' room walls to provide a clean surface for the projector's image, and set up the projector itself on the coffee table opposite the bare space.

"Bet that thing don't work no more. Film's too old." Ludwell said between bites of his burger.

"We'll see." I spooled the film onto the projector.

Right as I flicked off the light switch on the wall, Ludwell grumbled, "I need to hop in the shower again. Get all this mess outta my hair." He cleared his throat a few times.

"Sit down, daddy. I ain't seen these in years. You probably ain't, neither."

He cleared his throat a couple of times again.

"You chokin'?" I imagined havin' to pull an onion slice out of his throat.

"If you got to play it, just play it, Reggie."

I switched on the projector and that dark room bloomed with the old footage of the young Dunn family. Holidays, birthday parties and family reunions whizzed by, as did aunts long passed and uncles since gone senile. But throughout the snippets of extended family and mid-80s fashion there was my momma, healthy and feisty, lovin' the spotlight of the camera every chance she got. She danced and sang and played the piano for a festive Christmas gatherin', and her voice reached my ears for the first time in twelve years. She was in her prime, and her heart was as big as the world itself.

Various scenes flickered by, out of any real order. At one point I was filmin' momma and Ludwell in the kitchen. Momma was makin' a red velvet birthday cake and Ludwell grabbed a handful of flour and threw it at momma's face and laughed somethin' full, yuckin' it up for the camera. Momma took a lighter, lit a birthday candle, pulled open the top of Ludwell's britches and tossed in that flamin' candle. Ludwell danced and shouted and smacked the shit out of his junk tryin' to put out that thing. Momma and me just laughed. Modern day Ludwell cleared his throat a couple of times in a row after that.

The last reel was the oldest, and it ended with momma rockin' me as a toddler. Toddler Reggie in the killer blue pajamas stared up at his vibrant momma and never took his eyes off her. The camera got closer until I could hear her singin' gently as she looked back at her son.

She sang:

Yes, Jesus loves me
Yes, Jesus loves me
Yes, Jesus loves me
The Bible tells me so

She had comforted the toddler with her touch and breath, and she now comforted the adult through a coarse film image and an old speaker inside a noisy projector.

As soon as she finished the song, the film ran out and the livin' room went dark again.

Ludwell cleared his throat a few more times. I cleared my own, too.

Once I turned the lights back on, I looked everywhere in that room but my daddy's eyes. My voice seized up, but I managed to say, "Found some Andy Griffith tapes in the closet. Wanna watch the one where they meet Ernest T. Bass?

He mumbled a quick "Yeah", so we watched TV for a few hours until Ruby's ride pulled up in the driveway. I never found the strength to look him again in the eyes that night.

Clearin' your throat could only hold off but so much.

❖   ❖   ❖

Standin' in a t-shirt and dark blue underbritches, Ruby talked all about her rehearsal that day as she got ready for bed in the garage guest room. Even that toothpaste foam around her mouth didn't ward my lust away. Those legs of hers went on for days.

After she rinsed, she stepped out of the bathroom and took a serious tone. "Reggie, this might sound stupid..."

"Darlin', half the things I say are stupid." I said while foldin' up my shirts. "I think you're allowed one or two."

"Ever since that church lunch, I just can't shake that silly rumor about you...not believin'."

I kept messin' with the laundry like nothin' won't the matter. "Oh, I thought we discussed that. Just church gossip."

Ruby went over to the top of her little dresser in the corner. "I know, like I said, it's stupid."

I turned to her. "It's not stupid. Not at all."

She rubbed some lotion onto her hands. "It's just that all that talk got me thinkin', and you haven't been as...open...about your faith lately."

"Well, you know I've never been a very expressive man when it comes to God and church."

"True, but you don't offer to lead the prayer at our meals or even remember to pray before we go to sleep every night."

"That's just my bad memory," I said. "I'll never shake that, heh heh."

Ruby stepped closer. "God is the most important thing in my life, even if I let Him down from time to time. And I hope he's the most important thing in your life, too, cause I don't want to get to heaven and not find you there. If you ever have questions or doubts, I need you to share them with me, because we can't have anything between us and the Lord. We can't risk eternity."

She placed her hands on my shoulders. "I know this is silly, but please tell me one more time...are you a Christian?"

A vision of my momma singin' *Jesus Loves Me* zapped through my head, and I lied through my teeth. "Of course I am. I wouldn't hide somethin' that important from you." She watched me for a moment, as if waitin' for more. "Trust me."

She hugged me and said, "Good." Once she let go, she went into the bathroom and closed the door.

Goddammit, I was lyin' straight to my wife's face again. I was full of shame.

I needed to lighten the mood, to make her laugh, to change the subject. I saw a mesh sack full of taters by the mini-fridge and got an idea. I stripped off all my clothes and tied the tater sack's drawstrings around my waist, turnin' that mesh sack into a tater codpiece. I propped my right leg up on the bed and faced the bathroom so Ruby could be astonished by my wit and whimsy.

Ruby came out of the bathroom and I said, "I've only got eyes for you." I shot her a wink but she didn't even notice. She climbed into bed and faced the window.

Come on now, that bit was pretty good on short notice. But she won't feelin' it.

I shut off the light and cuddled up next to her in the bed. It took her a second to reach behind her and feel my new codpiece.

"Is that a bunch of taters?" she asked.

"Mmm hmm." I kissed the back of her neck."Wanna mash 'em with me?" I expected a laugh or a slap on the fanny. Some amusin' yet proportionate counter attack.

But instead she said, "I'm tryin' to pray right now. Did you remember to pray?"

Fuck me with a tater. I forgot a-damn-gain.

"And could you get those out of the bed, please?" she said without turnin' from the window.

I untied the taters and laid them on the floor by the bed. I rubbed her shoulder but she didn't respond. Eventually I stopped and turned my back to Ruby, too ashamed to look and touch her.

NINETEEN

AFTER I DROPPED RUBY OFF at the rehearsal studio the next mornin', I drove myself down to the Fat Bargain department store to start my newest temporary gig. With toolbox in hand, I was led to the manager's office in the back of the store. He was a young guy about Keith's age, and had the thickest arm hair I'd ever seen on man or beast. I stood in his office while he reviewed papers behind his desk.

"I saw you had some shelves that use a special type of Ludson bolt," I said. "Want me to start takin' those bad boys down first?"

"Uh, no, that's not necessary. I've already hired enough contractors to do the job. You aren't needed."

I chuckled since I knew the man was messin' with me.

He looked up and said, "Sorry about that. Thank you for coming in."

Fellar wasn't jokin'.

"Hold on, now." I held up my hand. "You hired me yesterday to work. And here I am."

He leaned back in his chair and sighed. "What can I tell you, man? This closing has made me sloppy."

I took a deep breath, maintained a cool head as best I could. "You gotta have somethin'."

The manager walked me outside to the front of the store. He lifted a twelve-foot tall wooden post off the pavement and stood that tall mother on its end. The post had five big signs nailed along its length, and they read things like 'STORE CLOSING', 'FIXTURES FOR SALE', AND '70% OFF EVERYTHING.'

"You need me to dig a hole for that?" I asked.

"No," he said. "I need you to stand by the road and hold it up for passing traffic."

I pointed to the post and said, "So I can spin it around and do tricks with it?"

"Nope. Just need you to stand there and hold it by the road." He pat the post a few times with his hand.

I shook my head. "You're going to pay me to do somethin' that could be accomplished by diggin' a three-foot hole?"

"Look, do you want a lesson on local ordinances or do you want a job?"

❊ ❊ ❊

For five hours I stood by the highway in the summer humidity and held that twelve-foot post upright. I didn't have suntan lotion, and the sun was shinin' bright the whole damn day, so I got burnt up a spell. Most of the time I sang to myself and considered all the life decisions that had brought me to the point where I needed to hold a signpost for a paycheck.

Around 1PM, the manager waved me back to the store's entrance. I brought the post along and kept it beside me as he squinted from afternoon light.

"I spoke with upper management for the past few hours and they think you're right. We should use a hole to support the post. The fine for putting a sign down by the highway is cheaper than paying you to hold it for the next week."

"So I'm gettin' laid off by a hole?"

"Yeah," he said through those stupid fuckin' squinted eyes and turned to go back inside.

151

"Hey, can I at least get paid?" I asked.

"Oh yeah." He reached into his back pocket and pulled out some wadded up cash. He counted out forty dollars and handed it to me.

"Forty? You hired me yesterday for sixteen dollars an hour."

"You didn't do eighty dollars worth of work today. You held up a post and earned forty."

I took the money and let the post fall and crash against the pavement, but the manager didn't seem to care. "Don't worry about the hole. I'll have one of the contractors do it," he said as he walked back into the store.

Forty dollars. That would almost buy us a tank of gas, I thought. That'll last us a week if we were smart. At least it's somethin'.

Right when I reached the minivan, I got a text from Ruby that read:

STEAM JUST GAVE ME $2000 FOR FRIDAY'S SHOW!
ASSDF341!@'OJAFNASDFASDFAVASDF@#%1

I assumed the gibberish was her randomly mashin' the phone buttons out of unhinged joy. She immediately followed up with another text:

I FOUND A FURNISHED APARTMENT NEAR THE DOWNTOWN
STUDIO. WANT TO MOVE TOMORROW?

Hot damn those messages knocked me back. The record company made good on their impulse buy after all and gave Ruby a windfall right when we needed it, and who knew where Friday's show could lead? My innards swelled with pride and excitement for her success. Her dream had become real.

I looked at the forty dollar wad in my hand and another part of me chimed in. The part that doubts and infests your heart and says you ain't worth the air in your lungs because you're a lay about. I knew they were idiotic thoughts, but I couldn't shake their twisted logic.

She didn't need me beside her on stage.

She didn't need my money.

She didn't want my lovin'.

And if she knew I didn't believe, would she need me at all?

❈ ❈ ❈

At least we got carnal that night. Ruby just couldn't get over the thought of that paycheck. She bit the love bruise on my left shoulder hard enough to draw blood. It was the best kind of hurt, and my darlin' sang her luminous erotic song. For that evenin', she put my petty doubts to rest and any hesitation about me faded away.

Ludwell had little reaction to the news. When Ruby told him we were movin' out of the garage the next mornin' for a downtown apartment on the third floor of some complex, he walked back to his house mumblin' "All right, okay, all right, okay" until he was inside. I figured he was ready to see us go, and wouldn't mind if we left earlier so he could watch TV in peace.

But the rib-rattlin' power of a diesel engine woke me up early that next mornin'. It rumbled from the side of the garage and travelled to the back of the building where it birthed a terrible racket of rusted metals clangin' against one another. The engine revved to a great speed and suddenly the garage itself shook as if somethin' had rammed into it.

Ruby and I shot outta bed still in our T-shirt/underwear combo and ran outside to the back of the garage and found Ludwell drivin' his old John Deere tractor, liftin' a front-end loader full of scrap metal. He shot a blank look at Ruby and I, then dumped the loader's scrap metal onto a pile of junk. The noise it made almost did me in.

Ludwell shut off the tractor. "What?"

"The hell you doin'?" Ruby's voice grew sharp.

Ludwell surveyed the trees and field behind him and said, "Since y'all are leavin', I'm gonna make a few changes. I'm gonna level this garage, clear this land out, then I'm gonna get some mobile homes out here and rent 'em out to migrant workers. Been workin' on my Spanish, too. Burro! Feliz! Como say llamas! Estado unidos!"

153

"You've had this garage for twenty years and you just decided to knock it down today?" I asked.

"Long overdue," he said.

Ruby raised her voice and said, "With us still inside of it?"

Ludwell fiddled with the knobs on the tractor. "Yep."

"Okay. I'm done." Ruby threw up her hands and tried to leave before I asked her to wait.

"I think he's bent out of frame because we're leavin'," I said.

"What?" She laughed at me like I'd turned into a gourd. "That man wants us to stay? That's a stretch. Maybe if he weren't so damn grouchy we'd want to see him more than once a year."

Ruby turned to Ludwell and said, "Thank you for lettin' us stay in the garage. Now you can get back to watchin' TV in peace." Before she walked back around the garage, she said "I'm gonna load the van."

Ludwell looked at me, his brow all bunched. "You knew this was temporary, daddy," I said. "I'll pick you up tomorrow so we can go to Ruby's show."

He cranked the tractor back up and drove toward the old soybean field at full throttle. Even when me and Ruby were pullin' out of the driveway, he was still back in that field, drivin' that tractor across that overgrown mess of land. I waved to him from the van window, but he didn't wave back.

TWENTY

RUBY AND I KEPT BUSY in the lead up to her Centennial Park show. Besides movin' equipment from the rehearsal studio to the stage, we hauled all our things into our new apartment on the third story of a little residential complex downtown. Every day, she would go and rehearse with her band in the studio across the street, and they would tear those songs straight out of frame. I mean they were musicians on a whole different caliber than the Ruby and Reggie duo. They simply got better and tighter every time they played.

Her band also brought out the best in Ruby's abilities. She owned the rehearsal stage with a killer charisma, demonstrated precise control over her vocals, and demolished the remnants of her stage fright. Ruby's band was hot, and she knew it with every downbeat and with every chorus. They were gonna go places.

On the night before the big concert, I stayed up late at the kitchen table, waitin' for Ruby to come home. I killed time with my acoustic guitar and played all the old tunes I knew by heart, all the songs that had fired me up over the years or got me to swoonin' about romance or the sweetness the world can show. I could always fall back on the classics.

But the music I played did nothin' for me that night. All I could think about was how most of my favorite songs were created by teams of condescending schemers.

So I strummed the first verse of *Paddy Wagon* instead, but I hated every moment. Then I played a little of *Tramping Ground* until I suddenly stopped and said, "This is shit." I put the guitar back in its case and turned on the TV.

The treatment by the record company was one thing; they were a business and I get why they didn't want me. Hell, I could even somehow learn to live without modern country music in my life. But seein' Ruby so happy with her own band, makin' music that just blew mine away... that just took all the heat outta my fire.

❉   ❉   ❉

Centennial Park outside of downtown Nashville was a warm sight to see that Friday mornin'. Paid for by the city, the concert was a free admission event that took place every month during the summer, and that open green space beside the Parthenon was gonna be packed with crowds of people driftin' through the merchant tents and eatin' from the food trucks parked every which-a-way.

The stage was an impressive rig, set with lightin' systems, video screens and an arsenal of guitars, drums, microphones and speakers waitin' for the chance to blow minds. Sure, people were probably gonna attend because it was free and because the headliner Randolph Suggs used to be a big draw twenty years ago, but any crowd for Ruby was better than nothin'.

When Ruby stood on the stage that mornin' and looked over that empty field, she hopped and squealed in delight. I got up on stage next to her and took in the view. Centennial Park was a handsome, natural space, and my imagination began to override the cold shoulder I had developed towards music. I couldn't help but pick up one of the acoustic guitars on stage and give it a strum. At first it won't amplified but a few chords later the sound suddenly rang out through the PA. I turned to the sound booth positioned just off the left wing of the stage,

156

and Hoover, the multi-platinum producer from the audition at Steam Records, gave me a thumbs-up. I waved back and shouted "Much obliged!"

I walked up to the front edge of the stage and stood by Ruby. "Wanna knock one out?" I asked.

She nodded.

With her on the microphone and me on the six-string, we tore up our old standby *Moonshine* for an audience consistin' of an empty field, the merchants settin' up their tents, and Hoover behind the sound desk. We played like we had in churches and coffee shops only five months prior, roused with fire and charm. Even though I had tempered my musical ambitions, we still filled that space with our sound, and our creation eclipsed the disconnect between us. In my heart of hearts, I was absolutely happy for three and a half minutes, and based on her smile during that song, I'd wager the same for her.

I never wanted that song to end.

❊   ❊   ❊

Ludwell and I stood next to a big ol' shade tree between the back of the crowd and the food trucks, givin' us a great view of all the goings on in the park. The air had finally cooled a little from the blisterin' heat of the afternoon, my sunburn from the signpost job had eased off, and the Parthenon was the epic backdrop Ruby's performance deserved. It was a good evenin' in the South.

"Goddamn there are some ugly people here," Ludwell said as he surveyed the crowd. "Some of these women should not be in daisy dukes."

It was five minutes to 6:30, and there had been no sign of Keith or any notice of his performance. He probably went back to Texas with a couple of his fan club girls, his mission to get laid and prove his hometown now fully accomplished. It had been several days since his sole text to me. It was a shame, really. I kind of missed him.

"I'mma get a Neptune from the beer tent. You want one?" I asked Ludwell.

157

"Make it a tall one," he grunted.

"They're sellin' tall boys for twelve dollars a cup. You could buy a case at the store for that much."

"You can afford it. You're makin' that signpost money now." He tried to keep a straight face but snickered anyway.

I was two people away from the front of the beer line when I heard a small portion of the crowd cheer. I turned around and saw four guys equippin' instruments on the stage. I genuinely wondered who the band could be until the frontman spoke into the microphone.

"Hello, my name is Keith Neck!"

Heartburn run up my chest in a flash. Keith wore a button-up plaid shirt, some nice jeans and the stage lights glistened off his acoustic guitar. He looked smart, I'll give him that. His band looked sharp, too. But why would Keith stay in Nashville and not tell me?

"Everybody say it with me...Keith! Neck!"

The crowd responded with a "Woo!" or two, but little else.

"Oh, that's all right, we'll work on it." Keith said and a sliver of the crowd laughed along. "We're gonna play y'all some songs. First one's called *Belt Loop City*."

The band sounded all right, but Keith looked to be havin' a ball on stage. He pushed his voice as best he could, and he pointed to various parts of the crowd throughout the song as if they were payin' attention. Today would be Keith Neck's greatest achievement, his apex, the day he gave a free admission crowd somethin' to kill time with. I'm sure he'd share the dramatic story of these ten minutes again and again over dinner with me and Ruby.

Keith received polite applause at the end of the first song, and his second song (whatever it was called) was a tired ballad that somehow tested the patience of a crowd that had paid nothin' for a Friday night concert. The crowd began to chatter above the music, and the shine of computer phones bopped up as Keith's second tune dragged to a close.

"Thank y'all for being so kind tonight," Keith said. "We've got one more song to play. I wrote this a few weeks ago when I was drivin' across this great country and saw the many wonderful ways we've been blessed as a nation."

I carried the two beers back over to Ludwell and handed him his tall boy. "That boy is hurtin' and he don't even realize it." Ludwell said after a gulp of Neptune. "Sad, sad, sad."

Keith turned his back to the crowd and yelled "ONE! TWO! THREE! FOUR!" The band kicked up a railroad rhythm with a simple chord progression that got the crowd's toes a-tappin'. The video screens showed an American flag wavin' in the sky while Keith strummed along and sang:

I'm like you
I work hard
I go to church
I drive a truck
Got mud all down the sides

Well I'll be damned if I almost shit my britches.

Every lyric he sang ran on the video screen with the appropriate backdrops of churches, workin' men and heavy machinery flashin' by.

Ludwell yelled over the music. "That sounds like that dumbass song you wrote in the backyard. Did you let him have it?"

I couldn't comprehend a response I was so shocked, unable to think of words or take my eyes off the stage.

And at the end of the first chorus, on the big transition back to G major, the stage lights shined on a shadowed portion of the stage and illuminated a three-man horn section precisely when they blared out the riff I'd written less than two weeks prior.

He had a fuckin' horn section.

Right where I had told him there should be a horn section.

Right where he said there shouldn't be one.

The crowd ate it up, and by the time the horns finished their riff, most of the crowd were on their feet. The song I'd written to mock Hilleman's insult to country music had brought people to their fuckin' feet.

159

My paralysis wore off and a shotgun blast of adrenaline rumbled through my beefy frame. With all of my heart I wanted to kick Keith Neck in the head.

I told Ludwell what Keith had done, but he'd already pieced it together. We set our beers on a bare table and moved through the crowd toward the stage, but the standin' crowd had thickened even more by the end of the second verse, and people were dancin' to every word. Ludwell and I couldn't even move after Keith finished the 'Hot dogs/fireworks...' portion because he asked the band and the video people to play it again so the frenzied crowd could sing along. All the lyrics I wrote? He kept almost all of 'em, even the verse about the crackin' skulls for Old Glory. The crowd liked that part, especially. Of course he changed the dirty bits of the bridge:

Hot dogs
Fireworks
Lovin' all the fine girls

Gasoline
Front yard
Everybody workin' hard

Blue sky
Big lips
Prayin' up to God with

And oh how that crowd chanted that second time around. With the lyrics on screen, Keith led them in a united sing-along. Even in my rage, I remember goose bumps on my arms when a few hundred voices sang my stolen work aloud. The creative slice of me felt as big as the universe, ready to eat the sun.

Me and Ludwell pushed through the singin', dancin' crowd long enough to reach the front of the stage right when the song ended on a big finish. Keith waved to the crowd he had won over in the past five minutes and left them wantin' more of the same. I leaned over the front barricade and hollered "KEITH NECK! LOOK AT ME! LOOK AT ME GODDAMMIT!"

But my calls were gobbled by the roar of the crowd, and Keith walked off stage with band and never glanced an eye upon me. As the cheers died down, one voice shouted above the quietin' chatter. He was a large man about ten feet away screamin' "YEEAAAAH!!" as hard as he could. His fists were clenched, his face was red, and his veins looked ready to burst through his skin as he hollered another five or six times at the empty stage. He didn't even look all that different from me, maybe a little bigger and sweatier. The music hadn't just touched him; he seemed ready to kill for it. A woman beside him leapt into his arms and they got to makin' out hard right there.

"Come on!" Ludwell led me along the barricade until we reached the curtained entrance to the backstage area. The security guard found our names on the list and opened the curtain for us. Immediately I saw Keith sittin' on a speaker case next to the sound control booth, talkin' to his bandmates. He stood up and tried to walk away, but I caught his shoulder and put my arm around him before he could get any further. His bandmates held out their hands and yelled "Whoa! Whoa!"

"He's okay. I know these two," Keith said to his band. "Don't worry, I'm not paying y'all to be bodyguards. I'll be in the food tent in a minute." I let go of Keith, and his band walked off, all of 'em lookin' over their shoulders every so often until they walked into one of the backstage tents.

"Good to see you guys." Keith said to Ludwell and I." How've you guys been?"

I grabbed Keith by the shirt.

"You liked the show, I take it?" He struggled to maintain a grin.

"I told you not to play my song," I said.

"No harm done, there, big man." He tried to wiggle out of my grip, just like Johnny had at Saddles weeks before. "But the people clearly like the song. So can I have it?"

"No."

"Are you even gonna use it?" he asked.

"Might. Might not. But that's my call to decide, because it's my song."

He looked over my shoulder toward the backstage tents, then he winked at me.

An incredibly familiar voice cried out "Reggie! Didn't Keith sound wonderful?"

Ruby almost skipped like a girl as she got close to the three of us. Hilleman followed her over. "I want to give him a big hug too!" she said. I took my hands off Keith and she hugged his neck for a good squeeze. "Oh bless your heart. I'm so proud of you!" she said when she finally let go, but Keith rubbed her back for an extra couple of seconds. "Keith, you remember Hilleman from Steam Records?" she asked.

"Of course!" Keith said as he shook Hilleman's hand. "I'm Keith, Keith Neck!"

"That last song sounded great, Keith." Hilleman said. "It literally got me throbbing."

"Thank you, sir."

"Well, it's a real killer with the crowd. Would you like to record and release that song through Steam Records?"

It's strange to watch somebody's mind work like gears in a factory. Keith's expression was pure shock and confusion until he oh so slowly turned to me. Joyful revelation suddenly overwhelmed him, and his smile went as wide as a Texas night sky, his eyes like a psycho killer.

"Absolutely I would!" Keith reached out to shake Hilleman's hand again, but I swatted it down.

"Keith, you left some important papers at Ludwell's house. I need to tell you where I put 'em."

Keith held up his index finger and said, "One second" to Hilleman. Ludwell and I stepped from the group and Keith followed.

"Did you hear that? Ruby said she's proud of me." Keith said with a grin.

I quietly replied, "You stole my song."

"It was a joke you wrote in five minutes."

162

"I wrote it in five minutes because I'm that damn good. It's not like I've been spendin' the last three years tryin' to launch a music career. Now stop this bullshit and tell Hilleman I wrote the fuckin' song."

"Did you write it down?" asked Keith.

"No."

"Did you ever record it?"

"No."

Goddamn the fuckin' smirk on that string of dick shit when he said, "Then prove it's yours."

If only I had lied, then life probably would've turned out incredibly different for a great many people. But I won't quick enough to come up with a bluff.

Ludwell stepped up to Keith. "I heard him write that song in my backyard, you damn varmint. All you did was listen and laugh and steal, after he helped you around town and I let you sleep on my property."

"What about all those people back home you wanted to prove wrong?" I asked. "The people who said you'd never be a famous songwriter. They'll be right."

"For all they'll know I wrote that song alone," he said. "They won't know the difference."

"If you even try to make a dime off my work I will hire a lawyer to kick your scrawny ass back to El Paso," I said, ready to raise hell.

Keith scoffed. "All you've got is the story of this old coot. That won't prove nothin'."

Ludwell jumped at Keith but I held my daddy back. He chose to walk away before he committed a felony.

"True," I said. "But how would it look if you were immediately sued for stealin' songs before your career even began? It won't matter if I win or lose. Nobody's gonna touch the little weiner named Keith Neck. He's too much trouble."

He looked and waved at Ruby. She waved back. Keith licked his chops and leaned close to my ear as he whispered, "If you or your fuckin' father do anything to stop this moment, I will tell Ruby that you don't believe in God anymore. She might not believe a bunch of church hags, but she will sure as hell believe me. I'll make sure of it. She'll be done with you and your lies."

A lesser man would've bit off the tip of his nose and spit it back at him. But honestly I didn't know how to react. I froze.

"I thought we were friends," I muttered. "I thought we were friends." Part of me still couldn't believe this was actually happenin'.

He stepped back and whispered, "Be a good boy, Reggie. This little weiner fucks back." He went back to Hilleman and shook his hand. Ruby applauded and cheered. Hilleman sparked up his plastic cigarette.

Ludwell came over and said, "You're givin' him the song?"

I could only sigh as I watched Keith and Hilleman walk together back toward the backstage tents, with Hilleman's fake cigarette glowin' green.

"What does he have on you?" Ludwell asked. "Does he have a knife? Cause I got a knife right here." He lifted his shirt and showed me a knife holder stickin' in his britches.

"He don't have a knife, daddy. I'm just...lettin' him have this one. Record people will discover he's shit before too long."

Ludwell grumbled. "That's a cartload of hocky, givin' it away for free. It's your song to give away, I guess. Ugh. I'm gonna go find our beers. I'm drinkin' yours." He passed through the heavy curtain back to the general public.

Ruby skipped over to me. "Ain't this neat? Keith is gonna be on Steam Records too! He really took our songwritin' advice to heart, didn't he?" She gave me a peck on the cheek. "I've gotta get ready. I'll see you in the crowd?"

I nodded. "You know it. Go get yours, darlin'."

On any other day I would've chased and smacked that adorable ass the moment it started walkin' away from me, but my zip was gone. Keith had me by the short ones.

The sound control guy came down from the stage and approached me with his hand out. "Mister Dunn?"

"Oh shit, hey Hoover." I shook his hand. "I've got to be goin'. Have a good night."

"One second, Mister Dunn," he said before I could walk away. He stared at feet for a moment, then looked up. "This is none of my business...but did you really write Keith's last song?"

I gazed past his head, toward the stage, reluctant to answer.

"This is between you and me," he said. "I won't tell a soul."

I chuckled. "What, did you listen in to our conversation with some crazy powerful microphone?"

He shook his head. "No, Mister Dunn, you have a big mouth. I heard you halfway across the stage."

I made sure Keith was gone and nodded. "Yeah, I wrote it."

"Mister Dunn-"

"Call me Reggie."

"Reggie...after overhearing your conversation with Keith, I assume there's a need for secrecy. Don't worry, I'm not prying for details. But if you honestly wrote that last song, I'd like to hear more of your work. Do you like barbeque sandwiches? The Farm House has a great lunch special."

"I'll be there," I said without even thinkin' about it. I just felt it was a good idea.

"Great." He started to leave but turned and asked, "Those lyrics...please tell me-"

"A joke. Total joke."

He smiled. "Good. See you tomorrow, Reggie." He saluted me with two fingers and climbed back up the stage to prepare the gear for Ruby's performance.

I went back out into the crowd and found Ludwell with a fresh beer. Ruby's show was everything she wanted it to be: fun, professional and appreciated by an engaged audience. It was an incredible performance of what I can remember, but to be honest, I couldn't focus on my darlin' person during what became the turning point of her life.

My thoughts and rage kept fallin' back to Keith Neck. What if *Thought About America* didn't sell and he had nothing to lose, or what if he got bored with keepin' a secret and told Ruby about my turn from God just for giggles? In a five-minute conversation he could set Ruby's mind on a track that wouldn't stop until she heard the bonafide truth from me, and then my best friend would cease to be just that.

TWENTY-ONE

TRIPLE-DISTILLED FURY kept me awake that night. I laid in bed next to a zonked out Ruby, and I ran the scenario through my head over and over and over and over and over. After givin' Keith Neck sanctuary in the middle of the night and helpin' him get on his feet in a new town, that little fuckin' weiner stole my shit-pissin' song and blackmailed me into silence. Son of a goddamn!

My anger ramped up faster and faster until rest was the furthest thing from my mind. At any second, Keith could call Ruby and spill the beans. And just like that, my life would be over.

I shot outta bed and put on my boots and walked out of the apartment with my crowbar in my hand.

I needed to use my hands.

Behind our building was a loadin' dock for a bakery, with dozens of wooden pallets stacked alongside its back wall. I walked up the loadin' dock ramp to one of the pallet stacks and let the crowbar slide down my hand until I had a firm grip.

I bashed and bashed and bashed the top pallet until half of it splintered into chunks, then I kept bashin' through to the next pallet.

My arms throbbed with every crack of steel against wood, and the pain only fed my rage.

The advice!

The help!

Why did I trust that fucker? Why did I tell him I didn't believe in God?

The curved end of the crowbar got wedged in the third pallet so I yanked as hard as I could and pulled half the pallets off the stack. I dropped the crowbar, lifted a fallen pallet above my head and threw it against the loadin' dock wall as hard as I fuckin' could. I hollered "YEAH!" when it exploded into wooden chunks.

"Reggie!"

I looked over my shoulder and my wrath cooled. Ruby stood at the bottom of the loadin' dock in a long t-shirt and slippers, but it was too dark to see all of the shock and worry on her face.

"Why are you smashin' pallets and hollerin' your lungs out in the middle of the damn night?" she asked.

I looked to our apartment building on the left. Lights had come on across all three floors, and people watched us from their windows.

My hands were cut all to hell, and my primal anger simmered down. I mumbled, "I thought he was my friend."

"What?" Ruby asked as she walked up the ramp. "What's botherin' you?"

I shook my head, unable to speak the truth about Keith or absolve my own lies. "I don't know." I said.

Finally, Ruby got close and held onto me. "Please talk to me," she said.

We stood there for a moment while I caught my breath. She wanted an answer to my strange behavior, this rabid outburst, everything. But if I said anything about Keith stealin' my song, then he'd know exactly where to strike me.

I sighed while I held Ruby and struggled for a safe reply that would ease her mind. All I could manage, though, was "I just...wish I could be a successful musician, too."

Yes, that was true. I really did wish I was playin' guitar in Ruby's band and sharin' those moments with her. And part of me still wanted Ruby to admit she cast me aside at the record company audition. But those weren't the reasons I started shatterin' pallets in the middle of the night.

My answer seemed to satisfy her worries, though, and she led me back upstairs without sayin' another word.

TWENTY-TWO

I KNEW HOOVER WAS A GOOD MAN once I watched him eat three barbeque sandwiches in a row. The Farm House had never hosted such a champion.

"Damn, I usually can't eat more than two without gettin' clammy," I said after he downed his third and final sandwich. "Plus I like to leave room for hushpuppies." I scooped a hushpuppy into a slab of butter and enjoyed one of life's minor miracles.

Hoover only nodded as he pulled several paper towels off the roll on our table.

"So, that last song Keith played...you wrote it," he said after he swallowed his food.

"Yep." I told him about the horn section riff, the goofy inspiration behind it, everything.

"But this wasn't the first song you've ever written?"

"Naw. I've written a notebook's worth of stuff. About ten or twelve of them are worth hearin'. The rest were just me cuttin' my teeth."

"And that's why I wanted to meet with you. Was 'Thought About America' a happy accident, or just one of many great songs you've got on you?"

I looked out the window, unable to shake Keith's threat off my mind.

"Don't worry, I don't want *Thought About America*," said Hoover. "It's not my style anyway. I want the music you've got beyond the jokes. I want to know if you've got something worth hearing."

"I ain't gonna lie, I got goosebumps when I heard the crowd singing my lyrics like some deranged mob. But after Keith finished, I saw a man consumed by those stupid fuckin' lyrics. And he won't laughin' either. He was yellin' like he'd heard a new gospel. It was weird and fulfillin', all at the same time, seein' a stranger love my work so hard. But honestly, I don't have the heart to make country no more."

Hoover chewed my rant over and said, "Yeah, there are a lot of nutty people out there. If you create something that's really good, then there will always be a few people who will run away with it. Doesn't matter what kind of message you put out there." He took a swig of sweet tea. "So you mainly listen to country?"

"Oh yeah. Some old-timey folk stuff, too...Leadbelly, Blind Willie Johnson, those Depression-era guys. Bluegrass is all right."

"Any other musical preferences?"

"Naw. Never saw a need for anything else. But after what Hilleman told me about the music industry, how everything is plastic, I don't really wanna listen to country now, either."

Hoover nodded as he ate a hushpuppy. "Hilleman was absolutely right about the manufactured aspect of popular radio. Sad but true. But every genre and artistic medium has a certain amount of 'plastic' material filling its ranks. Music, movies, books, paintings...all of these contain terrible creations that were made solely for financial gain, but these same mediums also contain a vast number of masterpieces and admirable works. Your job as a lover of music...hell, your job as a human being is to sift through the meaningless shit and discover the things that truly enrich your life."

"I know you're right," I sighed, "but the fire in my heart just done went out."

"Huh." He had another swallow of tea. "That's too bad. Music is one of mankind's greatest inventions, and I'm ashamed the industry tarnished it for you. Well, I was hoping to plan some way you and I could make music together, but now my afternoon is free. You want to go shoot pool and drink beer at my house?"

Aside from buyin' a new set of toenail clippers I didn't have much of anything to do that day, so I followed Hoover back to a suburb outside of Nashville. We parked in the driveway of a real nice brick split-level with a great yard and a handsome porch swing. Every good home deserves a porch swing.

❈   ❈   ❈

He had a state-of-the-art recordin' studio in his damn basement. It was a gorgeous chamber with microphones scattered all over and a baby grand piano in the corner just waitin' to get torn up.

"Now this is somethin'. Bet you've had some talent in here." I ran my fingers across the many acoustic, electric and bass guitars hangin' on the wall in the basement hallway, all of them in perfect standard tuning.

"Grab one of the acoustic guitars, and have a seat in the recording room."

I remembered I had just told him not an hour ago that I didn't want to make music anymore, and now I was about to take a guitar off the wall because I was so damn excited to play in a studio. It seemed I could be easily swayed.

I grabbed a dark green Martin and went into the main recordin' room. I sat on a stool in front of a expensive lookin' microphone and my imagination went to stirrin' amongst those foam-wedge walls. I'd never sat in a proper recordin' studio before that moment, and I immediately wanted to spend all day in that room, creatin', revisin', perfectin' my music.

Hoover appeared in the control room behind a window of soundproof glass. "Can you hear me?" he said through studio monitors.

I gave a thumbs up.

172

"You can talk through the mic. Let's hear what you've got."

"I'm a bit rusty. Haven't played in almost a week."

"All good," he said.

I strummed on the guitar a bit, eager but unsure how to impress a man who had produced a dozen platinum albums and heard millions of bad songs.

"We're just having fun, Reggie. Pretend you're Leadbelly on his last boxset. The one where he played every song he knew while sitting in a kitchen."

"Heh heh, I don't have five hours worth of material, but I'll give you what's worth givin'."

For the next hour, I sang every half-decent song I'd written and Hoover recorded all fourteen of them in one unbroken take. One more song was never enough. I didn't care if no one else ever heard it. I forgot about Ruby and Keith and God and country music breakin' my heart. Instead I focused on the sound.

When I finished, Hoover clapped from the control booth. "That was fantastic, Reggie. Well done. Come on out and we'll have a beer."

I met him in the basement hallway, and he paused before he opened a new door.

"If you call this next room a 'man-cave', I will kick you out of my house," he said. The both of us laughed. That's when I knew Hoover would be a friend for life.

Through that door stood a heaven any music lover would be happy to die in. It was a sittin' room dedicated to the consumption and worship of sound, and my mind nearly fizzled out from the sight of it all. There was a U-shaped couch in the center, a 9.2 surround sound system, and framed platinum and gold disc awards hangin' on the walls, not to mention the shelves and shelves of vinyl records and CDs. And the TV overlookin' that holy land? Made me wanna kick myself in the head it was so damn huge.

I spent twenty minutes gawkin' around the room. "You've got the banned version of Randolph Suggs' debut record from '92, the one with the sample of chaw stapled to the sleeve. They only pressed a few dozen of these."

"Yeah, Suggs swapped me years ago for the Beatle butcher album."

"I bet my daddy would try this chaw if you let him."

Hoover offered me a bottle of Neptune: Great Dark Spot and I sat at the crest of the horseshoe couch with a fancy beverage goin' down my gullet. He sat on the other end of the couch and flipped on the TV with a remote from the coffee table. "Two hours ago you didn't even want to make music anymore. How are you feeling now?"

"Feelin' great, actually. Playin' around in that studio was fun."

"Good, glad you enjoyed it," he said while flippin' through a near endless library of artists and discographies on the TV. "I liked what you played. I'm gonna show it to a few friends, if you don't mind."

"Sure. That's fine."

"You've got some talent, and you're definitely comfortable in a certain type of songwriting. The rhythms, the melodies, the themes are very country and folk oriented. It's a good foundation, but you'll need to grow if you're ever going to beat Keith at his own game."

"Whoa whoa whoa whoa whoa. What?"

He smiled. "At Ruby's audition at the record company, I watched you struggle for a chance to be heard. I saw how crushed you were when Ruby carried on without you. And now that I've heard over an hour's worth of your songs, I truly believe you wrote *Thought About America*. I once heard you say you're a songwriter, and now I know you're a damn good one. I believe there's an audience out there for you."

Unable to think, I took a few swigs of Neptune. "With all due respect, what's in it for you? You're in the big leagues."

"I've always wanted to foster my own talent and see where it goes. Try something different. Plus I think I heard Keith call me sausage paws yesterday. People that make fatty jokes are simple and I want to make them all cry. What do you say?"

"Well...shit." This offer was incredible, but I didn't know just how much it would take to lose Keith's silence. "I was, uh, plannin' on lettin' Ruby do her thing, you know? I don't think music is for me anymore."

"Okay, I gotcha. Again, I know there's something going on between you and Keith, but it would be a damn shame if you withheld

174

your talent." He paused for a second and nodded. "Actually, let's do this. I'm going to let you borrow a few albums you probably haven't heard. If they don't inspire you to play, fine. Live your life as a happy tour husband and play guitar as a hobby. But if the music blows your mind, will you reconsider?"

I finished off my Neptune. "What do I have to lose? At worst I'd listen to somethin' new for a while." I stood up and shook his hand.

"Great!" he said. "Before you leave, we need a palette cleanser for all that acoustic guitar. We can't get too sensitive, can we?" He scrolled the TV's library to an artist named DJ Tuna and hit play on a song called *Me? I Do It Big*.

"Do you dance?" he asked.

"Yeah, sure I dance. But what do you mean a palette cleans-"

An electronic hip-hop beat rumbled from the powerful subwoofers and an aggressive male chorus shouted:

ME I DO IT BIG!
ME I DO IT BIG!
ME I DO IT BIG!
ME I DO IT BIG!

Hoover got up and threw his hands in the air. His ample hips swayed and rocked to the heavy bass and rapid lyrics attackin' my brain from all sides. It was a lot to process.

"IT'S FUN!" he yelled over DJ Tuna's verse about sweaty club girls. He grabbed my arms and lifted me to my feet. His face exploded in glee when he pointed at the floor. "I SEE THAT FOOT TAPPING!"

Sure enough, my foot was tappin' in time, so I got up and bobbed my shoulders to the sides and got my neck weavin' to and fro. The hip-hop started to make me shuffle, so I gave into the beat and pumped my fist in the air while Hoover and I hollered along:

WHEN I GO TO THE CLUB
THE CLUB DON'T CLOSE!

WHEN I GO TO THE CLUB
THE CLUB DON'T CLOSE!

I dipped and contorted to the rhythm and found out how low I could actually go. (Pretty far, actually.)

A thin guy with spiked brown hair and an oxford shirt came down the stairs and tapped Hoover on the shoulder. Hoover paused the music and bearhugged the guy.

"Oh, is this your brother?" I asked.

Thin Guy kissed Hoover on the lips.

"All right," I said.

Hoover held his hand out toward the smoocher. "Reggie, this is my husband Everett."

I shook hands with Everett.

"Good to meet you, Everett. You've got a real neat house, here. Where'd y'all get hitched?"

"Maine, last year," Everett said as Hoover hugged him again. "I grew up outside of Augusta."

"Oh, Maine is one of my favorite places. The Saint Croix river is somethin' else. Too bad y'all couldn't marry here."

Hoover shrugged.

"I ain't never understood why anybody got quarrel with gay people," I said. "Ain't nobody's business. It's just as natural as anything. When I was little I saw these two longhorn steers pumpin' the hell outta each other in a pasture. They were havin' a big time and those other cattle minded their own business. Daddy told me won't nothin' wrong with man or critter doin' such a thing as long as it's good lovin'."

"Ah," said Everett.

"Well, I gotta head on. I didn't tell Ruby I'd be out this long." I shook both their hands. "But to be honest she's probably too busy to notice I'm even gone."

"You're married to an ambitious woman," Hoover said.

"I'm a lucky man, no doubt." I said. "We're good for each other."

"Oh, hold on one second." Hoover said and went to the music shelf and started pullin' out various CDs and puttin' them into a little plastic box. "Despite their convenience, I'm not a big fan of iPods or MP3 players. You don't always need 4000 songs at your disposal. Focus is incredibly valuable."

He filled up the plastic box and snapped a lid onto its top. "This is a very broad slice of classic rock. I threw in some evergreens and a few deep cuts. I recommend The Who for your initial leap. Many of these songs have been heavily overplayed on radio and TV over the years, but their core power has never been diminished, no matter how many car commercials have tried to corrupt them. I'm actually kind of envious of you, Reggie. You get to hear these albums in their purest form."

"Thank you," I said as I accepted the plastic box. "I'll bring 'em back safe."

They walked me up to the front door and I stopped right before I opened it, because I needed a second to process a thought.

The three of us were outsiders to popular opinion, and I felt a kinship with that parallel. But these two fellars were livin' and lovin' together without compromise, so far as I could see, and in these parts that couldn't have always been the easiest thing. And there I stood in their foyer, afraid to tell my darlin' person that my natural instincts had changed the way I saw the world. I knew Hoover and Everett were just two people tryin' to lead peaceful lives, but they were brave, because they had the nuggets to be themselves.

"If y'all don't mind me askin..." I paused as I made sure I had the words right in my head. "I'm sure it ain't easy thinkin' different around here...do y'all feel like you have to hide how you feel about each other?"

They looked at each other. "I don't feel like we hide, do you?" asked Hoover.

Everett shook his head.

"I was miserable before I came out," Hoover said. "I lived a lie just so certain people wouldn't be offended by my own beliefs. But then I realized I don't like those people anyway, and I'm far more successful than they will ever be, so why should I care what they think? I'm not going to compromise my own truth because a few people choose to be offended. As long as my loved ones understand and accept me, I'll refuse to let the willfully ignorant bring me down. Things are always getting better, anyway."

"Hell yeah," I said.

A big part of me wanted to tell Hoover about becomin' an atheist and hidin' it from Ruby. I wanted to tell him everything. The man seemed genuine, and I already knew he could offer a far more educated opinion on the subject than that little weiner from El Paso. But I didn't want to get burned again by somebody I thought I could trust, so I kept my yap shut.

"Talk to you soon, Reggie. Let me know what you think of the music!" Hoover said as he closed the door behind me.

※   ※   ※

Traffic was light, sunshine was abundant, my window was down. I put *Who's Next* into the minivan's Discman and expected to moderately enjoy a few songs before I put George Strait back on rotation. I mean, shit, the album cover had four fellars zippin' their flies after pissin' on a concrete block. How good could it be?

That opening electronic keyboard tickled my mind in some strange way. My first instinct was to shut off it and return to familiar waters. Reggie Dunn didn't play techno.

But Hoover said this new music would help me get an edge over Keith, though, and I would've done anything to beat him. So I rolled up my window and turned up the volume and let myself dive in.

A sunrise crestin' over a mountain.

Catchin' a catfish with your bare hands.

Gettin' your first tugjob in the back of a pickup.

All of life's most glorious moments were contained in the three chord piano riff of *Baba O'Reily*.

Before I could comprehend the music before me, the drums pounded in with wondrous guitar and a vocal born from a fiery soul.

178

The unpredictable structure made my own songs sound like nursery rhymes. I discovered The Who were four cosmic prophets that had journeyed into galaxies unknown and returned with the truth as they understood it.

I pulled over in the parking lot of a bank and gripped the wheel tight when the violin coda raged deeper into chaos.

After the song finished I shut off the van and stood in the empty parkin' lot and in the sunny heat. I felt powerful, like I'd been given the launch codes to a nuclear warhead. I felt godlike.

You could call me a believer because I was born again.

TWENTY-THREE

FOR THE NEXT COUPLE WEEKS I did little else but play guitar and listen to Hoover's music collection. *Revolver, The Freewheelin' Bob Dylan, Led Zeppelin IV, Definitely Maybe, Eliminator, Born in the USA, Let There Be Rock*...call me a goddamn those days were a revelation. Once I stopped accidentally rewritin' Who songs my songwriting notebook grew by one or two songs every day. The horse trot tempos of country were outshined by the variety of the Beatles, the aggression of AC/DC, and Bob Dylan's testament to the power of a clever man and his guitar. I discovered masterpiece after masterpiece, and virtually every single song was written by the artist themselves. I forced myself to take breaks every so often to let all this new information sink in. I'd leave the house for an hour, and in the middle of traffic or a hardware store a new melody or lyrical fragment would suddenly present itself. I saw potential in everything.

But don't get me wrong. If you get too complex then the music just ain't relatable anymore. If I wrote a two chord thrasher that was an absolute barn-stormer then I wouldn't try to fix what won't broken. A good song is a good song is a good song.

Some of the albums Hoover gave me were made in the 60s and 70s, and I didn't understand how the world had continued makin' chaos for itself. You'd think once *Yellow Submarine* and *Blowin' In The Wind* came into existence that everyone on the planet would collectively realize a lot of the bullshit in the world could be solved with a little talk, music and lovemakin'. If more people had been payin' attention back then, then the Earth would be several decades into global peace by now.

After dinner each night, Ruby and I would sit on the livin' room floor and I'd play all the rough drafts I had conjured up that day. She enjoyed most of what I created in that period, especially my use of songs that went beyond verse-chorus-verse. She recognized I had begun writin' songs that would be best portrayed with an electric guitar, what with the heavier chords and more abstract lyrics.

But she felt distant. Aside from the musical discussions, we didn't talk as much anymore.

One evenin' she asked me to lead the prayer before a meal of beef rice and green beans. I provided the standard list of gratitudes and prayer requests, but curiosity got the best of me. In mid-prayer, I slowly peeked out of my right eye, and those brown eyes looked back at me, wide open as if observin' for further study. I shut my eyes, finished the prayer, and started eatin' like my peek had never happened.

I had a mouthful of rice in my mouth when she said, "Saw you lookin' at me during the prayer." I had never seen her with a blank expression before.

I swallowed the rice and smiled. "Yep. You were kind of quiet. Wanted to make sure you were still there."

"Of course I was quiet. I was being respectful."

"Mmm hmm," I said chewin' my greens. "Then why were you lookin' at me?"

"Just wanted to." She gave a half smile.

I reached across the table and held her hand. For all the years I'd known her, I honestly couldn't tell if she was just being a strange kind of sweet, or if she genuinely suspected me of wrongdoin'. I took the optimistic route and assumed she was just tired from the constant rehearsals.

I never peeked during prayers again, and she never mentioned anything else was the matter, aside from her fatigue and the mild anxiety about her career. We were happy, I think. We even made love occasionally.

But she didn't bite me anymore.

One night before I stepped into the shower, I looked at my naked self in the mirror. Ruby's perpetual love bruise on my left shoulder had faded from deep purples into yellowish orange patches. I rubbed it but felt no pain for the first time in years. She was only in the next room but my heart trembled.

She had begun to cede her territory.

❊   ❊   ❊

The record company threw a party for itself due to that quarter's performance. Their main conference room hosted a dump truck's worth of free booze, catered food, and a hundred-some people dressed up all smart. Bikini girls served drinks from behind a makeshift bar in the back, and a green dinosaur mascot with a giant goofy head walked around takin' pictures with people and grabbin' their asses. Hilleman and Keith took turns doing tequila shots off an ice luge shaped like an acoustic guitar. If the record industry was dyin', nobody told Steam Records.

Ruby couldn't have looked more fine. She was in this tight red dress, makin' everybody salivate. She hung on my arm with a champagne flute in her hand. I'd been writin' songs and she'd been rehearsin', and we didn't see each other much. When we did, things between us weren't too chipper. But for the sake of appearances, Ruby granted me the privilege of seein' her smile for the first time in days.

About an hour after the party began, Bossman Riddle grabbed Ruby and Keith and walked through the partygoers to the front of the conference room.

182

"Clear some room, clear some room!" He barked over the music and chatter. "Or I'll take all your coke!"

People immediately spread away from the front of the room and created plenty of space. Bossman held up a wireless microphone and said, "Can someone shut off that music?" The DJ stopped the music seconds later.

"Hey! I wrote that song!" someone yelled.

"Oh, excuse me," Bossman said. "Can someone shut off that shit music?"

The party laughed.

Bossman cleared his throat into the mic. "Welcome to the celebration of another solid quarter!"

The gathering clapped and cheered.

"We've been busy," he said. "Our recent tours have posted record attendance, and digital sales have continued to outpace physical units, drastically reducing overhead. We've also welcomed the return of a legendary artist, Mister Randolph Suggs."

Polite applause followed.

"But in the past month we've also added two new artists into our fold, both thanks to the dumb luck of Mister Hilleman.

Hilleman yelled out "WOO!" with a mouth full of beer.

Bossman motioned for Ruby to step forward. "Only eight weeks ago, Ruby Naris was touring the country in a minivan with her husband, playing music at churches and coffee shops for little or no pay. But after a fantastic demonstration in this very spot, Ruby has charmed our hearts with a powerful voice and a gor-"

"FINE ASS!" somebody hollered out. The party laughed, of course. Ruby seemed plum tickled. I couldn't even get mad cause it was true.

"And a gorgeous smile, you freaks. A gorgeous smile." Bossman nodded to her. "She is now in the middle of recording songs for her debut album to be released later this year."

The assembled clapped and whistled for my darlin'. Her happiness outshined all the suits and commerce now tethered to her talents.

Bossman turned to Keith and put his arm around him. "And then we have Keith Neck, a friend of Ruby's. I knew from the moment I met him that there was more to this young man, and by hell he proved it a couple of weeks ago when he played a knock-out tune called *Thought About America* for the Friday night crowd of downtown Nashville. He finished recording the studio version only last week, but the response so far has been incredible. Radio stations around the South have sprinkled it into their playlists, and it's being considered as this year's official theme song for a certain professional motor sports organization."

Cheers, hoopla, you know the drill. Keith clasped his hands together and shook them above his head.

"But don't think success has warped him. Keith is one of the most polite and thoughtful young people I've ever met."

Chatter sprang up all around me. "He's such a nice boy," I heard more than a few say. "He's such a nice boy. A nice boy." My eyes couldn't stop rollin'.

"Where is Suggs?" Bossman called out. "Where is Randolph Suggs?" Moments later a short middle-aged man with a grayin' ponytail stood beside Bossman, Ruby and Keith. He looked like he hadn't slept in days.

"But the best news for these two young stars involves the magnificent Randolph Suggs." Bossman pat him on the back. "Now Randolph, your last four albums weren't so well received, were they?"

Suggs stared ahead like a broken soldier. He shook his head.

"And you've had some other bumps in the road these past few years?"

Bossman held the microphone up to Suggs. "Well, I keep having bouts of orchitis, and my ex-wife ran off with my accountant and now I owe three million dollars in unpaid taxes."

"What's orchitis?" someone yelled out.

Bossman said, "People, let's not dwell-"

Suggs took the mic and groaned, "Inflamed testicles. When I'm naked I look like an apple tree."

Out of the silence, somebody in the back of that party laughed hard as hell. I wanted to shake that guy's hand.

"Yes, well, but people still love those old hits, don't they?" Bossman said as he took back the mic.

"Yeah," Suggs said before the mic was back to his lips.

"And you're headlining a forty date concert tour beginning in only a few weeks, and many cities are close to selling out."

Suggs squeezed his face with his hand and nodded.

"But Suggs hasn't found any supporting acts for that tour...until now. Ruby Naris and Keith Neck will both perform as two parts of the triple bill Red Delicious Randolph Suggs tour!"

Cheers overtook the room. Ruby went into shock at the mention of the tour, her hands over her mouth. Keith held up a closed fist as Bossman spoke.

"We've also booked all three of you for Nashville's second annual Birch Bark Festival this October!"

The party provided more spirited applause.

"Your tour is officially ready to take the world by storm!" said Bossman. "How do you feel, Randolph?" He held the mic up to Suggs.

Suggs sighed. "I wish I was dead."

The party laughed and cheered. Suggs walked back into the crowd.

"Now for a teaser of things to come, we're going to have Ruby and her bandmates perform for us. One moment."

Everyone got to chattin' again while tech guys hooked up amps, microphones and guitars at the front of the room. Right before I went back to the drink table, Hoover tapped me on the shoulder. "Hey Reggie, hope you're well," he said after our handshake. "I want you to meet Michael Odom. He'd like to be your manager."

Odom was a shorter guy in his 30s with slick brown hair and what looked like a damn zoot suit. He stepped from behind Hoover and looked me up and down. "Wow, he *is* beefy," he said as we shook hands.

"Okay, I've got a little extra, but I ain't made out of sirloin."

Hoover and Odom laughed.

"I like your sound, Reggie," Odom said with a raspy voice. "Love your sound, actually."

"I showed him those songs you recorded at my studio," Hoover told me. "He digs 'em."

"They're like a twenty-first century version of Springsteen's *Nebraska*." Odom said. "You've got really fun songs, and based on that material, I would like to represent you."

Hoover smiled. "Do you wanna make music again?"

Two people that were not required to love me had told me they enjoyed my music. I could've been drownin' in a vat of Neptune I was so blissed out.

"Hell titty-fuckin' yeah, I do," I said quietly.

"Great!" Odom clapped his hands. "Here's my plan: We're going to start slow and cheap like a wholesome first date. I'm thinking we release the twelve best songs four at a time as a series of digital EPs. We'll push college radio, social media, music journalists big and small. People go crazy for the acoustic stuff. "

"This sounds great," I said. "What's the catch?"

"No catch," Hoover said. "This isn't a Steam Records thing. We'd be 100% independent and free to do what we want. In today's world you don't need a record deal to be a successful musician, but somebody's got to provide the startup capital. I've already paid Odom's initial fee out of my own pocket."

I started to balk but Hoover saw where my brain was goin'.

"This is an investment, not a handout," Hoover reassured me. "If this project makes money, I'll take my cut out of that."

"How much will all this cost?" I asked.

Hoover chewed his thoughts over. "$3500, give or take a C-note. That'll cover digital music retailer fees, cost of pressing a few promo vinyls for the college radio set, a professional website, plus legal fees for the Copyright Office."

"I especially like that last one," I said.

Hoover laughed.

"Don't worry, I'm gonna draw up the contracts to make all this kosher," said Odom. "And I only get paid when you do. We'll have everything in black ink before any profits split between us." Odom's tone got serious. "I know this is a lot to hit you all at once. You can sleep on it and call me-"

"I'm in," I replied. "Absolutely. Of course."

"Nice." Odom shook my hand.

"I need to put a band together first," I said. "The songs I've written lately are too big for just me."

"All right," Odom said. "If you've already got a name picked out we can go ahead and prep the promo material. Anything in mind?"

Nothing popped in. Despite all my musical daydreams, I had never scrounged up a damn band name.

"I'll get back to you," I said.

"Do that," Odom smiled. "Look forward to working with you, Reggie."

"Call me next week," Hoover said as we shook hands again. "I want to hear those new songs, and we can swap albums again. I'm giving you some classical stuff next. You're gonna love The Planets." Hoover and Odom vanished back into the herd of partygoers, hobnobbin' and what not.

I turned my attention back to the front of the room. Flanked on either side by her female bandmates, Ruby strapped on her guitar and led an acoustic rendition of a song that thankfully never made it onto her debut album. The chorus lyrics were:

There should be more threesomes in country
There should be more lovin' with comp'ny

The whole song was about famous country duets and how better they would've been if they only invited more people into the mix. Ruby and her bandmates all did a little dip move with their hips as they sang the word 'lovin'. It was fuckin' stupid so naturally the party loved it. Every time Ruby and her band sang the chorus, violent cheers sprouted up.

187

Right after they finished, the six-foot-tall A&R rep Erin Villeda bumped into me with a frosty mug of beer in her hand. It splashed back on her sparkly blue top, but she didn't notice.

"Holy shit," she said. "Do you ever just want to nail your wife sometimes?"

"That ain't none of your bus-"

"Uggggggh!" she groaned and swayed in place. "Singing about threesomes and I haven't had one in for. Ev. Er." She drank a quarter of her mug right there.

Keith walked up from behind her and put his finger in her beer. She swatted him away and called him an asshole before she slowly eyed him up and down. "Did you come here with anyone, Mister Neck?"

"I'm runnin' solo tonight," said Keith. "Why do you ask? Did you fall in love with me all of a sudden?"

She smirked as she sipped her beer. "I'm not in love with you, cutie."

"Same. My heart is spoken for."

"That doesn't mean we can't have fun." She raised her eyebrows a few times and took another swig.

I waited quietly for Keith to do his thing.

He leaned close to her ear and covered his mouth with his hand.

Villeda gasped and smiled and said, "Oh! I have a secret secret for you too!" She leaned down to his ear and whispered. Keith stroked his chin while she spoke.

"I like that. Quite a bit, actually," he said.

"In two mintues?" she asked.

He winked back. She blended into the party and disappeared.

"Congratulations," I said. "A drunk girl at a party wants to sleep with you."

"She's a good-lookin' woman. Bet she'll be a lot of fun. But I believe all the best girls are taken." Keith straightened his posture.

"You got somethin' to say to me?" I asked.

"No, not really," Keith smirked. "Just wanted you to see what a successful musician looks like."

"Gimme one reason not to stomp your ass all over this party," I muttered through my teeth.

"Whatever. I could kick your teeth in any time."

I set my mug on the floor. "All right. Let's go. Right now."

Keith held up his palm and said, "Wait, not here. It's too crowded. We might hit somebody."

"Fine. Let's go outside."

"No, there's people smokin' out there. They might try and stop the fight."

"Then we'll go to the eighth floor," I said.

"There's construction on the eighth floor," Keith grimaced. "I don't want to fall do-"

I grabbed him by the back of his shirt. "I ain't askin' you on a date."

Keith looked around the party for a second and started to grin. "You wanna dance? Okay. The big office at the end of the main hall. Let me get another drink and I'll punch you out in there."

I let go of his shirt and walked away before I broke his neck.

He stepped into the crowd toward the drink table, and I stepped out of the conference room and into the main hallway of Steam Records. The hall was fairly empty save for a few people by the bathrooms and reception area, and they all seemed plenty occupied by their intoxicated discussions. Light shined through the frosty glass door of the office at the end of hall. I planned to push any furniture against the wall to provide ample combat space. Oh, the little weiner had this whoopin' comin' to him.

I opened the frosty glass office door and froze mid-step. A woman sat spread eagle on the front end of the desk, her legs propped on the desk's corners, and her beaver starin' me in the face. Her hair down there was shaved like a playin' card spade.

Villeda picked her head up and smiled. "Hey there, Mister Man. Come here and show me your poker face."

"No, thank you," I said as I stepped back to shut the door and almost knocked over Ruby in the process.

"AAAHH!" I hollered. I couldn't get out any more than that.

"Hey, Keith said there was an emergency down here." She stepped around me and paused at the sight of Villeda's lady parts.

Ruby's eyes went mad as hellfire.

"I didn't know she was in here," I said. "I swear to you."

Villeda picked her head up again and giggled when she saw Ruby. "Oh hell yes. You can hop on too, you vixen. I need to get fucked haaaaarrrrd!"

Ruby pointed at Villeda. "Look skank, I'll punch you straight in the cooter if you say another goddamn thing!" Ruby slammed the door and crossed her arms. That recurrin' fantasy of Ruby and Villeda in the sex barn died a quick death.

I spoke carefully. "Me and Keith needed to discuss somethin' and we were gonna meet in here. I opened the door and discovered her five seconds before you did. I swear."

She just stood there, her arms still crossed.

"Wait a minute," I said quietly. "What made you come down here?"

Ruby's brow got cross as hell. "I told you. Keith told me there was an emergency. He was right."

Keith's true intentions crashed on me like a slab of Surry County granite.

His hugs with Ruby that lingered too long.

All the times I've seen him starin' at her.

And now he got Ruby to catch me starin' at Villeda's v-hole.

He had already stolen my song.

But now Keith wanted my wife.

I wasn't tempted by Villeda's flesh, but if I chose to speak the truth about his deception, Keith's scheme would have succeeded all the same, cause he would have surely ran his mouth to Ruby about my atheism as soon as she asked about his ruse. And then there'd be no turnin' back. I felt like a conspiracy nut.

Ruby focused on me. "We have always trusted one another, Reggie, and I need you to answer my questions right now. Did you sleep with or intend to sleep with Villeda?"

"Hell no."

"Did you really plan to meet Keith in here?"

190

Of course I did, cause I planned to kick the kid's ass. But instead I told her another lie, and a bad one at that. "Yeah, but I guess I heard him wrong or somethin'. I promise you, Ruby, all of this was bad timin'. That's it."

She rubbed my shoulders and her eyes damn near broke my heart. "Is that the truth?"

"Absolutely," I said.

Ruby sighed. "I believe you, and I trust you because you are my husband, but that doesn't mean I'm happy with you right now."

I nodded.

"Let's go home," she said.

Ruby and I gave quick goodbyes to a few people standin' outside of the conference room. For a few brief seconds, I saw Keith from across the room, standin' on a table and smilin' at me above all the party people. He raised his beer mug in a toast.

I could've filed legal action against him if he didn't toe the line, and his bullshit empire would've been easy come, easy go.

But he wasn't alone anymore. Steam Records dealt with lawsuits all the time, and they probably kept lawyers ready to fuck 24/7. His rendition of my song was about to cash in for everybody, and Steam would protect him and that money with everything they had. Keith knew I was outgunned.

Why didn't he just tell Ruby my secret then? If he sat her down and told her I didn't believe in God anymore she would piece everything together and she'd leave me. He could swoop in to bandage her broken heart and he'd still have his stolen song. So why would he hold back?

Either way, Keith had me up against the wall, and I had to take action. That little shit wanted a war? Fine by me. My wife wasn't some object to be conquered; she was my best friend, and I wouldn't tolerate any attempt to steal her affections.

"Ruby, can you come here for a second?" I asked as I stood by the doorway to the conference room.

Ruby walked back from the reception area and asked, "What?"

I took Ruby in my arms, and dipped her like we were salsa dancers. I gave her a big ol' smooch then pulled her back up. My, she was pissed when she got on her feet again.

"Ooooh, you might get punched tonight," she hissed as she stomped back toward the reception area.

She was mad, yeah, but it was worth it. I looked back across the conference room, and saw Keith still lookin' at me from the top of his table. There was no way he hadn't seen that dip kiss. For all he knew, his little trick with Villeda had turned Ruby on and now she needed to be serviced by her lovin' husband.

I gave Keith a salute, and that smirk of his faded away.

❋   ❋   ❋

Ruby said she believed me about Villeda and kissed me and got into bed with me that night. But not long after we shut off the lights, Ruby grabbed her pillow and went out of the room. For the first time in our relationship, she slept alone on the couch.

TWENTY-FOUR

HERE'S THE PART all you music nerds are gonna eat up: the formation of the band. I'm sure half of y'all got your birds in your hands after readin' that last sentence.

I played Hoover several of my new songs in the listenin' room of his basement a few days after I saw Villeda's long-legged snatch. After every song he never applauded or critqued. He would only say "play another one." I must've played seven or eight songs before he stood up suddenly and wiped his mouth. I figured he was three seconds away from throwin' my guitar across the room and tellin' me to stop fillin' his ears with shit.

But Hoover asked, "Have you found a drummer yet?"

"No. I haven't been lookin' lately. Ruby's been givin' me the cold shoulder and I'm tryin' to fix things betwe-"

"I want to be your drummer."

"Uh...okay. Yeah! Hell yeah!"

For some reason we high-fived. We were two grown ass men, and we high-fived.

"Reggie, these songs...I'm impressed. You've really embraced some different approaches to melody, structure and tone. They're big and

193

ambitious and interesting but they're still fun and they bash along when they need to. And once you get an electric guitar with some power behind it, and a tight rhythm section... holy shit, Reggie. I'm going to let you borrow one of the Rickenbackers. And an amp. And some effect pedals. We're going to be something special."

He paced back and forth around the room. "I don't mean to invite myself into the band, you know? I don't. I just want to be part of this. I haven't been in a band for years, and constantly sitting in the control booth has bored the shit out of me. Plus I don't have to produce another album for another six months, except the album our band records."

"I'd love to have you on board! Drummin' and producin'? Absolutely."

Hoover stopped and looked me in the eyes. "And yes, I know what you're thinking. I know I'm a little overweight, and I don't look like I would have the stamina to last ten minutes, let alone a full set. I'll never be Keith Moon, but I can-"

"You fuckin' kiddin' me?" I almost hollered. "You believed in me after overhearin' an argument and an hour's worth of songs. And I count fourteen platinum records hangin' on your wall. I think I'll take your word for it."

✸   ✸   ✸

I had to find a bassist before Hoover and I could ever rehearse as a musical unit. The local guitar shop always had a bulletin board full of want ads and resumes for musicians in the area, so I grabbed a bunch of phone numbers and scheduled meetings with bass players in Public Square beside the courthouse on a Sunday afternoon. I spent ten to fifteen minutes with each of them, listened to them play, talked to them a bit. They were all college-age boys or burnt-out metal guys lookin' for a hobby to pass the time. After two hours of bullshit, I figured I'd need Hoover's help to find a decent bassist.

Until I met Sadie at 3:15.

She swaggered up to my bench wearin' a green tanktop and denim short shorts covered in cigarette-sized burn holes. She was a trashy kind of hot: not my type, but I could see the appeal. Her shoulder-length blonde hair was stiff as hell, probably from all the product I smelled on her when she sat down. She shook my hand then adjusted her beat-up short shorts.

"My name's Sadie and I'm going to be straight with you. I'm tired of games. I want a man that's worth my time. I like hikin', paintin' and fuckin'."

Sadie shook her head and huffed. "I shouldn't have said that. Fuckin' is the name of my old band. I played bass and fiddle and kept drunks from walkin' off with my kid sister who sings."

She pointed at me with contempt in her eyes. "I'll admit, I'm 37 and a little older than most ladies, but if you meet my sister and sleep with her I swear to God I will stab you in the thigh." She pulled a cigarette out from the waist of her shorts. "Just like a damn man."

"Sadie, I think you've got the wrong idea," I said.

"Just be honest with me and I'll be honest with you," She said with an unlit cigarette dangling from her lips. "I'm really fun and I love variety. Sometimes I go to the Wendy's near Market Street, other times I go to the one by Wendover. I like to mix it up nowadays. I used to go to the one on Battleground everyday but I threw hot chili in the manager's face after she wouldn't give me an extra thing of barbeque sauce."

She took the cigarette out of her mouth and looked out at the park. "World's fallin' apart."

I chuckled. "Sadie, I ain't tryin' to date you."

Her eyes filled with fire. "Oh, so you just want the milk for free, huh?"

"Sadie, can you play bass or not?"

She got quiet and thought to herself.

"Wait...oh shit...this ain't my online date, is it?"

❄　　❄　　❄

You now know how I met the drummer/producer and the bassist, but I don't need to tell you much about the lead guitarist. I've already told you plenty about him. Only thing I need to add is that Ludwell volunteered to join before I had even finished askin' him.

Hours later, all four of us were down in Hoover's basement studio, rehearsin' and tryin' sounds.

"So...you're gay, right?" Ludwell asked Hoover as they sat behind the studio's big ol' sound board.

"Yes, I am." Hoover replied, his eyes on the sound board.

"And that handsome fellar I met upstairs, that's your husband?"

"Mmm hmm."

"Do y'all use condoms?"

"Goddamn, daddy, you don't ask people that," I said from the couch across the room.

Ludwell turned to me and hollered, "I don't know the physics of it! Hush, now."

Hoover spun his chair to Ludwell and held back laughter. "My husband and I are in a committed relationship. No, we do not use condoms."

Ludwell leaned back in his chair. "That's right. You got some sense about you. My daddy never used a condom neither, and I know that because I've got sixteen brothers and sisters. He always told me liberals wanted us to use condoms so we couldn't outvote 'em one day, so he fired live ammo all his life. Hell, he was 65 years old when I was born. Kept his prostate healthy enough to see me get married and have that youngin'." He thumbed over to me. "That's what longevity is all about. Keepin' your prostate busy."

Hoover laughed as he leaned toward the microphone by the sound board. "Okay, Sadie, take one."

Standin' on the other side of the glass in the recording room, Sadie listened to my acoustic demo for *Molecule* and moved her head in time to the click track. Her bass crawled from a purr to a steady groove and turned my little song into somethin' greater, into somethin' powerful.

I'll be damned if goose bumps didn't get over me again. That was the first time I heard a bandmate build off of my creation in an effort to make a better work. Sadie heard notes where I had heard none before, which led to a flood of counter melodies and guitar fills. I jumped off the couch with my hands up in the air, ready to burst with expression. As of that moment, I became addicted to inspiration.

✻   ✻   ✻

Hours into that same night, Odom texted Hoover askin' for our band's name so he could buy a website.

"Suggestions?" Hoover asked.

I stared at the grid of knobs and switches on the sound board, my brain primed to churn out a new lick or lyric every ten seconds, but still unable to deliver a decent band name. I wanted a name that was short and distinct, not some ironic bullshit like 'What the Cereal Hid Today' or somethin' desperate like 'Pussy Fart'.

"Hey," Ludwell said through the control room speakers.

I looked at him in the recordin' room with his old mahogany guitar strapped round his neck.

"How about your momma's maiden name?" he said.

✻   ✻   ✻

The first four-song collection, simply called *EP One,* was released on the internet a couple of days before Ruby left on her support tour with Randolph Suggs. Odom forwarded digital copies to dozens of music news sites and publications in hopes they'd review the thing out of sheer curiosity and the legacy of Hoover's production history. Even though the EP only contained those acoustic songs I'd made on my lonesome the first time I played in Hoover's studio, we still used our new band name: Delaney.

✻   ✻   ✻

Our early mornin' drive up to the tour bus was a quiet one. Ruby and I hadn't been exchangin' much information aside from the scheduled tour stops and her days off. She said "that would be nice" when I told her I'd like to visit her somewhere fancy like DC or Pittsburgh, but she kept on starin' out the window.

She hadn't gotten upset about Villeda's thang or quizzed me about my prayers for several days. Her rehearsals, studio sessions and tour meetings kept her so busy we never got a chance to talk even if she had wanted to. I didn't make much effort either. I spent so much time in Hoover's studio just to keep my mind occupied. I stopped askin' questions, stopped tendin' to her heart. We shared dinners and a bed sometimes, but not much else.

That parkin' lot behind the record company building was full of families sendin' off their loved ones on Randolph Suggs' two month tour of the US. The official caravan was a couple of tour buses and a few pickup trucks with trailers attached to their fifth wheels. I spotted a few familiar faces from the record company, such as Suggs dressed in his pajamas and Keith Neck sayin' goodbye to his fan club of young women. They all swooned over Keith like he was some legitimate musical heartthrob, but George Harrison he won't.

I loaded Ruby's bags into the bottom of the tour bus while she signed some documents with some record company bureaucrat I'd never met before. While she was busy, I went over to Keith's gaggle.

"And you're gonna watch my tour diary, right?" Keith said to one of the girls from my church.

"I'll check it everyday!" she replied.

"And I'll keep discussions going on the forum," said another church girl. "And I'll make sure all of my friends buy your song at least five times."

"Gotta get to number one somehow, don't we?" Keith smirked.

A chorus of affirmation and praise rained upon Keith just as he noticed me. He soaked up the attention for a moment and said, "Excuse me, ladies. Gotta talk to my friend real quick. Thanks again for being so wonderful!"

The girls each gave him a hug and they walked away from the loadin' area as a single chatterin' clump.

I made sure Ruby was still busy then I closed the distance between Keith and myself. "So now we're friends again?"

He smiled. "Of course. Don't friends set each other up with hot A&R reps?"

"Nice try, boner boy. Ruby knows I'd never betray her."

"Oh yeah? Not what I heard."

I ignored that. He wanted me to lose it in public.

"You're fuckin' lucky Steam has a dozen lawyers on their payroll," I said.

He sighed. "I'm so glad you figured all that out on your own. I was all ready to make this big speech on how your original threat had lost all its teeth since I was officially a corporate asset now, but you saved me the trouble of explainin' it all. Thanks."

I didn't give a shit about lawyers or copyrights no more, but I won't gonna let him know that. I leaned closer. "You stole my song, you're cashin' my royalty checks and you're tourin' the country with my wife. Then you try to fuck up my marriage with that naked Villeda stunt?"

"Okay," he said holdin' back laughter, "I got that idea as we were talkin' about our fight. I knew Villeda was tryin' to get laid that night and the pieces just lined up. It was nothin' short of perfect timin'. I'm clever, you have to gimme that."

"Isn't your fan club keepin' you busy?" I asked as I nodded over to the gaggle of late teens on the other side of the parking lot.

He shrugged. "I mean, the fan club is fun, but none of them are keepers. They lack a certain...fire. But Ruby? Now she's a keeper. Like a take-her-home- to-mom, hold-her-all-night-long, write-songs-about-her kind of woman. She deserves another dimension of love and affection. Hell, didn't you used to know that?

A lightning bolt surged through me. "Always knew you had a thing for her."

There won't enough shit in the world for the grin he gave me. Took all I had not to slam my fist through his head.

"Why didn't you just tell her about me in the first place?" I asked. "Would've saved you a lot of trouble."

"No shit. I thought that would be the easiest part." Keith spit on the parkin' lot. "I know Ruby said she believed you when you said you were still born-again, but she didn't mean it. Every time I've seen her after that church lunch, she's needed little excuse to go on and on about how she worried you might really not be a Christian anymore and how your soul was in jeopardy and blah blah blah. Found her cryin' in the rehearsal studio a few times. Her concern for your salvation overshadowed all else, and it became clear she still cared about you. I can't tell you how many tickle fights I tried to start with her. It didn't matter what I said or did, she couldn't stop worryin' about you." He ran his hand through his hair and smiled. "The only way to get you off her mind was to let you do it yourself, funny enough."

My steel-toed boots would've fit well in his stomach.

Keith started to say, "Now because I'm a nice guy-"

I couldn't help but chuckle.

"I'm serious!" He grinned. "I am a nice guy. I ain't forgotten how you helped me when I first got to Nashville, and I sure as hell ain't forgotten that great song you wrote. Granted, you wouldn't have been inspired to write it if I hadn't been there, so in a way you've always owed me that song, but that ain't here nor there.

"But because of your support, I'll propose a new deal." Keith looked from side to side and whispered, "Just walk away. Forget about the song, forget about the lawyers, forget about Ruby and just walk away. If you do that, I'll write you a check for $15000 after this tour finishes, plus I swear I will not mention a word of your betrayal against the almighty God, and when Ruby finishes fallin' out of love with you, she'll still remember you as a good man. That last part isn't true, of course, but at least she'll think so. Your marriage is in rough shape, Reggie. It's time to let it die, cause she deserves to be with someone who makes her happy. Someone who shares her faith in God's will."

My fury stuttered for a second. What if she did deserve someone better? What if my selfishness really was keepin' her from a new dimension of happiness? What if, after all my declarations of non-faith, leavin' her really was God's will?

I didn't realize I'd been caught in my thoughts until Keith slapped me on the shoulder and said, "Be sure to watch my tour diary. Take care, Reggie."

By pure instinct I wrapped him in a tight bear hug. His fan club all swooned a loud "AWWWWWW!" from across the parkin' lot. He smelled like three different kinds of cologne.

"I'm not perfect," I whispered as I held onto Keith, "and I may not worship God anymore, but I know I'm a good man. You've got some balls to think you can win me away from my wife with money. I will be your personal apocalypse, Keith Neck."

I let Keith go and he adjusted his shirt. "Good luck with that apocalypse, as she and I embark on a two month long tour, gettin' cozy on the tour bus. What are you gonna do? Follow her around the country like a hobo?"

Hold up.

That idea tickled my bird.

It seemed I could scheme too.

Keith picked up his duffel bag and threw it into the bottom of the first tour bus. When he reached the door, he looked back before he stepped inside the idlin' bus.

He didn't even know what he had inspired.

I went to my minivan and leaned over the driver's seat, starin' at the floorboard as if my answer could be found in mashed up fried chicken crumbs. The time for hesitation was through.

I ran up to Ruby before she got on her bus and asked her to wait. "Gotta give you somethin'," I said. She knew little about my sessions with Hoover and nothin' about Delaney, so she was right surprised when I handed her a plain CD case containin' all of the songs the band had recorded thus far.

She looked at the handwritten song titles on the insert. "Why didn't you tell me about this?"

"Well, I guess, I...you know, we haven't really been..."

She nodded. "I know."

"I figured you've got time to listen, I guess. You got the CD player?"

"Yeah." She went into her purse and held up the Discman from the minivan, the Velcro strips still on the bottom.

"Okay, good. You'll recognize a few songs on there, the rest you'll have to let me know what you think."

"Of course."

I held her hands and she gave me her first genuine smile in a couple of weeks. I savored her nose and cheeks and the little mole on the left side of her chin.

Ruby turned away before I could see more of her teary eyes. She looked back after she climbed onto the bus and blew me a kiss. I clenched my hand in the air and pressed it against my chest.

The buses and trucks rode off the parking lot and I waved until they were out of sight. The windows were too dark to see anything but faint shadows, but I waved anyway.

※   ※   ※

I sat in a plastic booth at a diner with a triple decker sausage biscuit in front of me but I couldn't force up an appetite. I watched traffic pass on Interstate 40 for at least half an hour and wondered.

Wondered if I should leave Ruby so she could live accordin' to her God's will.

Wondered how I would begin such a conversation.

Wondered if Ruby would resist or be relieved at the idea of endin' our marriage.

Wondered what the hell I was going to eat if I went back to livin' on my own. If I couldn't microwave my dinner then my options were either fast food or starvation.

I tried not to think about the worst case scenario. I had to hope for the best, and wait for my longshot idea to take root in Ruby's mind.

I had picked a corner of egg off my biscuit when my phone rang. I answered immediately.

"I love that CD you gave me," said Ruby over the phone. "You're really good, Reggie."

My throat got tight at the sound of her voice. I barely managed to say "thank you."

We talked for a good while and I couldn't stop smilin'. There was no hesitation in her voice, only genuine praise for the music I'd written. "I am so proud of you," she said. "You are a talented man." I wanted to hug her so damn bad, but she was so far away and gettin' farther with every passin' second. It was the first enthusiastic conversation we'd shared in the longest time.

Then I played my card.

It was a little strange and a little expensive, but I saw no other way to regain Ruby's deepest affections before she decided she didn't need me anymore.

"Ruby, I've had a crazy thought," I smiled. "And I bet you're gonna like it."

TWENTY-FIVE

"A TRAVELLIN' BAND?" Ludwell asked. "Playin' on the street like a gang of ragamuffins?"

"Yep," I said. "Odom already told me he can send me a list of good places to play in every city on the tour. If we need permits to play somewhere, he'll line 'em up. Other than that, we've got nothin' to worry about."

"Naw, nothin' to worry about," Ludwell said, "except for police, vagrants, power supply and the elements."

"They don't worry me," said Sadie, pickin' at her fingernails." I have a certain way with vagrants."

I had called the band to meet at Hoover's house not long after the Randolph Suggs tour buses left for Raleigh. The four of us sat around the studio control room, discussin' a plan barely four hours old. At first I felt like some dictator due to my requestin' a meeting in the middle of the day, but everybody admitted they weren't doing anything important anyway.

"As we all know, the album's not finished." said Hoover from the big chair behind the sound board. "Why do we need to follow this tour right now?"

I stood up and paced around the room. "Well, we need to play as a live unit, no doubt about that. We can try our songs in public, and we'll hear what works and what don't. Plus ramblin' is its own kind of fun. I'm an old roadhog at heart. But I ain't gonna lie. The biggest reason to do this is a personal one. Hoover, could you find Keith's tour diary on your computer?"

Hoover clacked on the computer by the sound board and found Keith's tour diary on his official website. Posted only two hours prior, the video began with Keith leanin' his head against the tour bus window, him holdin' the camera out beside him.

"Howdy everybody," the little weiner said. "This is Keith Neck, comin' to you from a caravan headed east to the Tar Heel state for the first stop of the Red Delicious Randolph Suggs tour. Of course we've got Mister Suggs-"

Keith lifted the camera over his head and caught a shirtless Suggs sittin' at a table, munchin' on an ice cream sandwich with nary an expression on his face. The table was covered in empty sandwich wrappers. "There's the hitmaker himself," said an off-screen Keith.

Suggs held up an ice cream sandwich and bumped the camera. "Want one?" he asked with a chocolate-stained mouth.

"No, thank you." Keith replied as he turned the camera to the seats across the aisle. Ruby stared out the window with headphones on, her CD player in her lap.

"And there's the lovely Ruby Naris," Keith said. "Say hey, Ruby!" She didn't respond, but her foot tapped in time to an unheard rhythm as trees zoomed by outside her window. "Ruby, can you hear me?"

She didn't notice.

Keith mumbled somethin', but I swore he said, "hottie".

He turned the camera back to himself. "Now I know everybody is all excited about my debut single *Thought About America*. People have been tellin' it's the greatest country song of the past ten years. Tell me somethin' network TV doesn't know." He chuckled to himself.

"But I've got more songs than just that one. One quite close to my heart is my follow-up single called *Where There's Smoke*. I wrote it for all the unhappy women that suspect their lovers are being deceitful, but they can't quite prove it. These women are neglected emotionally, and they deserve to be with a man that'll treat her goo-"

"All right, turn that shit off, please," I said. Hoover closed the video.

I faced my bandmates. "I have reason to believe that Keith is gonna try to pull a Johnny Cash on my June Carter during this tour. But the Man in Black didn't give service to that kind of shit and neither do I."

"You're positive he'll do somethin'?" asked Sadie. "He's got some fuckin' nerve."

"I've always sensed he's had his eye on her," said Ludwell. "I'd believe it."

"Ruby and I haven't been doing great lately, and Keith knows that. Plus he asked me to leave her right before they got on that bus this mornin'."

"Holy shit, that's brazen," said Hoover after he whistled.

"And Ruby's okay with this piggyback tour idea of yours?" asked Ludwell.

"Spoke with her a few hours ago and she approved. She'll be busy with promotional events at every stop, so I don't expect to see her much. But I'll take what I can get."

"So you'll be sleepin' on their bus then?" Sadie asked.

"Me and Ruby, uh, ain't quite there yet," I admitted.

The band thought everything over.

"I know this is my fight," I said. "And I know it's a strange, sudden request. But that woman is my darlin' person, and she's damn near the only reason why I think this world is worth a hang nail. I would walk on glass or army crawl through pig slop if that kept her by my side."

"I'm in," Hoover said after a brief silence. "I'll have to fly back here every so often for meetings and the husband, but yeah, I'm down. Sounds like an adventure."

"Thank you. Sadie?"

She pulled a phone out of her pocket. "Lemme call out of work." After she dialed, she said, "Hey, it's Sadie. I can't come in tomorrow...it's my birthday...yeah it was my birthday last week too...I celebrate birthday week...okay...that's fine."

She hung up. "I'm free from tomorrow till forever. Let's do this."

I turned to Ludwell sitting on the couch. "Daddy?"

He rustled his thick gray hair. "Who's gonna take care of the bees while I'm gone?"

"They're bees, daddy. They'll take care of themselves."

"Yeah, I know. Just bein' hard headed."

I know I thanked y'all a dozen times that day, but there ain't no harm in saying it again.

Thank you, Hoover.

Thank you, Sadie.

Thank you, Daddy.

Y'all are somethin' else.

❖   ❖   ❖

I'm a firm believer in not spendin' every wakin' second around the people you love, and the rest of Delaney agreed. We drove my minivan and Hoover's old SUV out onto the highways and swapped passengers and drivers often. This strategy kept all of us sane and prevented any road trip blowouts between the four of us. If you were hopin' for a tell-all memoir where I talk about how Hoover got so drunk he shit in the ice cooler, you will be disappointed. Those weeks of campin', travelin' and playin' music were a near-constant joy. Even Ludwell laughed for most of the trip.

Playin' in downtown Raleigh was tough. We went to the corner of Hargett and Wilmington where Odom told us to go, and set up beside a little parking lot. It was a time tryin' to find electric outlets for our gear, and though we never got too rowdy out of respect for the area, people didn't seem interested by our uptempo rock/country mixture. Ruby had told me she would try to stop by our street gig after her radio interview, but she had to cancel her visit about twenty minutes before we started playin' so she could get to her soundcheck.

No big thang. There were thirty-nine more cities on that tour itinerary.

207

Nobody paid any mind to us until this one young couple stopped by and shared a dance as we played an early version of *All The Women I Never Wanted To Kiss*. The couple gave us a dollar and the guy started recordin' us on his computer phone for whatever reason.

And right then I see this older fellar stroll across the intersection, headed straight for us. The man's clothes and face were haggard and he smelled like a shit cake but that didn't stop him from walking directly in front of me and starin' me dead in the eyes as I sang and strummed my electric guitar. I smiled once, but otherwise ignored him, thinkin' he was just a bit off. He stood there for the rest of the song, and once the band finished he said, "Five dollars" into my microphone.

I looked at our money collection in the open guitar case on the sidewalk and saw it only had the one dollar from the couple and the quarters I threw in to give people the right idea. "Sorry, we don't have five dollars." I said.

He kept starin' at me. "Five dollars," he said into the microphone again.

Hoover rustled through his travel bag and handed him a granola bar. The man glanced at it then stepped closer to me, his odor was a strong type of awful.

I tried to say, "Look, we don't have any-"

The haggard man suddenly reached into his pocket, and I prepared to swat away whatever weapon he planned to produce. But he instead pulled out a little baggie of marijuana.

Ludwell stepped forward. "Damn, you must've paid five dollars for that cause that's the dirtiest chronic I've ever seen. I can go buy you some rollin' papers if you're dyin' for a spliff."

The man grabbed all of the marijuana from the bag and shoved it in his mouth. He chewed and crunched and spit the stems back into the baggie. Then he put the baggie back in his pocket and walked back across the street.

None of us knew what to say. We kinda laughed, more cause it was strange than funny. Once we made sure everyone was all good, I got ready to bang the first chords of *Walrus Tusk* when I saw that young couple from earlier, still recordin' us on their phone.

208

We made friends and exchanged impressions of what just happened and watched the video of 'Weed Man' four times in a row. I had been so focused on Weed Man I never noticed how close the couple had gotten in order to get a better angle on the action. They saw and heard everything, even Ludwell insultin' the man's chronic.

I figured that video would just be that couple's souvenir of a bizarre encounter between a street band and a vagabond.

Never thought anybody else would ever want to watch it.

❋   ❋   ❋

I only got to talk with Ruby for a few minutes between the end of her show at the downtown amphitheater and the tour's departure for Virginia Beach. The number of fans waitin' for her around her bus genuinely surprised me in the best of ways. She had only released one single by that point, but she already had a bunch of young people askin' for autographs and pictures.

"It's the video for *Moonshine* that's doing the heavy liftin'." She told me after she met with her last fan of the night. "It came out last week but it's been watched almost ten million times. Have I not told you?"

I shook my head. An omission of that size did not put me at ease.

Her eyes got all big. "You need to watch it. You will definitely like it." She grinned like a devil.

"Before you leave," I said, "I gotta tell you what happened to us today. We were play…oh, hey Keith!"

Steppin' out of a gaggle of female fans, Keith walked toward the tour bus before I called out to him. His smile melted away once he realized it was me.

"Reggie," he said without expression. "You're…here."

"In person." I tipped an imaginary hat to him. "You look cute in them tight jeans."

He huffed and climbed onto the bus, grumblin' somethin' awful.

"Time to go!" hollered the bus driver. He cranked the bus to life.

"We'll talk soon," I said. "Drive safe."

"You too," she told me. "Sorry I didn't get to see your show today. I'll try next time!"

"All good, darlin'. You're a busy superstar. There's always tomorrow."

She climbed onto the bus and turned back to wave. I waved back. The bus door closed and the tour caravan rolled out of Raleigh.

❈   ❈   ❈

Hoover showed me Ruby's music video for *Moonshine* and immediately I knew why it was a hit. It was a mix of her lip-singin' in a studio and footage from that muddin' event several weeks prior. Ruby looked fit as fuckin' hell in those short shorts and mud scattered all over her legs. To be fair, it won't even raunchy, she was just that good lookin' for the camera. There was even a few seconds of myself lookin' like some local roughneck scratchin' my underarm and drivin' the four-wheeler with Ruby in the inner tube. But the best part? *'Moonshine'* was one of her compositions, only dressed up with some typical modern country production, like an exagerrated Southern twang and an overpolished vocal. It was a fun song, and I'm glad Steam carried enough confidence in her to release it as her debut.

I tried to watch Keith's video for *Thought About America* but I couldn't stomach his bullshit so I shut it off after the first chorus. It was mainly Keith playin' a black and red acoustic guitar in front of a giant American flag and some haybales. He kept pointin' at the camera after every fuckin' lyric. He looked like a USDA-certified asshole under that tan cowboy hat.

I did see the little weiner later that day when I went to try and see Ruby. He was in the backstage parkin' lot in Richmond, surrounded by a bunch of suits from Steam Records, all of 'em arguin' and shoutin' atop one another. All of a sudden Keith throws up his hands and shouted, "Shut the fuck up! All of you!" Them Steam people got quiet real quick.

"I don't need no songwritin' team!" said Keith. "I'm an artist and I've got somethin' to say that's never been heard before and I'm gonna say it all myself. My song is a few days away from goin' platinum again, and y'all are tryin' to chop off my-"

One of the suits interrupted and said, "Look, Keith, we're just tryin' to hel-"

"No, no you're not," said Keith. "I'm writin' my own songs and you're going to market the shit out of them. That's all I need you for. Period."

All them suits just stood there in silence.

"Get lost!" shouted Keith. "Get!"

The suits scattered, and Keith clapped his hands as he hollered out a victory yell.

❊   ❊   ❊

Ten days into their cross-country journey, the Randolph Suggs Tour took an official day off in Pittsburgh, so Delaney followed suit. Hoover flew home to see his husband and work on record company mess, while Ludwell hung out with Sadie and her kid sister who drove into town for a rowdy visit. All of us needed the rest from the annoyed pedestrians and traffic and sunburn. And despite the great music we were makin' together, the public never really seemed to give a shit. Richmond and Washington DC had better things to do than watch us play. In Philadelphia some dillweed tossed an open can of soda into my guitar case and another took off runnin' with our buskin' tips. Sadie ran after the damn bastard but no luck. Band morale wasn't fabulous.

On the mornin' of the break day, I drove up to the venue to pick up Ruby from the tour bus caravan for a fancy breakfast outside of town. Throughout the past ten days, I had yet to spend any real quality time with her, what with her sound checks and radio promos and what not. I needed to prove that she was my primary objective regardin' Delaney's street tour or else I could kiss my marriage goodbye.

When I got to the backstage parkin' lot, all of the tour personnel — a couple dozen musicians, roadies and record company people were gathered together in a few big clumps, apparently waitin' for the official signal to begin their day off. I had just stepped out of the minivan when one of the roadies hollered, "All right, everyone, let's join hands for prayer."

Aw hell.

The clumps of people began to join hands with one another until everyone made up part of a big ol' prayer circle, includin' me with some record people I didn't know. I saw Ruby on the opposite side of the circle and we both exchanged smiles. I was about to mouth the words 'you are fine' when I noticed Keith Neck holdin' her left hand and smirkin' all the live long day.

The holy roadie prayed for the Lord to protect everyone on their day off, and everyone closed their eyes in reverence, save for me and a certain song thief. Keith and I stared each other down as the roadie prayed for the Lord to keep us away from "marijuana cigarettes". Keith looked at his hand holdin' Ruby's, then winked at me. I knew he was tryin' to bait me into rage like a warthog with his nuggets caught in a gearbox, so I kept my cool.

I mouthed the word 'nope' and smiled back at him.

※   ※   ※

It didn't matter that I had gotten the food from Waffle House, cause Ruby enjoyed our picnic breakfast at Cedar Lake all the same. The view made the eggs and bacon and orange juice taste better anyway. We were tucked back in the woods, away from any walkin' paths or designated overlook areas. It was right nice, listenin' to the loon calls and what not.

Ruby and I talked about her tour, her new songs, Delaney, and all the shit in between. For the first time in weeks, she was sharin' a discussion with me and volunteerin' information about her life. She may have been on the other side of the picnic blanket, but progress is progress. It was a relief.

After we finished eatin', she stretched her legs out in front of her and reached for her toes. "Thank you for breakfast," she said.

"Thank you for comin' along," I said.

"It's nice to spend time with you again. I've thought about you a lot."

"Same here, darlin'."

She stared at the lake for a little while, and I just looked at her. Hell fire, she was a purdy woman. I thought about sayin' that very thing right then, but then I had a better idea.

"Wait one second," I said while I got up and climbed into the minivan.

I came back out totally nekkid with only my acoustic guitar strapped round my neck. Ruby clapped and whistled as I stood before the picnic and played a rousin' rendition of *Staple My Head Back Together*. She had a hoot over my bare ass.

That moment was the whole reason I went on that wacky street tour. All the sparse crowds and the Weed Man encounter and those nights sleepin' in the minivan? Worth it, just for that picnic breakfast.

We didn't make love that day, despite my obvious enthusiasm. But I sure as hell made Ruby laugh. I didn't care that I had to get nekkid in public in order to get that laugh. Fine by me. She was worth lookin' stupid for.

TWENTY-SIX

DELANEY ROLLED INTO CINCINNATI expectin' more disinterested passersby, but after we set up in a little courtyard I'll be damned if a dozen people didn't show up specifically to hear us play. We knocked out a few originals and an Oasis song to energetic applause and scattered shouts of "Yeah, Delaney!" I had noticed a few singin' along to my lyrics, so I finally asked our little audience, "How do y'all know about us?"

Half of them yelled back "Five dollars!" and the other half giggled. A young woman in bright purple dreadlocks walked over and showed us a video on her computer phone. It was titled:

HOBO EATS WEED FOR DELANEY BAND (FIVE DOLLARS)

That Raleigh couple had posted that crazy video online and even included our website in the description. It had been viewed over 100,000 times.

"Yeah, dirty chronic!" some guy yelled at Ludwell. My daddy pumped his fist in the air.

214

A few songs later, two young guys stumbled over from a next door beer garden, holdin' glass mugs full of draught.

"Hey gentlemen," I said into the mic. "Gettin' buzzed on a Friday afternoon, that's all right."

One of the drinkers shouted, "Hey Delaney, play *Paddy Wagon*. Please."

The other drinker repeated, "*Paddy Wagon*, yeah."

Paddy Wagon was no longer the acoustic track I had performed in Ludwell's backyard. Hoover's drums gave the one-two beat a real stomp, and Ludwell borrowed some of The Who's flamenco influences, but it was Sadie's fiddle that transformed the song into a barn-stormer. It was still a tune about bein' lazy and stupid, though. People dug that kind of stuff.

We obliged the request and fired up the tune. Sadie barely completed one round of her fiddle riff when one of those beer garden guys sucker punched the other one in the mouth. The band stopped playin' immediately and yelled "Whoa! Whoa!" in unison with the startled audience. The punched guy stumbled back but didn't spill his beer mug. He eventually faced his attacker, put his mug down on the ground and raised his fists. "Where's the music?" he hollered.

"What?" Hoover yelled back.

"It's okay, we're good," said the attacker as he set his own mug down on the pavement.

"We're all friends here," replied the punched guy.

I looked at the band. Ludwell shrugged, so Sadie jumpstarted her fiddle riff and we restarted *Paddy Wagon*. The audience all took a step back as those two guys charged one another and beat the drunken hell outta each other while we played the song that became their fightin' anthem.

The first guy got socked in the gut a few times, the other one took a hit to the nose and a kick to the ass. But the two fighters wore out quick and bear hugged for a few seconds before they started bobbin' their heads in time after the first chorus. With arms over their shoulders, the two fighters danced out a bloody and bruised rendition of the can-can, and a few of the bolder audience members joined them

215

just as everyone present chanted the final chorus with a violent power, as if their hearts would have stopped beatin' if they didn't sing as hard as possible. They hollered:

We're all going on the paddy wagon!
We're all going on the paddy wagon!

I had goosebumps for the rest of the day.

✻   ✻   ✻

I learned an important lesson on that tour: People. Are. Bonkers.

After video of the *Paddy Wagon* fightin' dance posted online, people crawled out from everywhere and started using our street shows as an excuse to lose their marbles. Thanks to Odom postin' our schedule on the band's website, we began to find crowds waitin' for us at whatever intersection or downtown courtyard we were planned to play at, and that turned our show into a circus. In Indianapolis, people organized somethin' called a flash mob and in the middle of *Molecule* everyone in the audience suddenly went to kissin' each other and swappin' partners like it was a square dance. In Peoria the audience actually did square dance in a nearby fountain. By Kansas City we had to apply for a permit to play in Mill Creek Park cause there were over a hundred people tryin' to see us play in a little courtyard downtown.

People used to ask us if we staged those scenes in Raleigh and Cincinnati to drive up publicity until the whole scene hit critical mass. I can confidently say there was no scripted conspiracy to get Delaney on the radar, cause you can chalk our explosion up to a truck full of nuts. Fans also started throwin' in five dollar bills in our collection case in honor of the Raleigh Weed Man. None of Delaney minded that one bit.

A few bloggers liked to approach Hoover after shows since he was a multi-platinum producer playin' alongside a bunch of roughnecks. Hoover always played up my songwritin' and his wish to be in a band again whenever he was asked if he was "above all this" or if he was

216

goin' through some mid-life crisis. All them bloggers and writers had the hardest time believin' Hoover was in Delaney just for the thrill of DIY rock and roll. Of course, their misunderstandin' got everybody talkin' about us that much more.

Sure, there was a fair share of crazy those days, but for every nut or attention seeker we'd always win over a few more authentic listeners. Usually they ranged from teenagers of all stripes to people a little older than me, but every so often somebody Ludwell's age would have a dance and sing-along. Aside from the crowd size, there were never any problems at our shows. Everybody had a good rowdy time at a Delaney street gig.

Okay, so the Des Moines cops did interrupt one gatherin' and threaten to take everybody's cheeba, but when they saw everybody was otherwise bein' ruly the law turned a blind eye.

But by Madison, Wisconsin, Delaney was flyin' high, and Odom had gone ahead and booked us with the proper permits to play in whichever public space would tolerate our growin' crowds. But what's rock n' roll without some hellraisin'?

Minneapolis was another tight show, with probably 150 people listenin' and dancin' and singin' along. We were playin' in this park with all these wacky sculptures, includin' one with a giant spoon scoopin' up a big ol' cherry. I couldn't imagine a more appropriate venue for our show.

Halfway through the set, a park security guard drove up in a golf cart and stopped between the band and the crowd. He was about my age with dark brown flat top, and a walkie-talkie in his hand. Once we finished our song, he looked at Ludwell and said, "Excuse me, sir. You'll have to stop playing."

Hoover pulled a paper from his back pocket and held it up. "We've got a valid permit for this show."

The guard shook his head. "Yes sir, but we've received a noise complaint-"

Our fans began to "BOOOOOOO!!!", and the guard held out his hands as if he were tryin' to signal them to simmer down. The whole complaint business was total horseshit. We had never gotten a noise complaint before, and aside from our audience, I couldn't even see another person in the area. We were hidden away by a picnic shelter in a little corner of the park, far from the more crowded areas.

"We've received a noise complaint and this music has to stop immediately," The flat-top guard said from his golf cart.

"What did you say?" Sadie asked.

"We've received a nois-"

Sadie thumped her bass and drowned out the guard. Then she muted the strings and the crowd laughed. When the guard tried to speak again, both Sadie and Ludwell hit their instruments and the guard's voice disappeared altogether. Hoover held up the permit as the guard gave Ludwell the stink eye and drove back down the sidewalk in his golf cart. Our fans cheered and the band leapt into a rowdy version of *Walrus Tusk*.

A couple minutes later, seven park security golf carts rolled around the far corner like a damn military column. They all surrounded the band as if they were makin' a wagon circle, and stepped out of their carts as soon as they had parked.

The Flat Top Guard hollered somethin' at me over the music. I pretended not to notice and kept singin'. Flat Top Guard nodded to his colleagues and they all moved in. Most of them started unpluggin' our amplifiers and the music suddenly went quiet. Two more guards grabbed Hoover by the arms and dragged him off his drum kit fightin' and screamin'. Hoover kicked one of his snares over and it knocked the high hat to the concrete, makin' a loud fuss. The moment Hoover got to his feet, the two guards sprinted back to their golf carts, cause Hoover looked ready to whoop some ass.

The Flat Top Guard smirked and spoke into his walkie-talkie: "Noise complaint has been issued and resolved." He put the walkie-talkie back on his belt and said, "Please enjoy your quiet visit to-"

I raised my fist in the air, stepped around that guard, and sang the final lyrics to *Walrus Tusk* at the top of my voice. Sadie and Hoover got next to me and chanted along as hard as they could. Ludwell banged on his acoustic with all his might, but the singin' voices of our audience overwhelmed all other sounds. Those people sang our lyrics back at us loud enough to stop a pacemaker.

I've always struggled tryin' to describe how that raw appreciation felt, so I'll call it like it was: It was fuckin' cool.

The guards got back in their golf carts and left, unable to argue with the consent of the peacefully assembled. And I never got a look at any paperwork regardin' that complaint, so I never knew who lodged it. But I did get a text from Keith right after our show ended, and it looked like this:

:-)

*   *   *

Keith's video diary of their tour became a frequent joke due to his arrogance and growin' delusion, and the diary got even better when he started broadcastin' live during his performance in Omaha. He started filmin' himself anywhere he could get a decent signal, so his brief five minute videos became hour-long rants on his favorite kinds of jerky or the merits of brunettes and blondes and redheads. Once he left that webcam runnin' while he took a nap. I still don't know if it was an accident.

Of course he broadcast the ceremony where he was awarded a framed platinum disc for two million sales of *Thought About America*. He had all his lackeys around him, his band, Hilleman and all the head honchos of Steam Records, everyone shakin' heads and smirkin'. I would've traded five years of my total lifespan for the opportunity to magically appear at the ceremony and fart in Keith's mouth.

During one of his video diary rants, he proclaimed, "I was hired for a Sassafras Burgers commercial that was due to air around Christmastime. They filmed me eatin' a big ol' beef burger then they wanted me to face the camera and say 'Happy Holidays!' You know what I said back to that director? I said 'I say Merry Christmas, not Happy Holidays. Not Season's Greetings. Merry Christmas.' The director said 'not everybody celebrates Christmas, Keith.' Guess what I told him? I told him that I'll pray for 'em."

We were settin' up in a park in Denver when Hoover loaded up the newest diary feed. Keith was backstage at his tour venue, sittin' in front of all the roadies rollin' gear onto the stage. In the background, Ruby crossed the stage to set a mic stand down.

"Come have a seat, Ruby!" He yelled across that busy stage.

I barely heard her say "I'm helpin' out, Keith. You should help too."

"Come talk for just for a minute," Keith said. "You don't get paid to set up gear anyway."

Ruby walked over to Keith but continued to stand.

"So tell the world of Keith Neck fans....what does Ruby Naris like doin' besides music?"

"Well, I like to hunt and exercise, and my husband and I enjoy travellin'."

Keith laughed at the camera. "Oh yeah, I know your husband. He works in pig lagoons, right?" A smirk followed, naturally.

Ruby smiled. "No, he's actually a musician too. He's the singer of a band and they're followin' our tour, playin' downtown scenes and havin' a good time. They're called Delaney."

Keith oversold a concerned look. "Your husband's band is followin' our tour? I don't know, Ruby...doesn't that sound creepy?"

"Actually I think it's sweet. He can't stand to be away from me for too long." Uh, her smile to the camera bout tipped me over.

"But I only see him around now and then," Keith added. "And me and you have been hangin' out almost this entire tour."

"Well, as you know, I've been busy with all the shows and the interviews and the travellin'. It's been tough to find time. But we're found times here and there to support each other. Plus his band have gotten busy themselves recently. They're really good."

Keith suppressed a smug grin. "But I remember a few months ago, when you auditioned for Steam Records, your husband tried to play alongside you and they immediately asked him to let you play alone. Then when he insisted on playin', you mashed your own hand against his guitar strings and asked him to stop. So if Steam Records rejected him, and you didn't even want him playin' with you, he must not be that good." Keith shrugged. "I don't know, I'm just callin' what I see."

Ruby stared off and got all worried in her brow. She walked away from Keith's sideshow, leavin' the maestro to make stupid faces until he thought of a new way to waste the earth's oxygen.

Hoover cut his phone off before Keith's mouth sent me into a grumpy rant.

I walked away and spit on the sidewalk and dug my heel into the grass with a hard kick.

I wasn't pissed off because Keith mentioned the audition. I was pissed because he was right.

Delaney played to a regiment of a couple hundred lively fans in Denver, half of them wearin' goofy clothes or barely anything at all. They sang, they danced, they gave us more than enough money to cover expenses. But I didn't put my usual gusto into *Caddo Mills* or jump into my fancy shuffle during the bridge in *Sun Keeps Burning*. Keith's tour diary video just took the fire outta me.

I got a text from Ruby near the end of our show:

COME TO MY SHOW TONIGHT? PLEASE?

We'd been on the road for a month at this point, but I had only seen her set a few times near the beginnin' of the tour. Delaney had started takin' up more of my time, despite the fact I was on this tour primarily to save my marriage.

I made it out to the Botanical Gardens amphitheater just after her second song. Ruby was a gorgeous creature in a red and white sun dress with an acoustic round her neck - hot damn I was married to a fine woman. She buzzed whenever she approached the microphone and surely made her audience throb cause they hollered and whistled every chance they could. "RUBY I LOVE YOUR LEGS!" one lady shouted. She had good taste.

"Much obliged!" Ruby replied and ripped through seven more songs to a crowd that was all about some of her country warblin'.

Before her final song but after her necessary plug for Randolph Suggs' impending set, she paused. "A friend reminded me today that I haven't been supportive of a special person lately. A person who has always had my best interests at heart, even when his own dreams took a back seat to mine. I let him down at the audition where I got signed because I didn't support him. I was also mad at him when I found him lookin' at another woman's cooter-"

The crowd oooh-ed and chattered.

Ruby smiled. "Don't worry, it was a crazy party. We found this woman at the same time and...whatever. Point is that I haven't been a good wife for the past few months, and I forgot to trust my best friend. So before we begin our final song, I would like to say that I'm sorry, Reggie."

My oh my how I wanted to squeeze that woman. I fought back the water in my eyes.

"Oh, and everybody check out his band Delaney. They're incredible." And then Ruby burst out with a killer rendition of *A Fantastic Color*.

I didn't wait for her to meet with fans after the end of the show. I moved past the throng of well-wishers and immediately found her by her tour bus and held her as tight as I could without puttin' her in an emergency room.

"I've prayed for you every night," she whispered into my ear. "I want us to be okay."

"Me too, darlin'," I said. "More than anything. I've...prayed for you too."

Did a liar like me have any business lovin' on someone as wondrous as Ruby Naris? No, and part of me felt like the lowest kind of dishonest shit for my claim of prayer. But the rest of me wanted my wife just too damn bad, and it was a lie I was willin' to live with.

TWENTY-SEVEN

ODOM FLEW OUT TO MEET us in Salt Lake City on our break day. We all rode in Hoover's SUV, and from the moment we picked him up at the airport, he had his ear to a phone and a giant grin across his mug.

"A lawnmower fell on Duane Mason!" he said away from the phone.

"Who?" asked Sadie.

Odom pressed the phone to his chest. "Duane Mason, the keyboardist for The Crimson Pachyderms. He was mowing his grass and the mower toppled over and he broke both of his arms."

"That's awful," said Hoover.

"No, that's wonderful," Odom said. "The Crimson Pachyderms pulled out of the Birch Bark Festival. I'm talking to the booking manager of the festival. I'm going to get you guys on as their replacement."

"The Birch Bark Festival?" I asked. "You mean Nashville, in two weeks time?"

Odom nodded and put the phone back to his ear. "Look, Mister Garba, The Wood Blocks are has-beens. You knew it when you booked 'em. Nostalgia act. Delaney, on the other hand, is burning up wherever they play. You could call them bubonic they're spreading so fast. Search for them online. Their videos are insane."

I leaned forward to Hoover's seat. "He wants us to replace an established act? I know we've had good crowds lately but we've never charged people admission. And we don't even have a finished album."

Hoover nodded.

Odom covered his free ear with his hand. "No, they don't try to incite riots. No, their fans will not burn the venue down..."

Ludwell shrugged. "You never know."

"Yeah, they've got country roots," Odom continued. "They do a fiddle thing...okay, this is the festival's second year, right? Wouldn't you rather be on the cutting-edge? Oh come on, climb off my ass, will you? If you are going to finger my butthole, could you at least...Wait, seriously? Okay, I'll ask them."

He put the phone to his chest and turned back to us. "Would you guys play for free?"

✾   ✾   ✾

The lead-up to the Birch Bark Festival were the fastest days of my life. In those last few weeks, Delaney's fan base exploded thanks to Ruby's onstage endorsement and her continued mentions of us in her show and interviews. Her support validated us with a slew of bigger publications that were already callin' Ruby Naris the next big force in country. Instead of more solo recordings, the third and final Delaney EP was a collection of songs not destined for our eventual album, and it received the best critical reviews we'd had up to that point. We got so many people at the shows we had to start using multiple five gallon buckets to collect money. We steamrolled through Boise, Seattle, Portland, California, Albequerque, Texas, Atlanta, Savannah, leavin' a trail of fun and fire in our wake. As we neared the end of the tour in Charleston, the band started to believe Delaney might actually belong in the six o' clock Saturday night slot at Birch Bark.

All of us were on top of our game. By the time we reached Charleston, Hoover must've lost fifty pounds thanks to weeks of drummin' and dancin'. Sadie damn near looked and moved like a pro athelete, since she insisted on carryin' the heaviest equipment by her herself on every stop. I had lost the belly pooch I'd had for years, and even Ludwell gained some muscle mass on his shoulders. Delaney was doin' things.

My daddy never said much about the concerns of his heart, and I suppose I inherited a bit of that stubbornness. But I understood him when he came up to me right before we left Charleston for the festival in Nashville. We were all standin' in a parking lot after loadin' the gear in the minivan, and I stepped away to admire Jupiter shinin' away in the night sky.

Ludwell held his hand on my shoulder for a good minute. I had heard him laugh and joke and carry on more in the last two months than I had in the past twelve years, and he especially got along with Sadie whenever they shared cigarettes and hellraisin' stories. He and I took in that night sky and didn't say a word.

I took it as his way of sayin' thank you.

❉　　　❉　　　❉

Ruby and I still couldn't find much time to share during the last leg of the tour, especially since she now overshadowed her headlinin' act, much to Suggs' relief. We always made the time every day to hug and kiss and joke around before other obligations crossed our schedules, no matter how brief our meetin'. We shared dinners when we could, and we even spent the night in a hotel on her day off in Pensacola. Both of us understood our unique opportunities and we promised we'd cozy up after the tour was in the past. But by the end of that tour, things between Ruby and I were purdy damn strong. We also prayed together every mornin' for at least a minute. It was so good to hold her hand again, to make her smile, to touch her skin, to hear her talk while she hoped for the best. I didn't mind fakin' prayer at all.

During each of our quick meet ups, Keith managed to work himself into the conversation almost without fail. Ruby would always mention how Keith made her dinner the night before, or how he bought her some toothpaste because she had a piece of collards stuck in her teeth for a whole day, or how Keith wanted to record a duet with her. It was annoyin' but I always played it off like it won't nothin'.

In Jacksonville he dedicated *Thought About America* to her, and after the show he found the two of us backstage and asked her what she thought about his shout out.

"Oh, well ain't that nice of you! That's the first I've heard of it," Ruby said, surprised. "Thanks, Keith!"

When Ruby walked off to the commode, I got close to Keith and told him, "She didn't hear your dedication because we were makin' love on the tour bus. In your bed. I loved your pillow, by the way. What's it made of? Memory foam?"

He turned and stomped down the hall towards his dressin' room, talkin' to himself all mad.

Those were good days.

❊   ❊   ❊

It was nice to be back in Nashville at the best part of the year, in mid-September when the brutal summer heat had finally relented its 24/7 assault and the breeze was a little crisper and easier to breathe.

The 2nd Annual Birch Bark Festival was a two-day affair that featured a couple dozen artists performin' at a number of bars, honky tonks and other venues around the city, with the biggest acts performin' at the Union Auditorium. Even for it bein' in its second year, the crowds arrived in droves to catch the latest music, and organizers were smart to include non-music events to shake things up, with foot races, beer tents, and what not.

I went with Odom and the band early that Saturday mornin' to sign the paperwork for the gig. The bookin' manager Mister Garba was all excited we were willin' to play for free but he was pissed off he couldn't find any staff willin' to fire the startin' gun for the festival 5K foot race that was due to start in twenty minutes. Once I told him about my firearm experience he volunteered me for the job and gave me a snub-nose startin' pistol loaded with blank rounds. Looked and felt like the real deal.

A hundred runners lined up near the entrance to Centennial Park, ready to roll. I fired the startin' shot and all manners of people passed me by. One fellar ran in cowboy boots with an American flag tied round his neck, another girl wore nothin' but a bikini, some swim goggles and a scarf three feet long, and I swear I saw that green dinosaur mascot from the record company party sprintin' as hard as it could. After two months of bizarre Delaney audiences, I expected a strict come down when I returned home, an abrupt shift in dress and demenor. But maybe Nashville had embraced the wacky after all.

The festival office was locked when I went back to return the startin' gun, and I won't about to walk around with a racin' pistol that resembled an authentic weapon. As I peeked through the office window, both Hoover and Sadie texted me sayin' they needed me at the backstage of the park amphitheatre. I tucked the pistol behind my back and told myself to remember to give that thing back as soon as possible cause my concealed carry license expired a year prior. Probably shouldn't have mentioned that, if any ATF are readin'.

Apparently Keith had a big event about to take place on his live web cam bullshit. He had been ridin' high since *Thought About America* got picked up for the upcomin' race season broadcasts, and his tour diary frequently featured his delight from the weekly royalty checks. His road crew, however, did not care for the young upstart's diva-like antics and behavior. By the time I'd met up with the band near the Parthenon, Keith's road crew had loaded up the live stream of his tour diary on a TV outside one of their tour vans. There was nearly a dozen of us standin' around, waitin' to see Keith's newest contribution to the world.

Filmin' in one of the many artist trailers stationed elsewhere in Centennial Park, Keith's camera sat fixed above a table adorned with lit candlesticks, a vase of red roses and a bottle of champagne. Although he wasn't due on onstage at the Union for another three hours, Keith had already dressed for his show in his faded American flag tanktop and slim leather jacket.

He sat at the table and sweet talked into the camera. "My dear fans, thank you for bearin' witness to yet another banner day in the official summer of Keith Neck. I'm so glad you could be here with me today. Now let me send a text real quick, and we'll get down to business." He took a deep breath and messed around on his phone. A minute later, sunlight poured into the trailer and Ruby walked through door behind him.

I leaned back. "The hell?"

One of the road crew said, "Keith told me last night he planned to make a move today. I figured you'd want to see before you kicked his ass in for us."

"The fucking balls on that kid," said another roadie.

Hoover frowned and turned back to the monitors.

"Hey Ruby, have a seat," Keith said as she sat by the table. "Have. A. Seat." He put placed two red champagne glasses on the table and launched the champagne bottle's cork into the ceiling with a pop.

"What did you need to talk about?" Ruby wiped sweat from her brow. "Whew, it is really warm in here, Keith. Is your AC broken?"

"You are here for a celebration of a few things." Keith poured the champagne into the glasses. "We're celebratin' the final stop of our incredibly successful tour together, your album debutin' at number nine on the country charts, and my song tearin' up everything it touches. I also wanted to celebrate...us." He sipped from his red glass before she ever touched her own.

Ruby held her eyes a particular way when she was both confused and intrigued by an idiot. The urge to barge into that trailer vanished the moment I saw that look. I'd witnessed it plenty of times myself.

"Oh yeah, we didn't kill each other on tour. I'll drink to that." Ruby downed half her champagne right there.

Keith laughed. "No, Ruby. I want to celebrate our friendship, our dear, dear friendship." He grabbed her hand restin' on the table. "Let's find out what else is between us."

Ruby looked at the webcam, then back to Keith. "Do I have lines?" she whispered. "I'm confused. I don't wanna mess up your show."

Keith leaned toward her. "There are no lines, no scripts. Only my passion for your every breath, your every step, and your intoxicatin' smile. Oh, I have loved you since I first saw you in El Paso months ago, and our late night talks on the tour bus only made my passion grow. I have sung my heart out for the chance to prove I am the successful, talented, lovin' man you have always dreamt of." He lifted her hand and kissed it. "And yes, it is hot in here."

Keith took off his tanktop and sat there topless, his little nipples pokin' out.

She stared at him, her brow cross as hell. Last time I saw that look was when I accidentally dragged deer entrails into the house after I hit one with my old truck. "Just so I understand, is this for real?" she asked quietly.

He looked her in the eyes and smiled. "Ruby, I've been dyin' to touch you and kiss you and give you unknown pleasures. I am deliriously in love with you. How long have you been in love with me?"

Keith tried to kiss her hand again but she cocked her head back and laughter rolled out of her like tidal waves. Keith slowly leaned back and let go of her hand, unsure whether to grin or cry.

Ruby looked straight at him and laughed, "Even if you didn't look and act like a fifteen year old boy with too much money in his pocket, we would NEVER share any sort of romance because I am happily married."

She held up her left hand for the camera, and the weddin' band I gave her in the middle of a fishin' trip three and a half years prior sparkled on.

Keith suddenly appeared like the child that didn't want to play with the mean kids anymore. He reached for the camera but Ruby slapped his hand down.

"Don't try to turn it off," she said. "You wanted a show."

He stared at the infinite bubbles risin' in his champagne glass as Ruby chuckled to herself. "I thought you and Reggie were done," he said. "You talked about your problems-"

"My husband is a good, God-fearin' man-"

Keith started to speak. "Actually, he-"

My heart stopped for a moment, but Ruby immediately countered with "Nope. Stop talkin'."

I dodged a bullet there.

She cleared her throat and continued. "My husband is a God-fearin' man with a big heart and a pair of arms the size of the Blue Ridge Parkway. He agreed to take you in when you mysteriously appeared in Nashville this year, and I know he regarded you as a friend. And now you have the gall to try and seduce me on your live webcam while you know he is somewhere within a mile of this trailer."

"It's the tan one by the John Thomas statue," said one of Keith's roadies.

Ruby took a second to breathe and continued. "And any problems in my marriage are nothin' compared to you broadcastin' private matters that I discussed with you in confidence and using them to trick me into makin' out with you in this hot ass trailer while your dime-sized nipples try to poke me in the eyes."

Ruby chuckled again.

Keith put his American flag tanktop back on in silence.

"Do you have anything to say before I leave for my show?" she asked.

Keith didn't dare take his eyes off the glass. Ruby got up and laughed her way out of the trailer. The moment she left Keith reached for the webcam and shut off the camera feed.

Holy shit did we all laugh. One of Keith's road crew guys got so tickled he banged his fist against the side of the van and knocked the TV down.

When Ruby found me before her show at the park ampitheater, she leapt into my arms and kissed me a hundred times.

Keith could keep my song and the money. I'd take Ruby any day.

✻　　　✻　　　✻

The band and I watched Keith from the balcony of the Union Auditorium. The crowd enjoyed the openin' number probably because a somewhat familiar name took the stage, but that energy fell hard after the first few songs, and the audience chatted and played on their phones for the next forty five minutes. All of Keith's set consisted of tunes he had written and they just won't no good. He debuted a new upbeat number called *Beaver Fever*, a desperate attempt to retread the blue-collar spirit of *Thought About America*. This new tune contained the eloquent lyric:

I work as hard as a beaver
don't matter if I'm sweaty or workin' wood

He sang that with a straight face, I shit you not.

Even before Keith soured on me, he was always too damn proud to realize his output needed a lot of work before he started paradin' his creations as masterpieces. Why the little weiner didn't accept any of the songs from the Steam songwriters to tide him over, I don't know.

His band clearly won't doing him any favors, cause they played with all the pep of a middle school band class. Of course the final song was the now white-hot *'Thought About America'*, and when that horn riff blared to life, the crowd immediately hooped and hollered along to their anthem of the day. But those big-screen monitors told a different story. Keith didn't seem as invincible as he usually did on stage. That smirk was nowhere to be seen, and he looked to be havin' a dreadful time.

It was lovely.

❧   ❧   ❧

Delaney waited in the backstage area of the Union. I was minutes away from playin' on the same stage as Cash, Dylan, Springsteen, Chet Atkins, Noel Gallagher, and a hundred more legendary musicians. I reminded myself to send Duane Mason of the Crimson Pachyderms a get-well-soon card and his lawnmower a thank you note.

I got a little nervous when I saw the types of people makin' up the crowd. I had expected a big ol' herd of our wacky faithful would be attendin' the show, but almost all of the pews were filled with more conventionally dressed festival goers. And I don't use the word 'pews' as some beatnik metaphor. Although there were 2362 marked places to sit, there were no individual chairs. All of Union Auditorium's seating consisted solely of solid-wood church pews, a callback to the Union's original purpose as a local Baptist church in the 19th century.

Minutes before we went on, I suddenly smelled fake strawberries as the band waited backstage. I turned around and there was Hilleman, sittin' on a crate, smokin' his damn e-cigarette. He blew vapor above our heads.

"Okay, so you call yourselves Delaney?" he asked.

"Yep," Ludwell replied.

Hilleman pointed to each of us and said, "Let's see...you've got an old guy on guitar, a butterface on the bass, sausage paws on the drums, and a weather-beaten hick on the mic. I don't know, guys, I think you really missed an opportunity to call yourselves Ugly Stick. He took another strawberry drag.

Ludwell stepped up to him. "Oh, that's one of them cyber cigarettes. How do they work?"

"Simple." Hilleman held up the e-cigarette and pointed to a port on its back. "The miracle of science."

Ludwell grabbed the e-cigarette and held it up. He looked Hilleman in the eyes and said, "You're already an asshole. This makes it obvious." Ludwell put the e-cigarette in his shirt pocket and we walked onstage not twenty seconds later.

❖   ❖   ❖

The mix of the audience itself was oil and water. Sure, we had some fans decked out in all sorts of colors, but they were sprinkled amongst the overwhelmin' number of cowboy boots and button up clothes. There was even a regiment of a hundred people from my church near the center front, all wearin' white T-shirts with our church logo splashed across the front. I spotted that old goat Miss Edna even before they shined the house lights on the audience.

Most of the crowd didn't dig our first few songs. Usually we killed with *Cosmos* or *Walrus Tusk*, but those festival goers were hungry for a pure country sound that we weren't providin'. The crowd won't rude or nothin', just bored. I almost felt like I was runnin' a Keith Neck show. I had planned for such a response, however. Three songs in, I played our trump card.

"Ladies and gentlemen, I am delighted to welcome the fantastic Ruby Naris to come play some guitar with us."

My, did that venue rumble upon the sight of her arrival from the wings. She was back in her classic green dress and cowboy boots, the same knockout combo that had bowled over the little weiner in El Paso. She waved to Sadie and Hoover, but gave a full hug to Ludwell. That shocked the hell out of me.

We launched into *Paddy Wagon* and then we were wetter than a prom date. Country or no, our tunes were tight and our energy was electric. Delaney + Ruby Naris were a flawlessly timed machine that floored the Union with melody after melody. Thanks to Ruby's endorsement, the more reserved members of the audience were immediately more willin' to give our sound a chance.

The crowd kept cheerin' hard after *Sun Keeps Burning*, our usual closer. I assumed they had loved our act so much that we might have had to do our first ever encore. I turned towards the band to discuss the idea, but my blood ran cold as I saw someone step out from the wings.

Keith stepped past Sadie and said into her the microphone, "Y'all may have heard of me. My name is Keith Neck." Oh the crowd ate that up and chanted his name like cavemen: "KEITH! NECK! KEITH! NECK!" These were probably some of the same people that were bored out of their minds when Keith played this same stage four hours prior, but they cheered regardless. *Thought About America* must've erased the memories of his shittier songs. Good endings tend to do that.

"For Delaney's final number," said Keith, "I propose a lively spiritual taught to me by none other than Mister Reggie Dunn. How about a round of *Let Your Light Shine on Me* in the style of Blind Willie Johnson?" Keith's black and red guitar glinted in the stage lights. I looked to Ludwell, Hoover, Sadie and Ruby, reluctant to let Keith hijack the biggest audience we'd ever had.

He started playin' before the rest of us could reach a silent consensus, and the audience approved of this old-timey hymn during an otherwise secular show. The church people in the crowd got into it far more than they ever would have in any Sunday sanctuary, clappin' and singin' and what not. The show nearly felt as if a Baptist revival were about to take off.

Keith stepped up close to me and started singin' into my microphone like we were a damn duet. His cologne almost made me forget the chords his stink was so offensive. On one particular lyric he stepped away from the mic while I sang the line about my religious pride. He winked at me as resumed singin' on the very next verse.

The end of that song couldn't have come soon enough.

We received a standin' ovation, and the rest of the band came to the edge of the stage to wave goodbye. As Delaney and Ruby soaked in our newfound tier of glory, Keith went back up to my microphone.

"Hold on, hold on now," he said, and the applause died down. "One last thing before we go. Not two minutes ago, Reggie Dunn sang a lyric about bein' proud of his religion." He looked at me and smirked.

Like a damn rabbit I lunged at Keith and tried to tackle him off that microphone, but he was too quick. He lifted the microphone stand and held the base out towards me like a lion tamer holdin' back a beast. Part of the crowd gasped when the stand thumped against my chest.

Before I could whip the mic stand out of his hands, he said, "I just found him singin' that lyric really funny, because Reggie doesn't believe in God anymore."

Everything went silent.

I stopped fightin' against the mic stand. The seed had been planted.

"Reggie is Christian no more!" Keith's words echoed and echoed and echoed through the Union.

I held out my hand and tried to pull the mic stand away before he did more damage, but a hand suddenly pressed against my chest. A hand I knew better than my own.

Ruby held me back from Keith.

Her eyes carried the weight of a terrible hurt. Her intuition had been vindicated in the worst way.

And now she wanted to hear the truth about me, no matter where it came from.

Keith smiled and said to the audience, "Reggie told me a few months ago, in the backyard of his father's home. He told me how Christians rationalize everything as God's will so they don't have to face reality," Keith almost chuckled. "He said he couldn't believe how intelligent adults can accept the creation story of Genesis as truth. Instead he believes astronomy and science explains where we came from."

Keith looked at me. "Where'd the Sun come from, huh? Explain that!" A few audience members clapped. "Can you believe it, folks? Some people don't have common sense."

He turned back toward the audience. "He said heaven is just wishful thinkin' and when we die, we're just gone. Forever." Keith took a deep breath. "This man said if God was real, He must be unwillin' or unable to help life on Earth, and because of that, God isn't worthy of Reggie Dunn's worship. Can you believe that arrogance?"

The audience chattered to itself. Heard a boo or three.

"Y'all have a good night!" Keith waved and left the stage in a hurry.

I didn't dare look at my bandmates, my father, or my Ruby. I could only focus on the microphone, beggin' me for a response. I didn't owe the audience an explanation, but the guilt inside drew me to speak.

"I...uh..." All of my wits left me, and I was exposed. I could've joked it off and left just as easily as Keith, but my heart told me otherwise.

Only the truth could get me out of there alive.

"I've been taught by the people I love that I should never compromise myself. And I need to embrace my own truth if I am to ever respect myself as an honest person."

I summoned the guts to look over my shoulder at Hoover, one of the coolest and bravest men I'd ever met, and then I looked at Sadie, the very definition of confidence. Both of them looked downright confused.

I looked to Ludwell, my evergreen source of incorruptibility. He was a blank slate.

I couldn't find the muster to look Ruby in the eyes.

I took a deep breath, and stared into the shadow of the audience. "I didn't plan on sharin' my personal beliefs with you today, cause it has nothin' to do with y'all. I've kept my thoughts to myself cause I didn't want to alienate the people I love. But I'm tired of lyin' all the time. I no longer believe in or worship God, or the Bible or heaven or church."

Some people hollered out, most of it sounded hateful or mournful. I was too nervous to remember what they said.

"Now I ain't tryin' to argue. We can talk about God and proof and faith until we kill over from exhaustion, but I know we should agree to disa-"

I paused. A song had taken over the silence. It was a lone voice somewhere out in the audience, carryin' a melody familiar to millions. The song gathered strength throughout the venue until there were dozens and hundreds of voices singin' a refrain I knew in the deepest parts of my heart. The song pierced any joke or defense I could have mustered.

They sang:

Yes, Jesus loves me
Yes, Jesus loves me
Yes, Jesus loves me
The Bible tells me so

It was an attack on the purest memories of my twenty-nine year old life. I pictured that home movie all over again, the one with my momma singin' me to sleep in a rockin' chair. I remembered the night Ludwell and I serenaded her with hours of music just before she passed. Those moments instantly became corrupted by a weaponized lullaby. Without a doubt in my mind, I knew I had broken my momma's heart, wherever she was.

I looked behind me, and only Sadie and Hoover remained. The singin' voices in the crowd grew ever stronger, so I ran off the stage, my fist gripped so tight I cut into my palms and bled.

TWENTY-EIGHT

BACKSTAGE HAD NUMEROUS EXITS and I had no clue where Ruby or Ludwell went. Sunlight suddenly burst from the loadin' dock doors on the other side of the building, so I ran across backstage, hopin' Ludwell would need a smoke after such a discovery.

Sure enough, I found him on the loadin' dock ramp, holdin' a lit cigarette in his hands, leanin' on the railin'. I waited at the top of the ramp, the evenin' sunshine givin' way to the slightest autumn chill.

We stood there so long in silence.

Finally, without lookin' at me, he said, "Who put those thoughts in your head, boy?"

"Nobody," I replied. "Came to those answers myself."

"Is that why you let Keith have your song? Because he knew?"

"Yeah," I said after a lengthy pause.

He took a drag. "You're a musician and a day laborer. What do you know about astronomy and faith and heaven?"

"I ain't tryin' to argue, daddy, I'm just-"

"Don't 'daddy' me."

I sighed. "It's just my own perspective. That's all. I've felt this way for a long time, and I only recognized it recently."

Ludwell took another hard drag. "I've had my problems with God, sure. I bout near broke in two when your momma passed. But I kept talkin' to Him. Every night I talked to Him, askin' Him to take care of her."

He paused and cleared his throat. "But to hear you've given up on eternity...on ever seein'..."

Ludwell flicked his cigarette against the brick wall beside us. "So I believed in heaven and your momma believed in heaven just to make ourselves feel better?" He faced me, his eyes swelled with tears. "And we were idiots for hopin' that we'd hold each other again?"

I could barely look him in the eyes, but I did. "I love you and momma so-"

"I ain't no damn fool, and neither was she! But you got it figured out! There ain't no heaven. No hell. Just nothin'!"

He stepped closer. "Tell me your momma's gone!" he shouted. "Tell me she's gone forever!"

"Daddy, I love-"

"SAY IT! SAY IT GODDAMMIT!"

My father stared through me, his stubbled face soaked in tears. I nearly forgot how to breathe, my chest stunned into absolute helplessness.

He walked down the ramp, cursin' his way toward Fourth Avenue. Nothin' I could've said would have helped.

TWENTY-NINE

I HAD TO FIND RUBY, but she could've been anywhere. I tried callin' and textin' her several times, but she refused to pick up, likely because it was my number. I needed a different phone.

I went back into the Union and found Hilleman backstage where we had left him. He was puttin' a new e-cigarette together.

"So now you're an atheist AND a hick?" he asked. "Jeez, nobody's coming to your birthday party next year."

"Give me your phone," I demanded.

Hilleman didn't move. "Is there a 'please' somewhere in there?"

"I'm not in the mood for your shit," I said. I could still taste the tears in my eyes.

He reached into his jacket pocket and pulled out his phone. "What do you need it for?"

I swiped it from him and said, "I need to text Ruby. Thanks."

I stared at it for a while but couldn't figure out what to do. I could text from a button phone just fine, but his phone had a thousand little icons on the screen and I was confused as all hell.

"Tell me how I can text Ruby," I said. "I don't know computer phones."

240

"You snatched my phone, yokel. I don't want to help you anymore."

Without lookin' away from the phone, I said, "Try that again and I might not hook you in the mouth."

He huffed and pressed a button on the phone. "Text Ruby," he said, and the phone responded. Hilleman motioned for me to speak.

"Where are you? I said, pronouncin' each word carefully. It typed my speech into written text.

I hit the SEND button without needin' instruction. Hilleman tried to take the phone back.

"Hold on," I said. "She has to reply first. Don't you ever get tired of bein' so ornery?"

"Hey, your dad stole my cigarette and you took my phone. You're the difficult one, hick."

"If you hadn't met me, you wouldn't have signed Ruby or Keith and you'd have been fired by Bossman Riddle months ago. You got lucky. And yet you've always been mean as a snake. And if you're gonna make jokes on Southern people, put some effort into it. There's plenty of material available, but you always go after the low hangin' fruit, what with the 'hick' comments and cracks on us bein' stupid or poor, as if the South had the monopoly on them things. That's just lazy, Hilleman."

As he chewed over what I said, the phone buzzed in my hand.

The text read:

IN THE EIGHT SECONDS HONKY TONK

I replied with "Stay there." The phone sent that text on its way.

Hilleman shuffled his feet. "Look, I know I can be an asshole-"

"You wanna show some damn decency for once?"

Hilleman looked down at the floor and nodded.

"Then don't tell Ruby I'm lookin' for her after I give you this phone back. Consider it your gift to me for savin' your career."

I pressed the phone against his chest and Hilleman put it back in his jacket pocket and mumbled, "Yeah, okay". The guy refused to look me in the eyes.

I ran down the street to the honky tonk as hard as my beefy frame could.

❄   ❄   ❄

That warehouse-sized honky tonk was jam packed with festival goers. The tiered, arena-like levels led almost all the way to the ceiling, while the dance floor at the bottom grooved along at full occupancy. Even though the music wasn't terribly loud, I still couldn't make head or tails out of the cowboy hats and twirlin' house lights and the chatter of hundreds of people line dancin' with their junk all up on one another.

I squeezed through the crowd and worked my way up to the top level and looked around.

By some trick of the eye, I caught someone that resembled Ruby sittin' at the far end of the dance floor. I pulled out my phone and called her. Immediately, that woman checked her phone then dismissed the call.

Gotcha.

Gettin' to Ruby was another matter. Almost every corner of that honky tonk was occupied by dancers or waitresses or drinkers unwillin' to lose their invaluable spot next to a beer-soaked wooden pillar. The only chance I had at reachin' her was to go through the dance floor.

I assumed I could dance my way through the masses, but assumin' made an ass out of me. I wedged my way through a few layers of sweaty people on the dance floor, but then the song changed and suddenly all of that honky tonk just had to dance at that precise moment. I couldn't sidestep or shuffle any which-a-way, and dancers pressed up against me from all sides. Short of shovin' people to the ground, I didn't know what else to do.

I reached for my phone and hoped I could call Ruby enough times for her to speak with me, but as a dancer pushed against my backside, I felt a warm metal on my skin. I reached behind my pants and shouted once I saw what was in my hands.

It was the snub-nose startin' pistol I had forgotten to give back to the Festival boss. I pressed it against my stomach and hid it with my hands. No one seemed to notice.

The longer I went without explainin' things to Ruby, the more likely my marriage would suffer irreversible damage. I needed to speak with her immediately.

So, in the name of love, I held up that pistol and fired two blank rounds, felony be damned. Unlike me, those dancers had no qualms about shovin' each other down to get somewhere else. Hundreds of people hollered and ran and panicked for every exit in that joint.

The DJ cut the music.

As the crowd vanished back onto the Nashville streets, several people all over the honky tonk stood in place and pulled out concealed handguns. Not ten steps from me, a mustached guy in a blazer and jeans kneeled on the dance floor and held out his 9mm, huntin' for a target.

"Citizen's arrest!" He yelled over the strange silence of the honky tonk. "Who the fuck shot that!?" Mustache pointed his weapon at me and said, "Did you shoot that?"

"Naw..." I said before I cut my eyes at him. "Did you shoot that?"

"No!" He double-checked his safety.

"Well, maybe he ran outside!"

Mustache got to his feet. "Good idea. You cover in here. Everybody, follow me!" He ran towards the main exit with all of the other concealed weapon fellars followin' suit. I put the gun in my pocket, and seconds later, that honky tonk was almost completely empty.

Almost.

Ruby sat in a chair against the back wall of the dance floor, her face turned away from me.

Only a few yards away sat my distraught wife, and now was the time to prove my worth as a husband. But with every step I took across that dance floor, my tongue went into spasm and all the tender, eloquent declarations I had thought up on my run to the honky tonk suddenly fell outta my head. Before I knew it, I was standin' in front of her with nary a thing to say.

Despite the gravity of the moment, I somehow managed to say, "Uh...hey darlin'."

She crossed her arms and turned her head away.

I took a deep breath and steadied my nerves. "Would you please talk with me?"

Ruby kept her arms folded and her eyes turned away. "If I don't, you gonna shoot me?" On any other day both of us would've laughed.

"Please look at me," I asked.

She stood up and tried walkin' off but I grabbed her shoulder. "Hey, hey, hey now," I said as I gently turned her towards me. "We're gonna talk about this, and we're gonna get through it. And you know I ain't gonna quit till we do."

Ruby hammered on my chest with her fist and said, "You lied to me!" through her teeth. "You tell me I'm your darlin' person and your best friend and then you lied to me! Over and over again! Every song we ever sang together was a damn lie! Every one of 'em!"

I tried to say, "our music won't no lie," but my throat seized up. All I could muster was a vigorous shakin' of my head. She pounded my chest several more times after that. I deserved those hits.

She stepped back once she finally stopped hittin' me, but she still refused to look in my eyes.

"How could you tell Keith about your faith and not me?" she asked.

"Tellin' him is officially the stupidest thing I've ever done," I said. "And I've done a lot of stupid things."

"And you lied to me for so long. How can I trust you?"

"I'm sorry I lied to you," I said. "I am so damn sorry I hurt you."

"Why didn't you trust me enough to talk with me about it?"

"I was afraid you'd leave if you knew. Every lie I told you broke my heart. Every single one is seared into my memory. I've been absolutely terrified to tell you the truth."

Tears ran down her kissable cheeks. "How do I know if you're still a good man?" she asked.

"I'm still a good man, darlin'. I'm still the man you married."

"Are you?"

That cut me deep, and I had to look away to maintain what little composure I had left. I won't gonna cry, cause if I cried then that meant it was over.

"Do you think I'm stupid for believin'?" she asked. "For believin' in heaven? Do you even respect me anymore?"

I held the side of her face. "Ruby, I love and respect you more than any person, place or thing in this universe. You're the reason I make music, the reason I worked so hard in shit jobs, the reason my life is worth livin'. You are the best friend I've ever had, and you are the most talented, intelligent, tender-hearted, fantastically gorgeous woman I could have ever imagined, and I swear I would rather die a thousand times than try and corrupt your faith. I will support and love you no matter what you believe."

Ruby looked away with a brief smile and wiped away her tears. "Reggie, when we got married, we signed up to be together beyond death do us part. We promised to love one another for eternity. I meant that promise with every corner of my soul, even the part about us gettin' old and dyin' together during sex." Her voice broke up on that last bit.

I swallowed hard, unable to speak.

I won't gonna cry.

"I'll go to church," I said. "I'll do mission work. I'll be an usher every week."

"I don't care about ceremony or appearances," she said. "If you don't believe in it, then you'd just be dishonest again. And I'd always wonder if you were lyin' to me again just to keep me around. Besides, what if we had children? How would we raise them?"

I couldn't answer.

"Do you really not believe in God?" she asked.

I summoned every ounce of courage within me. Honesty was my only option. "No, I don't," I said.

Ruby took a deep breath. "Nobody's perfect. I mean, we all sin and fall short of God's example. But if you don't even believe...oh, Reggie, I don't want you to go to hell." More tears dripped from her brown eyes. She leaned her forehead against my chest and gave a big sigh.

When she looked at me again, she struggled for strength.

"You are the love of my life." she said, "You have always given me abundant happiness. And ever since I met you, I knew I wanted to grow old beside you, spoonin' our way through life's joys and sorrows. But you are askin' me to choose between you and everlastin' God, between a lifetime of love with you and eternal heaven with the creator of the universe. I can't risk my salvation."

She took my hand and kissed it. Then she stepped back, with gobs of teardrops runnin' down her face.

Ruby Naris took off her weddin' band and held it.

"No, no." I shook my head. "We can solve this."

I won't gonna cry.

She put her weddin' band in my hand.

I won't gonna cry.

Ruby Naris turned away from me and began to walk away.

I won't gonna cry.

Impulse took over. I grabbed her hand and hollered, "Please don't go!"

She stopped but wouldn't face me.

"I can't take you leavin'," I called out. "I can't do it. Please don't go. I love you too fuckin' much, and I will always love you so long as I draw breath."

She didn't move, but she didn't pull away either.

I got down on one knee and held up her weddin' band with my free hand.

"Will you marry me, Ruby Naris?" I said as I fought back the tears. "We'll start anew, from right here. Please be my wife."

She turned around and faced me as I held onto her hand. I lifted the ring a little higher. "Will you marry me?" I asked with a tight voice. "Please marry me."

She put her free hand on my cheek and I looked into her brokenhearted eyes.

She tried to smile, but the tears wouldn't let her.

She pulled her fingers out from my grip, and turned from me and walked away.

My knee went weak and I fell back onto my foot, with my other knee still propped up.

I watched her walk across that dance floor toward the exit. I couldn't even find the physical strength to shout after her. Even from across the room, I could hear her weepin'.

To be sure she'd recall the life we shared together. The music, the travelin', the jokin', the lovin' we made in a soybean field. She couldn't turn her back on a legacy like that, cause at any second she'd remember we vowed to cuddle up on each other till we were old and senile. The religion and God stuff, those were just a buncha details.

I got overtaken with the thought of her body, her smell, her voice, her laugh, that mole right below her stomach that I always kissed before I went to town on her. I didn't want those memories stained by this nightmare.

My best friend needed to turn back so I wouldn't have to cry, then everything would be alright.

Instead my darlin' person opened the main exit of the honky tonk and never looked back.

Once she left, the honky tonk fell silent.

I crumpled to the floor and wept like a broken child.

THIRTY

LIKE A FINAL BOSS in some video game, Keith was waitin' for me when I walked through his trailer door. I was genuinely surprised by the size and quality of the trailer, especially since Keith's popularity hinged on a single hit song. He sat on a counter top far from the door, his black and red acoustic guitar across his lap, his hands in a bowl of produce by a sink.

"Hey, buddy." Keith picked up a grapefruit, tossed it up in the air and caught it. "Uh oh, somebody's been cryin'."

I didn't care how red my face was.

His webcam hung in the corner of the trailer, with a red light shinin' beside the lens, and I pointed to it. "You realize that's still runnin', right?"

"Eh." Keith grabbed a shirt from the counter and tossed it onto the webcam.

I kept my fury in check for the moment, as a loss of control would only please him more.

"What, Reggie?" he groaned.

"You're goin' to apologize to me," I said.

Keith chuckled. "Yeah?"

I nodded.

"Deep down," he said, "you wanted me to tell everybody your secret, because you didn't have the balls to do it yourself." He tossed the grapefruit up again and caught it. "I did you a favor. You don't got to compromise any more, right?"

"That won't your call to make. You fucked up my life today, all because your crush on my wife didn't pan out. So you pout like an adult-sized child."

"Reggie, I told you not to fuck with me. And I asked you to walk away from me and Ruby. But instead you tested my patience and started that freak show and kept Ruby involved in your LIES!"

He slammed his fist against the counter, and the shirt draped over the webcam slipped onto the floor. And he didn't notice the webcam's little red light, still burnin' bright.

"I've always wondered how you've justified the wrongs you've made against me," I said." I've wondered how you live with yourself."

"Oh quit actin' like I owe you somethin'. You've always doubted me, always doubted my ambition. You were just waitin' for me to fail the whole time."

I stiffled a shocked laugh. "What in the goddamn hell are you on about? I let you live with me and my wife when I didn't even have a home to my name. I introduced you to Hilleman and all them other Steam people. I helped you every chance I could and you know it. I had your back, you damn twerp!" I bout near shouted. "We were friends!"

"Okay, yeah, you gave me a shitty carpet layin' job for a few days and a place to stay for a while. I'll give you that. But we were not friends.

"Horseshit. We were friends. I wouldn't have confided in you if we weren't."

"Huh. I wouldn't have called us friends. More like associates. Or roommates. Besides, I'd never be friends with an atheist. I'm not gonna let you drag me down to hell."

He dug his fingers into the grapefruit skin and juice ran down his fingers. "You fuckin' disgusted me when you told me you didn't believe in God." He peeled off skin from the grapefruit and bit into its flesh. "It took all my strength to not throw up that night," he said through a mouthful of grapefruit. "I don't celebrate those who worship the darkness."

The champagne bottle was still out on the table, with the red champagne glasses still half full of bubbly. "You might want to put that champagne back in the fridge," I said. "Ruby might come back and change her mind about bein' attracted to man-boys."

Keith hocked a phlegm wad on the floor.

I smiled. "You tried your damnedest to fuck me over on your path to glory, but I flourished anyway. You, on the other hand, can't seem to engage an audience without playin' a song I wrote. And you know even *Thought About America* is gonna run outta gas before long, and your gravy train is gonna crawl to a dead stop. Then you'll have to find another talented sucker to leech off of.."

Keith threw the grapefruit at my head. I ducked and it crashed through the window behind me.

I turned back to him, amused I had finally gotten under his skin. He sat on that counter with the guitar still in his lap, cuttin' me some hateful eyes.

"All you know how to do," I said, "is copy and lie and steal. You are a self-righteous hack, you're a little stupid, and you are rotten inside. But most of all, Keith Neck, you are not talented."

Keith turned away from me for a second.

I leaned to the side and hollered "Hey! Look at me!"

He faced me again with tears wellin' up in his eyes.

With a strong, clear voice, I said "You are not talented, you little weiner."

Keith jumped to his feet and clutched the neck of his black and red guitar like a baseball bat. He stepped forward and swung it at me hard, so I hopped backwards and hunched down, my hands open and ready to move.

He clenched his teeth as he swung the guitar again and knocked the champagne bottle against the wall. Shattered glass and bubbly went everywhere. Due to his swingin' that guitar at me, I stopped payin' attention to my surroundings and backed myself against a dresser. Before I could move, his hands choked up on the fret board and he hollered out angry nonsense when he thrust the butt end of the guitar like a spear and cracked that damn thing against my right shoulder. It hurt like a goddamn.

I grabbed that guitar body as quick as a mongoose. We struggled for it in a dead heat, his cologne stink at point blank range. My height won out when I lifted the guitar up to the ceiling and yanked it behind my head. He stumbled back, and I grasped the fret board by the headstock. I stepped my right foot back and lifted that thing above me as if it were a sledgehammer. With all of the power and rage in my person, I smashed that guitar against the trailer floor, then smashed it again and again and again like a redneck Pete Townshend.

I tossed the broken hulks of the guitar at Keith's feet. My hands and arms were bleedin' from the shards of wood and frayed guitar strings, but it was a pain well earned.

Keith's war face showed up and his eyes went all ballistic and he hollered "AAAARRRGGHH!!" from the back of his throat.

Upon seein' him seize up with a new level of fury, my first thought was 'how cute, the little weiner wants to try and attack me barehanded.'

He charged across that trailer and spear tackled me hard enough to knock me into the back wall. The trailer rocked somethin' violent upon the impact. He got me good, I'll give him that.

I slipped while tryin' to stand back up and crumpled back onto the floor, with my shirt tail halfway up my chest, exposin' my belly. Keith got on top of me like some wannabe MMA fighter and punched my left side several times.

Now despite all the tears I had shed that day, I started to laugh as he hit me. "Your skin is luscious," I said. "Do you moisturize?"

Keith revved his fist back and socked me in the chin.

Ooooooohh, he wanted me to hit him now.

I shoved him off me and he stumbled backwards to his feet. I stood up and tried to put him in a headlock, but he slipped out like a salmon jukin' a grizzly. He leaned forward with another fist and landed another hit on my left ear. Immediately I heard a fierce ringin'.

"I'm tryin' to turn the other cheek here!" I yelled.

Tears swelled out of him and he hollered again as he cocked back another fist, but that joke won't funny anymore. I compressed my beefy hand and cracked it straight into his forehead like a pneumatic bolt gun. Keith went limp and started fallin' backwards . For the tiniest of moments, I savored that vacant look in his unconscious eyes like I savored every bite into a medium rare steak with pecan butter. But I noticed the broken husk of that champagne bottle stickin' up on the floor behind him, and acted on instinct.

I caught Keith's arm and held onto him before he crashed to the floor. If he had fallen another few inches, that broken bottle would've gone straight through his back.

While holdin' onto his one arm, I kicked all the loose glass and wood and guitar strings to the wall, and once the floor was free of debris, I dropped him. Keith finished fallin' with a thud. He didn't stir.

I kicked the heel of one of his leather boots for some reason. I should've said somethin' funny or a clever one-liner, but my damn ear hurt too bad to come up with anything worthwhile. So I did what I'd been raised to do: I told the truth.

"You throw a good punch," I said. "Apology accepted."

I walked out of that trailer and never saw Keith Neck again.

❖   ❖   ❖

When I got back to the apartment later that night, all of Ruby's things were gone. I couldn't sleep on the bed neither, cause her pillow still smelled like her, so I rolled one of the Mexican blankets under my head and slept on the couch.

THIRTY-ONE

HOOVER CALLED ME OVER to his house the next day to get my mind off the festival. He thought if I sunk my energy into finishin' the album I'd be able to turn somethin' terrible into somethin' productive.

I stood in the recordin' room with my electric guitar ready to fly, the headphones providin' me with the playback. But my mind kept driftin' back to the night before.

"Reggie, you missed your cue," said Hoover through the headphones.

I came out of my trance. "Oh yeah, sorry."

"All good," he said. "Take four."

He ran the song back and I pounded a dirty riff over *Starstuff*, an otherwise quiet song. I didn't even think about the chords. Just bashed out nonsense.

When I finished, Hoover said, "Hell, Reggie. That was good stuff. Didn't see that coming, but it works. Clever lad."

"I was tryin' to fuck it up, honestly," I admitted.

My well of accidental good ideas dried up fast.

Hoover cued up another song that needed work, and I fell into recent memories when Ludwell's recorded guitar rolled through my eardrums. I remembered the childhood story he had told us right before he played this particular solo, about some weird kid in his neighborhood that hid condoms inside a trumpet case, and how the kid asked Ludwell to be on lookout for adults so the kid could have sex with a tree knot. The memory of Ludwell gleefully demonstratin' the kid's thrusts drove me to unlatch my guitar and let it crash to the floor.

I paced around like a caged loon.

"Whoa, it's okay, Reggie," Hoover said. "Just breathe with me."

Sadie grabbed the control room microphone. "Reggie, your business is your business, and I don't care if you believe an ice cream machine is gonna save your soul. You are my friend and I've got your back. I can go kill Keith if you want me to."

I tried to laugh.

"I'm serious," she said. "I can make it quick or I can scare the goddamn hell out of him before I chop off his toes. Call it."

Hoover took the mic back. "I know you're a good person Reggie, and that's all that matters. Ludwell and Ruby just need to process everything. That takes time. Come on in here, there's a couple of Neptunes in the fridge."

"Probably shouldn't drink," I said as I stared at the studio rug. "I ain't eat nothin' today."

"Shit, Reggie, it's three in the afternoon," cried Hoover. "Let's go get some food."

My mind couldn't stop.

Momma makin' biscuits.

Ludwell smackin' his chops.

Ruby.

The vision of Ruby leavin' me in that honky tonk rattled me for the hundredth time that day.

"I can't do this," I said.

"We'll take a break, come on," said Hoover.

"I don't want to do this anymore. There's no point."

I opened the studio door and started down the hall before Hoover and Sadie met me.

"Reggie, I know you're going through some shit," said Hoover. "God, I know. We just want to help you. Let's go get some lunch and then we can just goof around in the studio or listen to records or watch a movie. Or we can watch that video of you knockin' out Keith again. It only gets funnier every time we see it. We'll do anything you want."

Sadie put her hand on my shoulder.

"I'm sorry, but I just want to be alone for a while." I walked past them, toward the stairs out of the basement. Without lookin' back I said, "Y'all can have the album. Do whatever you want with it. I don't care."

❅   ❅   ❅

In the days followin' the festival, I kept myself busy for the sake of my sanity. I went walkin' in the mornin', sat at a diner and watched TV in the afternoon, then went drinkin' at a bar where I knew no one would recognize me. I just needed to give Ruby and Ludwell some time to chew things over. They'd come around, cause I believed they still loved me. I could wait 'em out.

When I picked up my mail on the day after I left Hoover's studio, I could've sworn I was hallucinatin' off a gas leak. In our weekly church newsletter, I spotted my own damn name in the PRAYER REQUESTS section. And the official reason? HIS FAITH, accordin' to the newsletter. That alone didn't bother me much, but what did bother me were the eleven other copies of that same newsletter in my mailbox. I chucked 'em all in the trash.

The day after that, I walked down to the corner gas station to get a case of Neptune and the cashier started chattin' me up at the checkout. He looked just like George Jones, no foolin'.

"Excuse me, sir, but you're Reggie Dunn," he said as he looked over my ID.

His curious tone caught me off guard. "Uh, yeah." I said.

"I've heard that name recently." He snapped his fingers. "You're the guy that renounced God on stage at the Union last week!"

255

I quietly said "Yep," and handed him a twenty dollar bill. "Did you, uh, see the show?" I looked over his shoulder at the cigarette shelves, eager for him to hurry the hell up with my purchase.

"No sir, I hear talkin'. A good many people got upset by it."

"News spreads fast," I said with a sigh. "Didn't think somethin' like that would concern strangers. No offense."

"None taken," he replied. "Those upset people are usually the first ones to forget the true principles of Christ, and that's to love one another no matter what. Now I can't say I agree with you, Mister Dunn, but I accept you all the same."

He handed me my change and said, "God bless you, Mister Dunn."

Some people may have turned that moment into a battlefield on the grounds of his potentially snide comment, and strong tempers may have won over. But I thought better of it, and took his comment as the kind gesture I hoped it was. I smiled and said, "Thank you."

Aside from a total stranger knowin' my business, I felt good walkin' back to the apartment that day. My gut told me this whole episode would blow over before too long, and people would find better things to do.

I soon discovered people really didn't have anything better to do.

Everywhere I went from that day on, I kept gettin' the feelin' that people were goin' out of their way to come talk to me or confront me or stare me down. That Wednesday, I was sittin' at a diner and all of a sudden I saw Ricky Brown from church and he invited himself to sit down with me so he could talk about "the whole God thing". I told him I won't in no mood to argue, but he rambled on anyway.

Then twenty minutes after Ricky left, this young lady named Brenda from the church's college class sat down in my booth and just went to weepin' over my soul. She asked me, "Why don't you just believe in Jesus in case He actually exists? You've got nothin' to lose if heaven isn't real, but everything to gain if it is."

I handed her some napkins for her tears and told her, "Thank you for your concern, but I don't wanna live that way. I don't believe in God for my own reasons, and pretendin' to believe just to hedge my bets is dishonest and low."

Then when I tried to pay my check at the front counter, I met Jason Degree, the head deacon of the church, as he was comin' into the diner with his wife and kids. I greeted him but he didn't return the sentiment. He only stared me down while he took a seat with his family, his face stern as hell.

More things like that happened over the next few days. The grocery store, the park, Wal-Mart, everywhere. I got earfuls from (former) friends, acquaintances and church people every time I left my apartment. One tall stranger stomped up to me in the grocery store and yelled, "People told me about what you said on stage the other night and it's pissed me off!" They got down right wacky. Most of the time I knew the people that approached me. Sometimes I didn't.

One time this guy who looked about my age came over to me while I was eatin' a burrito at Queso Queso. He didn't introduce himself or nothin', just said, "I want to pray with you." He bowed his head and folded his hands while standin' over my table in a too-tight polo that made his nipples poke up. "Dear Lord, please help this man turn back to you so he may find contentment in you, Lord." I grabbed my chicken burrito and tried to leave, but the guy followed me out the door while keepin' his head bowed, his hands folded down, and his prayerful words flowin'. Even as I was pullin' out of the parkin' lot, he stayed in position, talkin' away.

People refused to shut the fuck up about me.

I don't know how they found me or recognized me all the time. I wasn't on the damn news every night, so far as I knew. Maybe they had some sort of phone tree goin', or a website called 'Reggie Sightings' where they reported my location whenever someone spotted me. Maybe I just had a really predictable daily routine. However they did it, this giant group of people knew how to track me down.

Usually I could shrug off all that harassment, but it started to eat at me when old Miss Edna invited herself over one early mornin' and got all ornery the moment I opened the front door. "Reggie Dunn!" she hollered while pointin' her cane at me. "You stupid man! Rubbin' your arrogance in our faces! Let me tell you, that pride of yours won't last a second in everlastin' hell! No one asked to hear your wickedness, and yet you're broadcastin' it to the world anyway!"

Keep in mind that Miss Edna stood before me wearin' a colorful T-shirt that read GOD IS AWESOME!, and I knew for a fact that her pickup had five of those Jesus fish glued to the tailgate.

Through my half-awake state, I said, "What do you care?"

Oh, her eyeballs just about exploded. "I'm being attacked for my beliefs yet again! God is gonna make you pay! How DARE you insu-"

I got bored and slammed the door in her face.

It won't just religious people neither. One of the clerks at the music shop got all excited when I tried to buy a pack of strings.

"Oh shit, man, you're the man," the beatnik-haired clerk said. "You spoke the truth. Religion is for sheep and should be-" He ranted on and on as he ran my credit card. I stared at his name tag the whole time, waitin' for the goddamn machine to dial up the credit company so I could leave. And for all that time I spent starin' at his nametag, I can't even begin to remember his name. Like everyone else I met that week, he sincerely believed I wanted to hear his bullshit.

I also received all sorts of mail, such as blank letters with no return address, envelopes full of Bible tracts and loads of poorly-written damnation requests, and they all went straight into the dumpster. Even had one letter that only read YOUR MUSIC SUCKS in giant block letters. Under it was a drawin' of a big ol' purple dick with all sorts of veins bulgin' out. That one gave me a chuckle for a second, I'll give it that. But overall I figured these people had to be gettin' bored of harassin' me all the time. It would only be a matter of time before some new distraction would come along.

Sadie and Hoover stopped by on Thursday for lunch. I warmed up some frozen egg rolls in the kitchen just so I wouldn't have to leave the apartment and risk a public scene. Unlike my other visitors, both of them had every right to resent me for abandonin' the band and the album, but they cheered me up and stuck by me all the same. I asked them about my daddy and my wife. Neither of them had talked to Ludwell since the show, nor had they heard anything about Ruby.

I called Ruby a couple of times that week but it went straight to voicemail. On my third attempt her guitarist Vanessa picked up Ruby's phone.

"She's safe and staying with me," Vanessa told me. "But she doesn't want to speak with you."

"Well, I'd really like to talk with her," I said, fightin' the urge to cry. "Gimme just a minute, please."

Vanessa sighed. "Please don't make this more painful than it has to be."

I stopped callin' after that. If Ruby needed more time then I had to give it to her. I could wait.

I drove by Ludwell's house Friday mornin' and hoped I could catch him before he left for any job he might've lined up. I could hear the TV goin' as I stood at the back door, waitin' for a response to my knocks.

"Hey daddy, it's Reggie," I hollered through the door. "How you doin'?"

The TV kept blarin' its noise.

"I just came by to visit. If you got the time, that is."

I thought I heard him move inside, but it may have been what I wanted to hear. I opened the screen door and tried to turn the back door knob but it was locked.

The TV's volume grew louder and louder, till I could understand every word out of the newscaster's mouth.

"Guess I'll be goin' then!" I shouted at the door. "Call me if you wanna get supper sometime."

Part of me hoped...no, all of me hoped that the man who raised me would come runnin' out the back door and chase my truck down as I pulled out of his driveway and try to talk with me. Talk some sense into me, as he'd probably say. I kept on hopin' all the way back to my apartment.

I didn't know what I was gonna do with myself. The music was gone, my money was runnin' low, my hometown was makin' me go crazy, and my family wanted nothin' to do with me. For the first time in my life I didn't know what to do.

I even drove down to me and Ruby's ol' house outside of town. Well, there won't a house there anymore, just a vacant lot surrounded by woods. There won't no AUTOMAX COMING SOON banner, no construction equipment or any real estate signs with that son of a bitch Lonnie's face. Just a wide patch of dirt where our home used to be. Where Ruby and I used to spank and plank one another under the moonlight. Now it was just a big ol' patch of dirt with no proof I was ever there.

#

Early Friday evenin', I stepped out my door to go pick up a pizza from Pizza Hole, and as I was walkin' across the lot to the minivan, this red truck rolled into the far side of my complex's parking lot all slow, with two ugly fellars in the cab and three more sittin' in the back. They were young, rough lookin' guys, haggard as hell. All of them stared at me as the truck circled the lot. Right when they got drove close to me, one of them guys in the back spat at my feet and grunted. I stood my ground and kept my eyes on 'em till they drove back onto the main road. There won't no license plate on the back of that truck, either.

Same thing happened the very next day, and the day after that. Same truck, same fellars wearin' the same ugly faces, all payin' me a visit in the early evenin' time. While I was in the parking lot again on the second night, on the third night I stood at my window on the third story and watched them circle around that parkin' lot just as they had been the nights before. Right before they pulled back out onto the road, the three guys in the back stared up at my window. One of them waved.

I started carryin' my knife on me whenever I left the apartment, and considered gettin' my concealed carry license back up to date. Part of me knew I should've moved when all the mass mailings started, and especially when the drive-by staredowns happened, but I refused to be terrorized.

The next afternoon I went to a few pawn shops to see how much I could get for my guitar. The best offer I heard was thirty bucks and some free DVDs, so I kept it for sentimental reasons. I figured I'd just keep it in the utility closet, leanin' against the wall behind the vacuum cleaner.

I never got that chance though, cause I came home to a kicked-in front door. In broad fuckin' daylight.

I pressed up tight against the outside wall and gently opened the broken front door enough for me to slip in. With knife in hand, I stepped into my dark apartment and listened for anything.

Silence.

I flicked on the light and saw my habitat flipped to shit. The few things I still owned were scattered all over the place. The kitchen cabinets had been bashed open, heaps of food was across the floor and thrown against the ceiling, and there were dozens of boot-sized holes in the drywall. But the centerpiece was the bold red graffiti sprayed across one of the livin' room walls.

It read:

REPENT, ASSHOLE

To tell you the truth, I almost smiled when I read that. That comma avoided any confusion over the vandals' intentions, otherwise I might've thought they were condemnin' my anal fixation. But my smile failed when I wondered about what could have happened.

What if Ruby had been home?

I knew she was safe with her bandmate, but a terrible imagination still got under my skin. Until that moment, I could've laughed at the hypocrisy of vengeance in the name of Jesus, but them boot holes in my wall made me take stock. Shit had gotten real. It was the only time I was ever glad Ruby left me when she did, cause things could have been much worse.

The police took fingerprints, witness statements from neighbors and what not, but nothin' came of it. I mentioned that unlicensed pickup truck creepin' around, but a suspicious vehicle wouldn't prove anything even if I had seen a plate number.

Hours later I cancelled the lease on the apartment, and the landlord had the decency to not take the damage out of my security deposit. I thanked him and didn't look back.

I spent that night in a truck stop parkin' lot about fifty miles down Interstate 40 East, and slept in the minivan with my Mexican blankets keepin' me warm. I didn't know where I was goin', but I made sure I was far from Nashville before I fell asleep again.

Honesty sure is the best policy, huh?

THIRTY-TWO

SPRING IS MY FAVORITE SEASON, mostly cause it reminds me of sex. It also don't hurt that the world's in bloom, and you tend to get a hopeful feeling more often than not. Spring is also when Ruby and I started our musical journey across the country. That was a damn year ago.

Huh.

I moved up to the Blue Ridge Mountains a couple of days after the apartment got busted up, with the thinkin' I could get away from all that Nashville mess by becomin' some mountain man, explorin' valleys and tamin' undiscovered varmints. But all the hills and uncharted territories I thought I'd find were usually filled with fast food and an Auto Max every other mile, so I spent my first few weeks hikin' around the state park, singin' to myself for the sake of the bears. Them bears don't like gettin' sneaked on.

My little house was a comfortable place, somewhat isolated near the top of a mountain, with a long driveway off a gravel road, overlookin' a little valley. It had a nice porch with rockin' chairs overlookin' a purdy view. I didn't have a computer or TV up there, and my phone got bad signal until I went to the other side of the mountain, so I lived a hermit's life for a time.

I had a radio for a little while, though. One day I was on the porch, listenin' to some local country radio, when I heard an unfamiliar song with a far too familiar voice. It was this midtempo ballad with lyrics about holdin' your women tight from the men that don't treat 'em right. I couldn't believe my patience actually lasted long enough to hear that boring tune reach its conclusion, but I wanted to confirm the singer was who I thought it was.

"And that was *Where There's Smoke*, the new single from Keith Neck, the artist behind the megahit *Thought About America*", said the first disc jockey. "What did you think about Keith's followup, Blake?"

"What did I think?" Blake the disc jockey asked himself. "Mmmm...you want me to be honest?"

"Of course," the other disc jockey replied.

"Well...uh...I have to admit I'm a little scared to be honest over how I feel about this new song."

"Why's that?"

"Cause if I tell the truth I'm worried Keith is going to burst into this studio and attack me with a guitar."

"HAHAHAHAHAHAHA!" laughed both of them disc jockeys.

"Folks, in case you haven't seen it," chuckled the first disc jockey, "there is a video online of Keith Neck getting into a fist fight with the singer from a little Nashville band called Delaney. Keith's people removed it from his website a few hours after it happened, but you can still find it elsewhere if you know where to look."

"Keith went down from just one punch. One. Punch."

"Guess Keith didn't have all that much fight in him, did he, Blake?"

"Nope."

"Do you know what they were fighting over?"

"I don't know for certain, but I've heard it was over the Delaney singer's wife."

"Ooooh!"

"Yep," said Blake the DJ, "Keith had recorded his attempt to win over the guy's wife and posted it on his website. That video isn't up there anymore, either, by the way. Seems this Delaney guy had had enough of Mister Neck's mischief. I would've tried to knock Keith out, too."

"And the Delaney guy's wife isn't just some pretty young thing, is she?"

"No sir, in fact she is Ruby Naris, the same Ruby Naris that has been scorchin' up the charts. In fact, let's hear Miss Naris right now. Here's *A Fantastic Color*."

And from hundreds of miles away, Ruby's voice found me on that porch in the mountains. It was sweet and electric and far too much for my heart to bear. I yanked the power cord from out the socket and tossed the radio in the garbage bin behind the house.

❊ ❊ ❊

So long as I kept my mind and hands busy, I was all right. Hikin' around or goin' into town tended to occupy me for a while.

One Sunday, I had a brilliant idea and went walkin' around the valley, tryin' to enjoy the sunshine before the winter took over. I must've gone past half a dozen churches as they let out for the end of their mornin' services. The congregations were always smilin', laughin', huggin' one another in those courtyards and parkin' lots. A couple of churches were havin' potlucks under a shelter or in their fellowship hall. Several more rang out their bells in celebration of another peaceful day. There were countless couples out, holdin' hands and showin' each other off, their love all too obvious, and I wanted to crawl inside a mountain for a few centuries. I was livin' a damn Kristofferson song.

My free time bout near killed me. Sometimes I took a shower simply to be in the heat. I'd just stand there and watch the water run down the drain. Wouldn't even wash. Every time I stepped back out I'd stare at my left shoulder in the mirror for the longest time. Ruby's love bruise healed completely by mid-October. After I'd seen my bare shoulder too many times, I took that mirror off the wall and put it in the crawlspace.

265

On almost every winter's day I shoveled snow from my driveway, but beyond that one task I didn't have much else to do, so my diet turned to shit. I lived off blueberry muffins from this nearby gas station for a good four or five days. Then I just ate those microwave vegetables with that nasty cheese sauce for a solid week. By Thanksgiving I barely left the house. I'd just sit on the couch and eat grated parmesan cheese straight from the can and stare out the window.

Most nights I'd sit outside and admire the sky. I'd watch the planets and stars up there, things that will continue to exist long after I fade away. Can't tell you how many times I'd sit on that porch and wonder if I should have kept my damn mouth shut at the Union. Yeah, I spoke my truth and finally quit bullshittin' people, but was it worth all the heartache and death threats? Was it worth losin' people?

Yeah, it was.

Didn't matter how much it hurt, how lonely it left me. I won't a liar no more, and I wouldn't be holdin' my gorgeous, talented, and devout wife captive no more.

I reckoned Ruby could find herself an honest Christian man, now that our relationship had run its course. Hopefully Keith won't harassin' her.

I bet myself that she was datin' somebody by the end of November, though. She was too damn special to be ignored.

I won't seein' nobody then, and I won't tryin' to neither. Besides, I was pushin' 30 and hadn't been on a first date in six years. I wouldn't know what I was doin' with a new lady. And I couldn't use the same schtick I did when I was 24 and expect to get anywhere. Grown women don't have time for bullshit.

❖   ❖   ❖

By December I got fuckin' tired of feeling worthless all the time, so I got a job. I apprenticed with a plumber in Asheville and earned a good enough livin' to afford a pickup truck I saw for sale in a flea market parkin' lot. There's good money to be made in the plumbin' trade so long as you don't mind fixin' frozen pipes in ten-degree weather and dabblin' in hocky all day.

Christmas came and went. It's funny. Despite not believin' in God any more, I still looked forward to Christmas and the singin' and family times and what not, even though I'd probably never be close with my family again. And I didn't have a tree cause it reminded me of Ruby too much. I couldn't stomach decoratin' the thing when the only person who'd see it would be me. I did make myself a real nice ham and turkey sandwich on honey wheat bread, though. It was good for a sandwich, but a let down of a Christmas dinner.

I finally picked up my guitar again around mid-December and wrote my only song during that seclusion. I tried writin' a big ballad regardin' the key subject on my mind, but it sounded all soppy and if Delaney had still existed there was no way they would have ever allowed such syrupy mess, so I gave those lonesome lyrics little more of a bounce.

That idea became the song *Anorak*. Anorak was a fancy name for a coat I heard around the mountains from a plumbing customer. It's a sad but boppy song about Ruby always bein' welcome to my mountain house, and how I always daydreamed about her walkin' up the driveway in a warm anorak full of goose down. Amidst one of my more primal mind sets, I almost included some lines about my favorite parts of her body, but I thought better of it and kept those to myself. The details of her chewable inner thighs won't nobody's business anyway.

On New Year's Eve, I mailed the handwritten lyrics of *Anorak* to Steam Records Headquarters in Nashville and instructed the mail center to forward the letter to Ruby. If she wanted to hear those words put to song, she knew where to find me. If she didn't, then she knew where to send the divorce papers.

I still carried her weddin' band around with me. Kept it in my front right pocket all the time. Felt like a hobbit, wanderin' those mountains, daydreamin' about times long since gone. Daydreams were about the only thing I had. I did grow a pretty good beard, though. A solid mountain man type of beard, with a slight red tint mixed within my dark brown hair, like I was some Scotsman hidin' out in the Blue Ridge Mountains.

Tennessee only required sixty days of separation for a divorce, so by late January I assumed the mail had gotten lost somewhere because I had yet to receive some big packet from a lawyer. I figured they were just being slow in gettin' their papers together. Or maybe the Steam Record mail people tossed it in the trash without even givin' it to Ruby.

When I checked my mail that Groundhog Day, I bout near fell over into the ditch. It was a postcard of an alligator showin' off her chompers in a swamp, with MIAMI, FLORIDA blazed across the bottom. I flipped the card, and I read the postcard's only message. All it said, in tight black script, was the name 'Ruby'.

❊   ❊   ❊

On a crisp April mornin', a worn-down blue Chevy pickup clunked its way up my driveway as I sat on the porch. The driver stepped onto my footpath and lit a Marlboro.

"Goddamn, boy, you ain't easy to find," Ludwell said with cigarette a-burnin' from his lips. "Been in that truck for five hours. I gotta piss right quick.

He turned toward the mountain valley and unzipped his britches. I stood up and held out my hand in a 'be my guest' motion that he didn't see.

"How'd you find me?" I asked.

"Ruby told me your address after I irritated her a little. Didn't take long. I figured you've had enough time on your lonesome, judgin' by that beard. Been keepin' busy?"

"Plumbin' mostly. Also helpin' a beekeeper down the mountain."

"Plumbin' is a good trade. Smart." He zipped up and stepped onto the porch, his face a little older than I remembered. "So how about this? I drive to the middle of nowhere and find you livin' on your own, lookin' miserable and bored, and I'm the one that has to kickstart you back to your senses. What a difference a year makes, huh?"

I smiled. "All I need is a few beehives out back and then I'd be just like you."

"You're damn right." He cleared his throat and took the cigarette out of his mouth. "Listen...I, uh..."

He cleared his throat again and looked me dead on. "I lost my temper after that festival show, and the thought of hurtin' you has been eatin' me up ever since. You chose not to compromise your truth, just like I raised you to do, and I couldn't be prouder of the man you've become. I know you'll always love your momma, and so did she. I shouldn't have taken your decisions as an attack on my grief. You're a good son, Reggie. I'm sorry."

For the first time since my ninth birthday, I hugged my daddy.

"Thank you," I said. "You explained yourself right smart. You been goin' to therapy?"

"Naw, just drinkin' a lot."

We sat down on the rockin' chairs, and I told him exactly why I moved out to the mountains in the first place, and then he updated me on Nashville.

"Everyone is doin' well," he said after he lit another cigarette. "Hoover's producin' an album with some electro band from Iceland called The Local Trolls. I met them a few weeks ago. I liked the way they talked. And me and Sadie have been seein' each other here and there."

"I knew it!" I slapped him on the back. "I always knew there might be somethin' between y'all. Two hellraisers like y'all couldn't help but get together."

"Heh, yeah, well she ain't gonna be your stepmother or nothin'. We're just havin' fun, lookin' out for each other, you know. She's a live wire."

I couldn't have nodded harder.

"And how is...uh...Ruby...doin'?"

"She's fine. She's doin' just fine. She's on tour right now, up in Canada, I think. Gettin' that free health care."

I didn't need to know any more. My mind couldn't handle details.

We looked out at the mountains in the full bloom of spring. "Don't worry, I went and checked on her as soon as I could after the tornado," he said.

I sat up in my chair. "What tornado?"

"Hit last week, went through the area somethin' fierce. You didn't hear about it? A few hundred injured, hundreds more homes tore all to hell. The town got beat up."

"Is, uh, everyone okay?"

"Yeah, everyone we know is fine."

Ludwell stood up. "Come back to Nashville with me for a few days. It would do you good, and there's still plenty work to do around there."

"Daddy, Nashville ain't exactly my favorite place. They may as well have run me out of town on a rail."

"I'm aware."

"Hate to be hardheaded, but I don't know if I want to help that town out." I looked out to the mountains and rocked in my chair.

Ludwell sighed. "Tell you what. Ride back with me, spend some time around the house, then I'll bring you back. A little vacation from your vacation."

He slapped me on the back, and I smiled. Aside from torturin' myself over Ruby, I had spent many nights in that mountain cabin worryin' if I had forever lost the affections of the man who had provided for me and raised me up in his own gruff style. But I can't even begin to describe my relief once he and I began to joke and talk again on my mountain porch, cause it proved Ludwell Dunn still loved me after all.

❊   ❊   ❊

Twenty minutes later, we were on Interstate 40 West, rollin' back toward Central Standard Time. Ludwell showed off his fancy new truck radio by playin' somethin' off his fancy new computer phone. "Take a look at this," he said.

Right there on his phone was the cover to Delaney's debut album called *Pale Blue Dot*.

"Well, shit on me," I cried. "Y'all finished it?"

Ludwell grinned.

The cover was one of the many we took in Hoover's backyard with some crazy color filters thrown on top. We were a motley crew, no doubt, but the music itself proved we were the shit. The album sounded fantastic, with all the crunches and soft bits and sharp edges where they needed to be. That rough yet professional sheen turned *Sun Keeps Burning* into a legitimate anthem with a keyboard solo I had never heard. *Walrus Tusk* stomped along to a set of fuckin' war drums, and the rerecorded *Paddy Wagon* captured all of the glory of its live counterpart. All ten songs were fun, singable and energetic despite the incomplete work I left behind.

I loved every fuckin' note.

"It's sold pretty damn well, too," Ludwell said. "Once that video of you fightin' Keith got big online, oh holy hell our whole situation blew up. You think our early videos were popular? You ain't seen nothin'. People just loved how you cold-cocked that kid. Good job, by the way."

"Thank you," I said, but I couldn't take all the credit. Keith's webcam did the heavy liftin'. All I did was punch out a little weiner.

271

THIRTY-THREE

DOWNED POWER LINES. Houses with fallen trees still crashed halfway through roofs. People pickin' up mess and destruction at every turn. Even five days after the storm, my hometown looked right haggard.

"Damn, daddy, this is bad," I said from the passenger seat. He had to drive slow to avoid all the debris still on some roads.

"Yeah, that twister got us up the ass," he said. "Still no electricity in some places." Ludwell drove us by the churches, the barbeque place, the Grand Ole Opry, the apartment Ruby and I once shared. Despite the city's recovery effort, I constantly saw more work to be done.

A tiny part of me struggled for sympathy. Did the city want my help? And if it did, did I want to contribute?

Ludwell flipped on the radio and we listened to various interviews with Nashville residents, and they all used some variation of the phrase "it looks like a warzone" or "it looks like a dadgum bomb went off." One guy even claimed "it looks like a tornado went through here."

Nashville ain't known for its trees, but you'd think it was in a rainforest based on the fallen trees lyin' around the Saddles parking lot.

"I gotta pull in here for a spell," Ludwell said. "They need me to help 'em fix the generator I let 'em borrow."

We walked past the workers runnin' chainsaws in the parkin' lot and entered my favorite honky tonk to survey the damage. One massive hole in the roof made part of that low ceiling into a skylight, but I'll be damned if the place won't open for business. It wasn't packed by any means, but there were just as many drinkers as there were people doing repairs. Most of the tables and chairs had been stacked on the stage so workers could reach the damaged areas easier. Even the bartender alternated between servin' mugs of beer from a keg with a hand-powered tap and pickin' up debris from behind the bar.

"Come on in," the bartender said. "Some of the kegs still got a little chill, believe it or not."

After I took a sip of lukewarm Neptune, a friendly face sittin' on the only chair at the bar caught my attention. "Good to see you, Wild Bill," I said and we shook hands.

"Well, hot damn," said Wild Bill, still a disheveled mess of a man. "Reggie Dunn, the music man himself. You bout to make any new stuff?"

"Naw, I'm not really doin' music any more. I'm a plumber now. Around Asheville."

"Huh." He sipped from his mug, and a little beer foam stuck on his stubble. "Plumbin' is a good trade and all, but I really enjoyed your music. Your show at the festival was a damn hoot. Whenever I hear you on the radio, I get all proud."

"Radio, huh?"

"Yeah, every now and then," he said. "So why'd you move to Asheville? It's cause of all the ruckus after your festival show, ain't it?"

"That's part of it." I took a long draw from my mug.

"Hmmm. That ain't fair. You were honest in a time of accusin' and people got bent outta frame over nothin'. Sometimes I think people get upset over things cause it gives 'em somethin' to do. They had no right to harass and terrorize you like they did just because you didn't agree with 'em. One of those college beatniks at the drywall protest told me that's called tyranny of the majority. And anybody that hadn't ever doubted their faith is a liar or a fool. Nobody's got it figured out."

I was taken aback. "Well damn, Wild Bill. I'm gonna start callin' you Guru. Got some wisdom on you." I saw movement by the legs of Wild Bill's stool. "Holy hell, is that the dog you talked about?"

Wild Bill smiled and bent over to pet the black and white mutt sittin' on the bar floor. "Yep. Found him again a few months ago. I led him back to my house, bathed him, fed him. Named him Samson on account he's a strong boy. Guess some things are just meant to be. I bet he was bred to be a bird dog. He's real smart."

Samson suddenly bit Wild Bill hard on the forearm. I mean that dog really got a deep hold. Wild Bill reached his hand into Samson's muzzle and unclamped those teeth off his arm. He smiled up at me. "Yeah, he's a good boy. They're just love bites."

I pointed to his forearm. "You're bleedin' bad."

Wild Bill stared at his gushing bite wound. "Well...goddamn."

He grabbed a fistful of bar napkins and slapped them all over his bloody arm, then rubbed Samson's head.

"It's okay," he said. "He's my best friend. We'll work it out, move on, do better for next time. Ain't that what best friends are for?" Wild Bill stroked Samson's back, and the pup sat there grinnin', probably anxious to strike again.

"I wish that were the truth." I downed the rest of my beer.

The bartender put a fresh mug of Neptune in front of me.

"Oh, no thanks, I'm about to leave," I said.

The bartender pointed to a couple of maintenance guys walkin' toward me from the other side of the bar. "A gift from some of your fans," he said.

The two guys couldn't have been more than nineteen, one with a buzzed head and the other blonde as hell. "Excuse me, are you Reggie Dunn?" the buzzcut guy asked.

"Yeah, that's me."

Both of them got giddy. "Told you it was him." Buzzcut said to the blonde fellar. I shook both their hands.

"I heard a rumor you went crazy and started making homemade deodorant," Blonde guy said. "Was that true?"

I smiled and shook my head.

"I saw you guys in Kansas City," Buzzcut said, "where those guys made that human pyramid, and of course I saw your show at the Union. You were incredible, even at the end with the ranting. That part was pretty bad ass."

"Oh yeah, thanks." I said.

The blonde fellar said, "I play your album during sex all the time."

I laughed. "As long as it keeps you up, brother."

"So you're back in Nashville to get the band back together?" Buzzcut asked.

"Well, no. I'm done with music. I'm here visitin' family. I might help clean up or somethin' while I'm here. I'll be like you guys."

Those two gave each other a worried look. "That's great you wanna help clean up, Mister Dunn, but everyone can help clean up," said Buzzcut. "Not everyone can do what you can, though. When Tennessee State got power back the other day, the first song they played was *Sun Keeps Burning*. Your song. Everyone with a battery-powered radio got fired up. I know I did."

Blonde guy nodded along. "I mean we've got workers and aid groups here, but we've gotta have a fire behind us to keep us going. We need somethin' to sing. We need Delaney."

Ludwell came up behind me and tapped me on the shoulder. "All right, let's go."

Of course those two guys freaked out all over again when they realized it was him, shoutin' about how Delaney really was getting' back together. Ludwell pretended like it wasn't a big deal, but I know for a fact he ate that rock star shit up.

Those guys' request stuck with me as Ludwell and I drove past more of the devastation. I saw national news vans throughout the city, but I knew the attention wouldn't last forever. Soon the country would find some other story to follow and Nashville's open wound would be forgotten.

I couldn't let that happen.

❧   ❧   ❧

I've forgotten most of what happened at that press conference a few days later. All the attention caught me off guard, what with the cameras and reporters all up Delaney's noses. I stood with my band mates and Odom by a pile of rubble in the parking lot of closed down Fat Bargain department store. On Odom's advice, I shaved my beard back down to my usual stubble-length shadow.

Right before we started the conference, Odom took me aside and told me how Delaney could be the next big thing if we followed through on all this momentum with a legitimate tour and a killer followup album. He also wanted me to get started on my memoirs right away. I made my muff-divin' donkey joke a little too close to the microphones and all the reporters laughed. After Odom told me to stop bein' a jackass, he just shook his head and slammed this voice recorder in my hand.

"Is this the only benefit planned for tornado relief?" asked a long-haired reporter.

Odom stepped forward to the herd of microphones. "It was one of many concerts being organized until Delaney here consolidated a number of smaller benefits into the extravaganza we've announced. In addition to Delaney, we've got Randolph Suggs and The Opossum Brothers on the bill, as well as a slew of local artists, all playing for the benefit of Nashville's recovery. This entire process has been like asteroids coalescing into a planet."

Of course someone asked where I had been and if I had gone crazy due to mad cow disease, but I said little more than "I had to figure myself out." A music journalist asked about *Pale Blue Dot* and I admitted, "I left near the end of the sessions, so these guys-" I pointed at Hoover, Sadie and Ludwell- "finished it without me. I just heard it the other day and I absolutely love it. And while I'm here..."

I turned toward my bandmates. "Sorry I left y'all in the lurch. That won't right of me." I had already apologized once to them in private, but they deserved a proper recordin'.

Hoover leaned into a microphone. "Well, I spent all your money from the album on a home theater, so apology accepted."

Everyone laughed and Hoover slapped me on the shoulder. Sadie hugged my neck. Ludwell cleared his throat.

"Will Keith Neck be performing at this event?" asked a reporter.

Sadie leaped at the closest microphone and almost shoved it in her mouth and said, "No, because if I see him I'm gonna slit his throat and watch him die!"

Most of the reporters looked horrified. Ludwell burst out laughin'.

Odom yanked the microphone from her and smiled. "We're going in a different direction for our festival. We're interested in booking artists, not one-trick ponies. The country music world has long since proven it is tired of his lone good song. Can anyone name a Keith Neck song besides *Thought About America*?"

Several hands in the gaggle of reporters shot up.

"Can anyone name a decent Keith Neck song besides *Thought About America*?" Odom emphasized.

All them hands came down and the gaggle murmured amongst itself without givin' up an answer.

"Exactly," said Odom as he looked at me and grinned.

Another reporter raised her hand with a question that I had waited all day for. "Will Ruby Naris be performing as well?"

I stepped forward to the microphones. "We haven't heard back from her people, as she's on tour at the moment. But I'd love to have her there...I mean we, the benefit concert and the people of Nashville, would love to have her there. But for the record, yes, I'd love to have her there, too."

THIRTY-FOUR

OVER THE NEXT TWO WEEKS the hype for that benefit concert blew up. That three act show became a five-hour telethon to be broadcast across three major TV networks. Even bigger names joined the bill: Jerome Deloatche, The Everyday Boys, plus Myra & The Queue. The response was fantastic.

Delaney only had a few days to get back into fightin' form, so I was forced to hot glue my fingertips to repair the callouses I wore off during the intense rehearsals. We weren't quite as good as we were on that two month street tour, but we were still an impressive unit. We talked about maybe doin' another tour, but for payin' audiences this time. It sounded mighty temptin'.

The Union Auditorium volunteered their venue for the telethon, providin' me with plenty of memories to stir. Despite the purpose of the concert and our new fanbase, I still seized up backstage before our set. A single pulse of vomit threatened to rocket out of my tremblin' gut everytime I recalled our first Union performance.

As the band sat backstage waitin' for our set to begin, I wondered if the buildup to this benefit concert was all a giant practical joke. I imagined I'd get on stage and suddenly thousands of people would yell the same thing:

You are shit.
Your songs are shit.
There's no home for you here.

I couldn't take my eyes off the floor. "I don't know if I can go out there," I said to the band. "I don't think I can do it."

And then Sadie gave me a hug.

And so did Hoover.

And so did Ludwell, his second hug for me in as many weeks. He smiled and told me, "If anybody gives you static, just tell 'em to go to hell. You ain't goin' there anyway."

"All right, show time! Let's fire it up, cuties!" Sadie hollered and smacked Ludwell on the ass. She shot him a wink and walked down the hall towards the stage.

Ludwell chuckled as the rest of us followed behind her. "That's a woman, right there," he said.

I'll never forget how the crowd popped when the four of us walked out on stage. Sudden mass praise from a couple thousand fans is one of the absolute greatest highs on this planet, better than anything that comes in a baggie or bottle. Either my detractors had forgotten about my onstage declaration from last year, or the couple thousand Delaney fans drowned them out with glorious singin' and dancin' in the aisles. The power chords and fiddle riffs were out in force that night.

We played that benefit for the recovery of our hometown, and we played for the fans that kept our engines hot. I played to make my momma and daddy proud. I even played to prove I was willin' to forgive my hometown if they were willin' to do the same for me. But secretly, selfishly, I played in the rare hope that Ruby might notice me and miss me and see I really was a good man and realize that my britches only got crowded for her. I still kept her weddin' band in my pocket like a good hobbit would do. I knew such a move was delusional and maybe a bit unhealthy, but a sliver of me refused to give up hope. I even played *Anorak* on my lonesome with my acoustic. I couldn't believe how quiet the whole venue got as I played that song. If you were there, I appreciate the reverence.

I ain't a scientist or a preacher or a poet. I can't tell you why Noah got drunk and hollered at his youngins, or how blue shifts determine motion from objects light years away. I can't tell you why people sometimes do horrible things to one another, or why good hearted souls suffer from the likes of time and bio-mechanical breakdowns. Don't make sense to me.

Music makes sense though. It can be as simple or complex as you like, and as long as it makes you smile or dance or sing or swagger then it has succeeded. Music gives you strength. Soothes your heart. Gives your daydreams a better place to play. You don't need an instrument or even sound itself. You only need a melody in your head, a driving force that makes you want to face the world despite all its infinite nonsense. So long as the music lasts, life is good.

So Delaney made music that night, and for the duration of that show, everyone could dance and sing the bullshit away for a little while.

But music ain't perfect. You can't cuddle it or marry it or make it dinner. Music is only the soundtrack of life, not the purpose. I believe everyone's purpose is defined by their own doin', but for me, love wins that one, no contest. Ain't love what music is usually about, anyway?

Throughout the night I could've sworn I saw Ruby in the front row or in the aisle or the side of the stage, but I reckoned it was only wishful thinkin'. I pretended she was out there, though. Gave my music a destination. It kept me peppered up.

When the noise of the crowd swelled to a massive roar before our last song, I assumed my pants had split or Sadie had flashed her boobs again.

Instead the crowd roared because I had stepped into a daydream, the caliber you conjure when you're fallin' asleep alone in a mountain cabin five hours from home. I knew that moment was more than a daydream, though, because reality had finally trumped fantasy. I knew that moment was real because I had never imagined a couple thousand people would cheer their praise while I laid eyes upon my estranged wife on stage.

Hot damn her body looked toned under that blue dress. Looked like she'd spent the last seven months shoulder pressin' boulders. Made me wanna do pushups right there.

She got close and whispered into my ear and raw lightnin' crackled through me. Songs, albums, rock operas, anthologies of music spawned from that hushed declaration, the galactic hinge of my life.

Did she and I kickstart a full-band barn-stormer to close the set? Hell yeah. You can watch it all you want on the online, Delaney + Ruby Naris smilin' all the way through the best version of *Paddy Wagon* ever played.

When the song ended, all of us went up to the edge of the stage and took a bow to the thrill of the crowd. Then she turned to me with those brown eyes of hers, and my heart bout went haywire.

I didn't know why she reappeared.

I didn't know if she only performed for the benefit of Nashville.

I didn't know if she only wanted to save my soul from the fires of an eternal hell.

I didn't know if she would ever let me witness and squeeze and worship her body and heart again.

She gave me an answer a few minutes later, though.

I still got plenty of space left on this voice recorder. I could go into detail.

You'd probably like that.

But you know what?

How I made love to my darlin' person ain't none of your business.

APPRECIATION

Vanessa, my darlin' girlfriend, found the inner strength to read four different drafts of this novel. Her excellent story sense and feedback showed me things in my narrative that I hadn't even considered. She held my work to a higher standard and motivated me to write something worth reading while giving me a dump truck's worth of emotional support. Ain't she somethin'?

Many thanks to my other beta readers:

Tyler – You gave me feedback worthy of a doctorial creative writing workshop and told me what I needed to hear. Thanks for the encouragement all these years.

Amy – Can you believe it? I finally wrote a story that didn't have a talking animal.

Rynette – You proved that a reader didn't have to live in the South in order to 'get' this book. Thank you, cousin! I owe you seventy pounds of Reese's cups.

Mike – It's not HRN-caliber, but what is these days?

Blake – I'm relieved you were willing to read this story after suffering through my aborted sci-fi novel six years ago. Hope this one didn't read like another psych report.

I am forever indebted to Jennie Rawlings and her spectacular cover art. It wasn't until I saw her work that I finally knew that my novel was real. Check out her material at serifim.com

My Mom, Dad, and two brothers provided a wealth of love, anecdotes, and history that weaved their colors into my story, and they've always had my back despite the irreverent things I've created. Plus I wouldn't be who I am today if I had never heard the phrase "pert near".

I'm also grateful for the love and support of the entire Ray family, who believed in my abilities before they ever read my work.

Rhonda, Brian & Lake hosted Vanessa & I during our 2014 pilgrimage to Nashville, and drove us all around that wonderful city. Y'all are so much fun. I seriously considered using Mason as a pseudonym.

Nick showed me the wonder of Rebel Radio.

BNIZ, BMAS, and MARO of RK: You're all jabronis.

I'm heavily inspired by the work and spirit of Noel Gallagher, Jimi Goodwin, David Bazan, Carl Sagan, and Neil deGrasse Tyson. Craig Ferguson's delightfully vulgar novel 'Between the Bridge and the River' stood as my comic novel gold standard.

Finally, I owe a great deal of credit to the mind and misadventures of my late grandfather Horace Williamson, who served as the template for Ludwell Dunn. He was a comic genius, even though he never knew it.

MUSIC

This novel being a celebration of all things music, I've been asked to list a few of the albums I listened to throughout the writing of REDNECK. While working, I listen to instrumentals or albums I don't know well, since I usually refuse to sit still if I'm listening to familiar classics. Most of the albums below eventually reached singalong status, but I learned to love those brief distractions.

Electric Warrior – T.Rex
Angels of Darkness, Demons of Light – Earth
...Like Clockwork – Queens of the Stone Age
Same Trailer, Different Park – Kacey Musgraves
F#A#infinity – Godspeed You! Black Emperor
Odludek – Jimi Goodwin
...and they have escaped the weight of darkness – Ólafur Arnalds
Oblivion Hymns – Hammock
Hag: The Best of – Merle Haggard
Screamadelica – Primal Scream
The Best of – Blind Lemon Jefferson
Kind of Blue – Miles Davis
Days Are Gone – Haim
Ultimate – Dolly Parton
Dark Was The Night – Blind Willie Johnson

ABOUT

Clayton Williamson is Clayton Williamson, surprisingly. Past endeavors include songwriting, filmmaking, and video game item descriptions. Future ambitions include owning a beekeeping yard and posting a nude pic of himself on the Internet. He also unironically loves *Invisible Touch* by Genesis and *Kickstart My Heart* by Mötley Crüe. In fact, if you get him started, he'll ramble on about obscure English bands until you just want to go home. He tends to have a bad memory, but he always drinks the recommended daily amount of water.

He currently lives in Raleigh, North Carolina, with his girlfriend and their two pups.

Photo by Vanessa L Photography

Start: Nov. 5, 2013
Finish: Sept. 5, 2015

18197538R00172

Printed in Great Britain
by Amazon